THE RETURN
OF THE
KNIGHT TEMPLAR

TULIO ALBUQUERQUE

Order this book online at www.trafford.com
or email orders@trafford.com

Most Trafford titles are also available at major online book retailers.

Translation by: Jack Liebof.

Printed in the United States of America.

ISBN: 978-1-4669-8822-4 (sc)
ISBN: 978-1-4669-8824-8 (hc)
ISBN: 978-1-4669-8823-1 (e)

Library of Congress Control Number: 2013905672

Trafford rev. 04/02/2013

www.trafford.com

North America & international
toll-free: 1 888 232 4444 (USA & Canada)
phone: 250 383 6864 ♦ fax: 812 355 4082

CONTENTS

AUTHOR'S NOTES

This book deals with very diverse matters. One of them is a rather controversial topic: returning to the past through dreams, regression.

Regression exists and has been the subject of study by renowned specialists. When I envisioned Reinaldo's return to the past, by means of his dreams, I knew very little about this phenomenon. Books such as "The Interpretation of Dreams" by Sigmund Freud, and the work by Dr. Brian L. Weiss, "Many Lives, Many Masters", helped to open the way to knowledge of this interesting experience. And my daughter, Renata, who already went through this experience, collaborated in my obtaining an understanding of this process.

Previously, I used to believe that regression could only take place under the effects of hypnosis, induced by a qualified professional person, such as a psychologist or a psychiatrist. However, I discovered that this was not quite the case. Awake or asleep, in certain circumstances, we can enter into a hypnotic state and penetrate the subconscious, where the most remote memories of our being are preserved, which can be associated with a distant past. Regression includes not only the return to the past within the scope of a single existence, in which we are allowed to recall happenings which occurred starting from our earliest age. It is also related to the return to previous lives, which gives rise to a complex idea of reincarnation.

The human mind and spirit are areas practically unexplored by modern science. Man has succeeded in discovering and traveling through the regions of our planet and is already starting to investigate outer space, without having progressed hardly at all in the discovery of his own inner universe.

As to the Knights Templar, the famous warrior monks of the time of the Crusades, a topic also covered in this book, a great deal has been written up to now about their existence, with some writers associating them with an image of heroic saints, and others describing them as bloodthirsty inquisitors. Nevertheless, I believe the truth lies somewhere in between. I believe in the good aims of the Order, mainly during the first century and a half of its existence, when it fought heroically to defend the holy sanctuaries of Christianity. The Order of the Knights Templar was created in the twelfth century, several years after the first crusade, when Jerusalem was conquered. Its headquarters was founded in the place where the ancient Temple of Solomon was located, in Jerusalem, nowadays the Al-Aqsa Mosque, with its golden dome. It lasted for almost two centuries, but, according to some scholars, was never extinguished and is still present, until today, in the masonic lodges of modern times.

Religious intolerance, a generator of relentless disputes and sentiments of hate, has always existed and continues latent among us. Catholics against Protestants, since the reform movement of Luther and Calvin; Catholics against Jews, up to the Inquisition; Catholics against Moslems, Moslems against Jews, Hindus against Moslems. After all, we are living in a world of intolerance and prejudice. One aspect of these struggles is shown in our story.

The struggle against the drug traffic, one of the problems involving our country's borders which are the entry point for a major part of the drugs consumed in the large cities, today is part of everyone's daily life. The scourge of drugs, the black plague in today's social context, is spreading throughout all the countries in the world, killing people and destroying families. This struggle is a cause that involves the entire planet, and its repercussion inspired the episode narrated in the book, which on a much smaller scale, really occurred.

We are mixing fiction and reality, many of the happenings and people mentioned really existed. The account of the battle of Hattin was recreated based on various books of Medieval History.

Thus it was that Reinaldo could embark on that fascinating journey, stretching across the centuries, in search of the answers to the crucial issues of his existence. Let's go along with him in his search, which could be the search of all of us who yearn to discover the reason for and the meaning of our existence.

Natal, Brazil—May 2003.

INTRODUCTION

T he night was hot and humid. Whenever he was on the border, after sunset Reinaldo used to go sit in the same place, on the fallen tree trunk. It was located on a high cliff, at the edge of a creek, a few meters from the camp. He had arrived that Saturday afternoon, August 12, 2000, to celebrate mass for the 4th Border Platoon, that had taken its position along the banks of a small tributary of the Auaretê River, on the border between Brazil and Colombia, in a region known as *dog's head*, because of its shape on the map. Always protected by a generous layer of insect repellent, he felt at ease—the place was safe and barren—from there the entire horizon could be seen on all sides. What most impressed the priest was the sky, which displayed an infinite number of stars. He had never seen such a spectacle. The first time he had observed it, he even decided to study a little astronomy in order to identify the constellations. He was in the northern hemisphere, he who had spent almost his entire life in the southeastern part of Brazil, under the sky of the southern hemisphere, which was quite different. He looked again. The weather was favorable for observing the sky, there were no clouds. He succeeded in identifying several constellations: Andromeda, Aries, Canis Minor, Cassiopeia, Swan, Draco, and Orion, visible in both hemispheres, with its star Betelgeuse, Pisces, Sagittarius, Taurus and its Aldebaran. He thought about how long a time those small twinkles would take to reach his eyes. Light-years. In those moments he would feel, as never before, God's proximity. How was it possible for us, such primitive minuscule beings, to comprehend His purposes? He would end up by praying contritely, and then return to his tent, thrilled by so much beauty and such magnitude.

THE ATTACK

Reinaldo was almost hit by the first shots. He had awakened around half an hour earlier and, after breakfast, was busy choosing a spot, near the river bank, for celebrating mass.

The problems with the Revolutionary Armed Forces of Colombia (FARC) began when a few groups of guerrillas crossed the border with Brazil fleeing from attacks by the Colombian regular army. Since then, the Brazilian government had ordered its army to move toward the probable border-crossing points.

The group of FARC guerrillas had attacked at 7:00 a.m., rapidly crossing the creek at a shallow point. The surprise was not complete only because of the warning received from the two sentinels who were guarding that point on the bank of the creek. The attackers opened fire with their AK-47 rifles in an intense barrage. There were around twenty men who took part in the attack, notwithstanding the Brazilians' numerical superiority, with thirty-two soldiers. The sentinels were killed by the first bursts fired by the guerrillas' Russian-made arms, but not before they could fire their FAL rifles and wound three attackers, who were lying, moaning, on the far bank of the creek.

At the same moment, the other members of the Brazilian platoon, who were having breakfast in the clearing near the river, improvised as a provisional campsite, grabbed their guns, which they kept until then at arms length, and sought protected positions to face the attackers.

The shouting was intense on both side. Reinaldo, a Brazilian Army Chaplain with the rank of Captain, was preparing the small altar on the folding table, well behind the place occupied by the dead sentinels. The first bullets hit his suitcase containing the religious trappings to be utilized in the mass. Instinctively, he threw himself on the ground, saving his life by a fraction of a second. The heat was suffocating at that point of the Amazon jungle so close to the equator. He was perspiring abundantly. A sergeant and a soldier came running and remained at his side, all of them being protected by some cases of provisions.

"Father, keep down and don't raise your head", the sergeant shouted to the Chaplain.

In the intense firefight, attackers and defenders looked alike in the small clearing, making for a tremendous confusion. The bursts fired by the handheld weapons made a thundering noise. At the next moment, on looking around, Reinaldo witnessed a terrible scene: the sergeant's head had exploded in a cloud of blood and the soldier had been hit in the chest by various shots. The two men's blood bathed his uniform, turning it dark red. Without thinking about what he was doing, through pure instinct, he grabbed the rifle which had fallen from the sergeant's hands and, with a strange calmness, he began to take aim and, with incredible precision, to mow down the attackers who were moving through the campsite. His shots hit their mark and brought down five Colombians.

The Chaplain's intervention neutralized the impetus of the attack. Some guerrillas were able to flee, going back across the river. Alves, the First Lieutenant who was the platoon commander, was wounded, shot in the chest, and a sergeant was in command of the small group that had escaped unhurt from the attack. While a medic tried to help the wounded, Reinaldo began to administer the last rites to those who were breathing their last breaths. His thoughts barely allowed him to concentrate on the prayers. How could he have dared to take up a weapon and shoot his fellow men? How had he been capable of committing a deadly sin, taking the life of those whom he should love, going against all the laws of God and the Church? It would have been a thousand times better if it were he who was stretched out there, dead, fulfilling the holy duty which he had assumed on accepting the priesthood.

The military base in São Gabriel da Cachoeira, which was alerted by radio, sent two helicopters with medics and reinforcements. The casualties were high: six dead and seven wounded, on the Brazilian side, and eight dead for the guerrillas, who took their wounded with them when they withdrew. The entire action lasted not more than five minutes and the destruction in the campsite was considerable, with most of the tents showing bullet holes. Reinaldo was evacuated without even celebrating mass. The commander thought it best to cancel the mass, fearing a new guerrilla attack.

When he arrived at the base, where the 12th Border Battalion was headquartered, Reinaldo prepared his report and had lunch in the officers' mess hall. There he had to tell several times what had happened, for those who were on duty and for those who had been called following the attack. At last, when the meal was over, he was able to remain alone in the small room that he shared with another officer and reflect on the tragic event. He couldn't understand his behavior during the attack. It didn't make any sense. Not for him, a priest. He had never fired any gun before. It's true that, being with the troops, he had already handled some small arms, out of mere curiosity, and he knew something about their operation. But shooting his fellow men, in such cold blood and with such excellent aim, was something he wasn't able to face. With a great effort, he tried to put his thoughts in order. He would celebrate the 6 p.m. mass, in the battalion chapel, when he would confess his sin to Father Francisco, who always came to help him. On Monday, he'd go talk to the Bishop, tell him what had happened and ask for counsel. The rest of Sunday passed rapidly. Lieutenant Colonel Peçanha, the battalion commander, came to congratulate him on his courage in combat that morning, without even noticing the priest's embarrassment and shame.

"Chaplain, your intervention at the border decided the combat in our favor."

Father Francisco himself treated him in a strange way, as if he were seeing him for the first time.

Finally, night fell. Sunset in the Amazon region is an indescribable spectacle. The sky in the west displays a myriad of dazzling colors. The green of the tropical jungle becomes darker and the enormous horizon, which is unveiled in all of its 360 degrees, takes on the grandeur of a divine temple. It's a moment of great spirituality. Reinaldo walked to the chapel with the enormous burden of repentance for the lives he had taken that morning. He was anxious to ask forgiveness from God for the sins he had committed. Finally, the hours went by, mass was celebrated, and he found a little peace in confession. Later, in his room, he fell into a deep sleep, which was a refuge for his torment and doubts.

Then the dream came. It was a dream that was different from all the others that he had had before. More realistic, more colorful, everything more intense, as if he were actually living through the events of the dream and feeling the real sensations himself. Suddenly, he found himself visiting a strange land, in a far distant past . . .

THE YEAR 1186

The month of November, in the year 1186, was unseasonably cold. Autumn was reaching its height and in the region of the Duchy of Anjou, it was exacting its annual toll of the foliage in the woods that bordered the Loire River. Jean de Saumur was traveling in the company of his squire, Pierre, with the only material assets that were left to him: the horse, the weapons that he had inherited from his father and that had never been lost in combat, his war horse, Valiant, led by Pierre, mounted on a third horse. The day before, he had delivered to the representative of the Grand Master of the Knights Templar, Sir Robert de Fontaines, his castle in Mont-Rémy, his lands, two villages with their respective vassal tenants, various property improvements and all the movable property, which were donated to the Order of the Knights Templar. The following night, they would arrive in Orléans, where, after Sunday mass, he would take the oath of initiation to enter the Order, together with four other knights, in the presence of the representative of Grand Master Gérard de Ridefort.

They rode along the road that following the river's course, constantly on the alert for any signs of an ambush, since that region was the frequent target of robber bands. By nightfall they intended to arrive at a small monastery of the Carthusian Order, where they would ask for lodging.

The rest of the day went by without any difficulties until they spied, shortly before dark, the small hill where the monastery had been built. They were welcomed by the abbot, a monk with very white hair and a severe look, and they said their evening prayers with the other members of the small brotherhood. After a frugal meal, composed of rye bread, beer and lamb, they went to sleep.

Very early the next morning, they took leave of the abbot, thanked him for his hospitality, and resumed their journey. Pierre continued to worry about highwaymen.

"Sir, we must remain on the alert so as not to be surprised by bandits."

At that moment, Jean felt a strong emotion, caused by the memory of the attack on the small chapel of Our Lady, built by his grandfather in the woods near the castle. Two years had already gone by since the misfortune which had beset his family. On that distant morning, while he was visiting the Duke of Anjou, his wife, Melissande, went to pray in the chapel, accompanied by little André, her two-year-old son, who was being carried in the arms of his nursemaid, Constance, and by a young page. It was only possible to know what had happened afterwards from the report of a peasant, who was working for the monk in charge of the chapel, at that moment. Even though he was seriously wounded, the peasant was still able to tell the castle guards about the attack, just before dying. The guards came running immediately, on seeing the flames which were rising above the trees in the woods. A group of around ten highwaymen, armed with wooden lances, knives and bows and arrows, emerged from the woods and invaded the chapel. The poor peasant, who was performing his duties in the yard behind the chapel, on hearing the shouting, took haste to flee, but while he was running, he was hit in the back by two arrows. After looting the place, the evil-doers locked the monk, the page, Melissande, Constance and André in the temple, and immediately afterwards, set it on fire. The castle guards did not arrive in time to avoid the tragedy, since the building contained a great deal of wood, which rapidly caught fire. The hunt for the assassins, carried out by a group of knights on horseback and another group of guards and archers on foot, was unsuccessful, after a day of intensive searching. Pierre's voice interrupted Jean's sad memories.

"Sir, the abbot told me that right after our entry into the Order, we will be sent overseas."

"Pierre, the Order exists for this very purpose, which is the defense of the Holy Land and the pilgrins. We will certainly be sent there. We are going to swear to defend those holy places, so dear to our religion, and to fight to the death, if need be, against the Saracens. Why do you insist on following me, even after I relieved you from your duties as a squire?"

"Sir, when you were born, I was ten years old and lived with my parents in the castle of your father, Marquis Mont-Rémy. I will never forget the day when we were all celebrating your birth, the birth of your parents' first son. It was then that the Marquis called me and said, 'Pierre, you shall be my son's squire. You shall start your training in the use of arms tomorrow. You must serve him with your complete loyalty and protect him with your own life until the end of your days!' And I replied, 'I swear I shall do so, Sir.'

"I shall never abandon you, Sir Jean, unless death prevents me from following you."

With his voice choked with emotion, Jean was only able to say, "Thank you, my friend. Your company and friendship lighten the burden of my pain."

They continued on their journey, now under the timid autumn sun, reflected on the waters of the Loire, which flowed just below the path. When the sun was on high, they stopped in the shade of a large tree, whose golden foliage still resisted the constant wind. There they sat down to eat the bread which they had brought from the monastery, with a few pieces of lamb, and drank water from their canteens. They took care of the horses and resumed their journey, after a brief rest. A few hours later, it became intensely cold, and the two travelers were anxious to arrive at the monastery of the Order. At last, before nightfall, they spied the walls of a large city. They crossed through the Saint-Marceau gate and finally arrived at the monastery of the Templars.

THE DOUBT

Reinaldo awoke at the sound of reveille played over the barracks loudspeaker system, at six o'clock in the morning. The sun was already strong and the heat was unbearable. He recalled all the details of his dream. It seemed like he was watching a film. He had neither read nor heard anything in the last few months referring to the Middle Ages. That dream didn't make sense. He got ready quickly, since breakfast call would be at seven o'clock.

During the morning he asked to speak to Colonel Peçanha. "Colonel, I'm asking your permission to go and talk with Bishop Dom José, this afternoon, in the diocese."

"Of course, Reinaldo. I also want to inform you that I'm forwarding to our headquarters in Manaus a decoration request, recommending that you be awarded the Distinguished Service Medal for your bravery in the combat with the FARC guerrillas on the border."

Reinaldo made no comment and asked permission to withdraw. That afternoon, he was received by the Bishop of São Gabriel da Cachoeira, Dom José Mendonça de Oliveira. The Bishop, a cleric born in the state of Bahia, very pleasant and kind, was over sixty years old, and had spent many years in the Amazon region. He was curious to know the reason for that unexpected visit. The Chaplain then told him about what had happened on the border and the dream of Jean and Pierre. And after a brief interruption for coffee, served from a thermos bottle in small plastic cups strategically arranged on a table alongside the Bishop's table, Reinaldo said, "I thought that, above all, I needed to come here and tell you what had happened and seek your counsel."

Dom José remained pensive for some time before replying. "Well, my son, what happened to you was really a traumatic experience. From the Church's point of view, you committed a deadly sin. However, the situation in which you found yourself was out of the ordinary. Your action was in defense of your own life and that of your comrades in arms. Furthermore, you repented, confessed and was forgiven by Christ and the Church. Your dream, however, may mean something more profound, some doubt regarding your real personality. Are you absolutely sure of your priestly vocation?"

It was Reinaldo's turn to remain pensive before replying. He looked in the direction of the window in the rear of the room, through which one could see the beautiful view of the Negro River, with its dark waters contrasting with the dark green of the dense forest on the opposite bank. He sighed at length and said, looking firmly in Dom José's eyes, "Bishop, I've always had doubts. I see them as doubts that could possibly occur to any Catholic, in moments of weakness. Perhaps the most important, which involves the very basis of our belief, concerns the Resurrection of Jesus. However, what has been tormenting me, in recent months, is doubting whether I'll be able to devote myself, with all my soul, to the work of the Church, without wishing to do other things. Living through other types of personal experience. In short, the answer to your question is, no. I'm not sure of my priestly vocation. What do you advise me to do?"

Dom José arose and walked to the window, where he remained for some time looking at the distant forest. "Our religion is based on dogmas that are difficult to accept. And many of them don't make sense. Just as life doesn't make sense. Where do we come from, where are we going and what are we doing here? A French philosopher, who died a little while ago, wrote a book entitled *My Philosophical Will*, in which he comments on these doubts. Jean Guitton wrote this book at the age of 97 and died at 99. In one of its passages, he states, "I believe in God because I have difficulty in believing in Him. If God were easy, he'd be within reach. He wouldn't be transcendent and He wouldn't be God. But if God is God, there's an unbalance between Him and us. It's not surprising that, in order to perceive Him, we must make use of the tip of our mind."

Regarding the Resurrection, which was also one of his doubts, he found the truth he sought in the testimony of the apostles. He argued that, if twelve men witnessed an event which was so difficult to accept as true, and they didn't change their accounts in the Gospel, even suffering torture and faced with the violent death that befell most of those men, in different times and places, it's obvious that, no matter how extraordinary this episode was, it really happened. They were people from all the different social classes, some rich and well-educated, like Phillip, others poor and illiterate, like Peter. All of them, nevertheless, maintained the same version of the event they had witnessed many years before their death.

The Bishop turned around slowly and looked at Reinaldo with a tired expression on his face. "As to the vocation, I think you'll have to find your own truth. I know you're entitled to go on leave from the army. I suggest that tomorrow you ask the

Colonel's permission to travel to Rio de Janeiro, your home town, to find there the answers to these questions. When you return, we'll talk again."

Feeling more relieved, the Chaplain rose, took leave of Dom José and returned to his barracks. The next day he would ask the Colonel's permission to go on leave. That night he slept peacefully. He had some dreams, nothing special, recalling only a few details of them on awaking, but he certainly hadn't returned to the Middle Ages.

At ten o'clock the next morning, he obtained the Colonel's authorization to travel the following day, on leave, to Rio de Janeiro. That same afternoon he'd go to Santa Tereza Church and ask Father Francisco to replace him in the barracks during his absence. After all, he'd already filled in for Francisco during his two-month trip to Rome on a pilgrimage. He'd make use of the remaining hours to search, on the computer available in the Officers' Recreation Room, for information on the Order of the Templars, which had appeared in his dream. Surely he'd be able to find lots of research material on the Internet. His knowledge of the Order was superficial. He knew that it had been created during the Middle Ages to fight against the Saracens, defending the holy places in the Middle East, and that it was active during the crusades. It was a religious military Order, which had been excommunicated and abolished in the 14th century, after a trial initiated by King Phillip IV of France. The good faith of this trial has been under discussion until today, and many believe that the Order was a victim of a great injustice.

The rest of the day went by according to schedule. His friend, the priest, agreed to replace him, and back in the barracks, he obtained some important information regarding the Templars from the Internet. At night, tired, he went to bed earlier than usual, and fell into a deep sleep. A dream, which was already familiar to him, had begun, after the sensation of a brief journey through a dark tunnel, from which a bright light emerged, drawing him toward a door which opened onto the ancient distant world that awaited him . . .

THE ORDER OF
THE KNIGHTS TEMPLAR

After a night's sleep in the cubicle frozen by the autumn cold, Jean awoke on being called by his squire, who had slept in the sergeants' lodgings. "Sir, you should be present in the chapel for the morning prayers and then in the mess hall for the meal. The oath of initiation ceremony for the new knights will take place immediately afterwards. The sergeants' ceremony will follow."

With the help of his faithful friend, the knight put on his coat of mail over his shirt and breeches, buckled his wide belt with the heavy sword, handing the iron helmet and the heavy shield to Pierre, who, in accordance with his duties as squire, should carry them.

Later, in the stone hall capped by an immense dome, the secret ceremony for initiation and swearing allegiance to the Order of the Knights Templar was held. The four knights to be accepted into the Order vowed to maintain poverty, chastity, obedience—vows similar to those of the Benedictines, and also never to falter in the struggle against the Saracens. The representative of Grand-Master Gérard, Bernard de Barusseau, solemnly officiated over the formal and religious ceremonies, helping each knight to put on a white mantle with a scarlet cross on the chest over his coat of mail, thus adopting the symbol of the knights of the Order.

Jean was the youngest of the four knights, of whom two were French, coming from Brittany, apparently around forty years old. The fourth, he found out later, was Portuguese, around thirty, and was named João de Tovar. After the knights' ceremony, there began the ceremony for the squires and sergeants, who received brown-colored mantles. They numbered sixteen. Once the ceremonies were over, mass was celebrated with the presence of all the knights of the Orléans brotherhood. Following this, the knights were invited to "dinner", where they partook of rye bread, pie, roast hare, roast pork, soft pears and wine. The meals were taken in total silence. After dinner, the new knights were led to a hall, accompanied by the Abbot, who also performed the duties of provincial master, and by Bernard, the knight. The Abbot then commented, "My brothers, our meals are habitually more frugal. However, on such a special day, we decided to interrupt our routine, to celebrate your arrival."

After the Abbot's comments came the instructions of the Grand Master's representative for the new Knights Templar.

"My fellow knights, we shall be traveling early tomorrow to the Holy Land. We shall ride to the south and shall embark in a Venetian galleon in Marseilles. You will stay in the Order's castle in Acre. As you must know, we have a truce with the Saracens for four years. This period has been devoted to strengthening our castles' walls in all the Latin kingdoms. Your arrival and that of the other knights that took their vows in Paris and Dijon is anxiously awaited by our brothers."

One of the Breton knights asked permission to speak. "Sir, I heard that good King Baldwin IV is very ill. Do you have any news of his condition?"

"The king died in March. His seven-year-old nephew, the son of his sister Sybil, has succeeded him. Raymond of Tripoli became his regent."

All of them deplored the death of the monarch of the Latin Kingdom of Jerusalem, a victim of leprosy. After a few more minutes of conversation, the meeting was closed and they returned to their duties. The new knights were taken to a place outside the walls where tournaments were held, and received instructions to practice *quintaine*, an exercise with horse and lance, which consisted of hitting the chest of a dummy mounted on an shaft, whose purpose was to imitate an armed knight. Its arm was tied to a club. When the knight hit the dummy in the wrong way, it swung around and hit the careless knight. The four knights hit the dummy correctly in all their attempts, thus demonstrating excellent combat technique. At the end of the afternoon, it grew much colder. All returned to the monastery and after evening prayers and supper, went to bed.

They left early the next morning, after saying their morning prayers and eating bread with a glass of beer diluted with water. They were a group of fifteen men, all on horseback: five knights, their squires and five more Templar sergeants. Five battle horses were led by the squires and four other horses carried baggage, provisions and weapons. They rode all day long toward the south, stopping briefly for a meal at noon. At night they arrived in Bourges, where they spent the night at a Benedictine monastery. The trip was long and very tiring. Nevertheless, as they advanced toward the south, the weather improved and the cold diminished.

In the afternoon of the fourth day, they arrived in Marseilles and went directly to the port, where they located the Venetian galleon, chartered by the Order, which would transport them to the Holy Land. At sunrise the next day, they put to sea. The voyage was dangerous, since that region of the Mediterranean Sea was infested with Saracen pirates. If they were attacked and defeated, the majority would be killed and the survivors would be enslaved. Fortunately, the days went by without any break in the routine on board. Even the weather, with clear rainless days, collaborated in their calm voyage. The constant winds contributed to their progress and alleviated the task of the oarsmen, almost all of them Saracen slaves. Jean made friends with João de Tovar, a cheerful knight who spoke French well. João had been in France for two years and had been brought by Knights Templar who were fighting against the Saracens in the north of Portugal.

"Why did you come to France, my friend?" asked Jean.

"'My parents' castle was taken by the Saracens and almost everyone was killed. I was saved because I was away seeking reinforcements from our relatives, who lived more to the north. Then I decided that my destiny was to take up the cross and the sword and go fight overseas. And here I am."

"We all have our sad stories, my friend." And it was Jean's turn to tell the Portuguese nobleman about the tragedy that had fallen on his life, culminating in the loss of his wife Melissande and their son André.

The two friends had lost their dearest ones in a tragic way. This fact contributed to bringing them together, solidifying the bonds of friendship that were beginning to spring up. After six days with good winds, the vessel neared the Isle of Cyprus and made port in Limassol. The Order possessed a monastery in that city, and the men could replenish their provisions for two days. In the morning of the third day, they put out to sea again heading for the Holy Land.

THE TRIP TO
RIO DE JANEIRO

The day was dawning in that far corner of the Amazon region. Reveille hadn't been played yet in the barracks. Reinaldo, already wide awake, was thinking about the events which that night's dream had revealed to him. Something told him that all those things had really occurred and that the dream must have been a manner of revealing the facts. What could he do but wait and see the outcome of all that madness? When he heard reveille, he rose and started to prepare himself for the long trip to Rio de Janeiro. He phoned his mother, telling her about his going on leave and that he would spend some days with her.

"What a nice surprise, my son. I'm going to tell your cousin to wait for you at the airport."

Reinaldo said that wasn't necessary since he was going to take a bus.

At nine o'clock, he left for the airport and succeeded in getting a ride on a Brazilian Air Force plane which was going to Manaus. It was a pleasant flight, and he conversed at length with two Air Force officers who were also going to Manaus. He was able to arrive there in time to buy a ticket for a commercial flight headed for Rio, with a stop in Brasília. Before boarding, he phoned his mother again to let her know that he'd arrive home late, since his arrival in Rio was scheduled for 10 p.m.

At last he was flying home, after two years on the border. The plane wasn't full. He'd be traveling with two empty seats alongside. As he always did, he recited an Ave Maria, asking Our Lady to protect everyone during the flight. He closed his eyes, and at random his thoughts turned to the past. His childhood in Copacabana, his colleagues, his father who had passed away at an early age, betrayed by his heart, and the school, run by Catholic priests. There he had acquired his belief in Catholicism and had decided, as time went by, to become a priest, who would struggle to save souls, including his own, in a world dominated by materialism. His thoughts were interrupted by a voice, "Would you like to read a newspaper, sir?"

The flight attendant's smile was captivating. Reinaldo also smiled and accepted a Manaus newspaper. A very pretty young girl and the situation reminded him that the fact that he was wearing ordinary civilian clothes—blue jeans and a white shirt with short sleeves—almost always caused him some kind of embarrassment or misunderstanding in his relationship with women. He found it amusing, and in a certain way, even enjoyed the situation. His physical appearance complicated things even more: he was relatively tall, five feet eleven, weighed 165 pounds, with an athletic bearing, light brown skin, dark hair and a face with manly features. He always had to explain why he had decided to become a priest instead of enjoying life. Undoubtedly, it had been a difficult choice. Maintaining his vow of chastity was an arduous challenge and fighting against temptation was a daily exercise. From the very beginning, temptation had always been present in the lives of Christ's priests: constant battles in the war for preservation of their religious vocation, during their entire lives. Until then, he had been concentrating his efforts on the goal of being a pastor of souls.

He had entered the seminary at the age of eighteen, soon after his father's death, very probably influenced by the impact of this great loss. Little by little, his vocation continued to gain strength and he ended up by becoming a good priest. When he was twenty-five, he was sent to a parish in the interior of the State of Rio de Janeiro, in Cachoeiras de Macacu. He remained there for two years, until being assigned to a parish in Campos, a city in the north of the state, whose parish priest had died. He had taken advantage of the opportunity to study Pedagogy at the local university. A year after his graduation, at the advice of the Bishop of his diocese, he had entered the Brazilian army as a Chaplain, with the rank of Captain. He was immediately sent to the Amazon region, from where he was returning now, on his first leave. Once again, the same voice interrupted his thoughts. "Would you care to have lunch?"

Reinaldo was hungry. After praying, he ate with a great appetite. Compared to the food served in the barracks, the meal seemed excellent, despite the small quantity. He dozed off for half an hour after lunch. He awoke when the pilot was announcing that they would land in Brasília in thirty minutes. The afternoon was beautiful and the sunset's dazzling colors outlined the horizon. Then he recalled his dreams. That was certainly not a normal thing. He'd talk to his cousin Luís, who was a psychiatrist and would know how to give him some guidance in this regard. One detail which he thought was curious was that the dream took place in France but the people were speaking Portuguese, all the better because he knew almost nothing of the French language. He had never been to Europe. The only time he had left Brazil, at the age of seventeen, was to play on the state all-star high school volleyball team in a tournament held in Argentina. He had spent two weeks in Buenos Aires, and that had been his only international experience. Something especially intrigued him about this dream. The knight named Jean reminded him a lot of his father when he was young. However, it didn't make any sense that his father could be Jean's reincarnation. In this way, the possibility that Jean was his ancestor could better explain the resemblance. Except that his family was of Portuguese descent, not French. This fact complicated all the reasoning.

Announcing that they would soon be landing at the International Airport in Brasília, the pilot's voice brought an end to his meandering thoughts. The bold architecture of Brasília, with the large lake, was already visible through his small window. He closed his eyes and awaited the landing. A few minutes later, the plane was already parked on the tarmac, waiting for the passengers who would be embarking for Rio de Janeiro. This time the plane would be full. The empty seats were being occupied, and a young blonde girl with an attractive figure sat down beside him.

"Reinaldo, don't you recognize me?" the girl asked.

Looking more attentively, he noted in her face something that was vaguely familiar, but he wasn't able to recall where he had met her.

"I was your brother Eduardo's girlfriend, remember?"

With this explanation, the past came back to him rapidly. "Of course. How could I have forgotten you?"

It was in 1983, he was seventeen and his brother Eduardo was twenty. Eduardo was attending the Catholic University in Rio de Janeiro, where he was in the fourth semester in the Law School. Josephine was his classmate and they had been going steady for six months. They both were the same age. Reinaldo also had a girlfriend, and the two couples went out together several times, in his brother's car.

"Did you get on the plane here in Brasília?"

"No, I'm coming from Manaus. Are you living here?"

"No, I came on business for the law firm where I'm working. I came to attend a trial in the Supreme Court involving one of our cases. We haven't seen each other for many years, have we?"

Jô's father was a diplomat and, in the beginning of 1984, had been assigned to the Brazilian Embassy in Rome. Then she broke up with Eduardo and had to interrupt her law course. There hadn't been any further contact after that.

"That's true, Jô. Can I still call you by your nickname?"

"Of course you can. And what about you? As I recall, your plans were to study engineering, right?"

"I changed my plans, Jô. Or better still, it was God who changed my plans. Isn't there that saying, man proposes and God disposes? As far as I knew, you ended up graduating in law."

"That's right, after two years in Italy, I returned to Rio and finished my law course. My former classmates had already graduated by then. I lost all contact with your brother. What's he doing?"

"After graduating, Eduardo took the civil service exam for Federal Police superintendent and he's working in Foz do Iguaçu."

"Is he married?"

"Yes and he has two kids."

"But you haven't told me what were God's plans, Reinaldo."

"He's my boss, Jô."

"What do you mean, your boss? Are you a priest?"

"Yes. I entered the seminary while you were in Italy."

He was already accustomed to the perplexed glances that people gave him on these occasions. The stewardess interrupted the conversation by serving a light snack. The flight time to Rio would be approximately two hours.

They ate in silence. After remaining silent for a few moments, Jô asked, "Is your parish located in the Amazon region?"

He didn't fail to note that Jô hadn't resorted to the usual platitude of asking why he had chosen to become a priest instead of an engineer. He admired her for this.

"In a certain way, yes, Jô. I'm an army chaplain, serving on the Colombian border, in São Gabriel da Cachoeira. I've been there for two years."

"Are you going to stay in Rio very long?"

"I'm going on leave, I should stay there for a month."

"I thought priests didn't take vacations. I'm sorry, I was only kidding."

"As a matter of fact, it's rare that we go on vacation, but it can happen."

They remained silent for some time, each one immersed in thought. When the stewardess came to offer some coffee, Jô broke the silence. "I have two invitations for a concert by the Brazilian Symphony Orchestra on Wednesday of next week. I guess you haven't been to the Municipal Theater for a long time, would you like to go?"

"That's true, the last time I went was when I was still attending the seminary. Yes, I'd like to, thanks for inviting me."

"Where are you going to stay in Rio?"

"In my mother's home, in Copacabana. I'll give you the phone number."

They each noted down the other's phone number. Jô was living in Ipanema, near Our Lady of Peace Square.

"I'm living alone. I've been divorced for two years and I didn't have any children. I've been devoting myself exclusively to my work. So I think it would be very good to recall the happy times of our youth."

Reinaldo thought that this really wasn't what he had come to Rio for, but it would be discourteous on his part to reject Jô's company.

Some time later, the pilot's voice was heard, announcing that they were arriving in Rio. In the pleasant cloudless night, he could contemplate his city's beauty, which he always used to admire every time his plane landed there. After picking up their bags, Reinaldo turned down Jô's invitation to share the same taxi en route to the south zone of the city. He explained that he preferred to go by bus, because then he could again enjoy at greater length the Rio scenery.

In a little more than an hour, he was arriving at his mother's apartment in Copacabana. Mrs. Sofia Cunha Mendes Tavares was in very good shape for her age of sixty-two and was quite happy over the arrival of her youngest son. After curing their nostalgia for each other, they sat down at the table to eat a pizza and chatted until one o'clock in the morning, when they went to bed. It was very good, sleeping in his old room. And Reinaldo then returned to his habitual tunnel and dreamed . . .

IN THE HOLY LAND

T he favorable winds that accompanied them on their passage to Cyprus gave way to a heavy rain which lashed them for three days. Living conditions on board were very precarious. The filth, the seasickness, the inhospitable conditions affected everyone's morale. On the afternoon of the fourth day they spied the coast of St. John of Acre, which displayed its distant imposing walls. The city was located on the extreme northern point of a large cove, from which the fortress of Haifa could be seen on the other extreme. Shortly before sunset on December 2, 1186, the Venetian galleon docked in the port. The Templars' fortress, surrounded by thick walls and moats, was in the southwestern zone of the city, which had a population of around 40,000 inhabitants of various nationalities: mostly French, in addition to Germans, Englishmen, Venetians, Pisans and Saracens. The climate there was mild and there were almost always very pleasant sea breezes.

The stone installations occupied a large area that extended from the sea to the walls. In the spacious halls, the knights were lodged in large dormitories. The local routine was subject to austere rules and strict schedules. The time was divided precisely between hours devoted to prayer and to seclusion, and periods of military training and patrols in the city. The religious rules were the same as those of the Benedictine or Cistercian monks. They awoke at four o'clock in the morning, said their morning prayers, took care of the horses and went back to sleep. Then they awoke again and recited the prime, terce and sexte before breakfast. At two thirty in the afternoon, they recited the nones. Meals were eaten in silence while one of the monks read from the Bible. After reciting the complines, the knights went to bed, remaining silent until the following day. Orders were customarily issued after each prayer session; this was followed by military training, done in groups that took turns in the instruction, and patrols in groups of two knights.

Jean had no difficulty in adapting to the Templars' austere system. In fact, there was little time left for thinking about himself, and in the rare moments in which this was possible, he took advantage of the opportunity to recall the happy moments with Melissande and little André. He only met Pierre in the morning, when taking care of the horses, and possibly during the military training and on patrol. João, his new friend, whenever possible conversed about the most varied topics. The devotion to the Order by the only Portuguese knight in Acre was admired by all. The truce with the Saracens continued to be observed by both sides, and up to then, the knights performed the role of monks more than that of warriors.

The celebration of Christmas was thrilling due to their proximity to the land of Jesus. Held in St. Paul's Church, Midnight Mass was celebrated with pomp and fervor by all the brothers of the Order. New Year's Eve was the occasion for a great party in the city, to celebrate the arrival of the year 1187.

It was during a morning at the end of January that the two knights at last had the opportunity for a comfortable chat, far from the rigors of the monastery, when they were taking their horses to be shod.

"João, you are so young, why have you not married and raised a family?"

"Since I was very young, I was prepared by my parents to follow an ecclesiastic career. I have two other brothers and a sister, all older than me. My sister married a knight from the court of the Duke of Almourol and today has two children. My oldest brother died defending our castle. The other brother was wounded, survived with the help of his squire, and was taken to the land of my uncle, who took care of him until he recovered. When I left Portugal, my brother was preparing to return to the struggle against the Moors. And I am here in accordance with my destiny; I intend to do whatever God decides."

They were returning along the tortuous streets of the city, after obtaining new horseshoes for their mounts, seeing with surprise the teeming trade in items from the Orient: spices, sugar, silks and jewelry, among other types of merchandise. The Latin Kingdoms had their own currency, the bezant, which circulated widely. On arriving at the fortress, they stopped for a few moments before the beautiful image of Virgin Mary sculptured in stone. There they prayed for their protection. The Templars were especially devoted to Our Lady and in all their buildings, there were images of the Virgin.

Right after the nones, they received orders from the Abbot, the commander of the fortress, Robert de Touville. In the morning of that day, two galleons of the Order had arrived, bringing two hundred pilgrims. They would be escorted by 15 knights and 32 squires and sergeants during their trip to Jerusalem. Jean and João had been assigned to the escort.

They set out the following day, after breakfast. The pilgrims went on foot. Four knights and eight squires formed the vanguard, flanked along each side by four knights and eight sergeants. In the rear guard, there were three knights and six sergeants. Eight donkeys carrying provisions and water, led by two sergeants on foot, went in front of the rear guard. An experienced knight named Albert Lagéry, with ten years overseas, was in command of the escort. Shortly before beginning the trip, Albert had called the knights to assign them their respective positions, telling them, "Brothers, we shall travel during the day and we shall only stop for a meal and a short rest, at midday. We shall spend the first night at the Saffran fortress, the second at *Le Petit Gerin* and the third in Nablus. These three fortresses belong to our holy Order and are garrisoned by templars. We should arrive in the Holy City, God willing, in the afternoon of the fourth day."

He paused, and looking firmly in the knights' eyes, continued, "We can be attacked starting on the second day by a group of renegade mamluks that hides in the caves near the Sea of Galilee. We have news that around 80 bandits frequently attack the Christians in that region. We must always be alert if any group approaches."

These words were followed by the order to begin the journey. The pilgrims made a lot of noise, some prayed; others conversed and laughed, overjoyed at the prospect of getting to know the holy places.

João and Jean were together on the right flank. Pierre had managed to join them, asking permission to exchange positions with an Italian sergeant. The day was hot and already during the first hours of the trip they began to feel thirsty and tired. They occasionally encountered Moslem travelers and their mules loaded with varied merchandise. They looked at them with curiosity, but without any hostility. For more than a century, Christians had been traversing the paths of the Orient, and they were no longer a novelty for the local inhabitants. At midday, with the sun well above their heads, they were able to reach a small woods, where they took shelter and had a meal. Jean, João and Pierre sat down in the shade of a tree to eat bread, cheese and a piece of lamb. They drank a little water and rested, until the order to resume the journey. A few hours later, they arrived at the small castle of Saffran, garrisoned by knights of the Order, where they spent the night.

Very early in the morning, they continued their trip. The landscape was always the same since they left the coast: semi-desert land, with few hills. The scorching heat was even worse for the members of the Order, with their heavy dress. It was a great relief when they reached the shore of the Sea of Galilee and halted under the shelter of the dense trees, which had existed there since the time when Our Lord Jesus Christ preached the word of God to his faithful followers. At that place, they had a meal and rested. Pierre seemed more animated than usual. "Sir, I must tell you, I found among the pilgrims a friend of my cousins who knows my uncles and was born in the same village that I come from. The village is near the city of Nantes. With your permission, I am going to seek him out in order to receive more news of my relatives who live in that region."

"Yes, Pierre, go and greet your friend on our behalf!"

João also smiled on seeing the squire's joy at meeting people from his region.

"It is a pity, but I did not know of anyone from Portugal among the pilgrims. Indeed, people ask why I did not stay there to fight the Moors that occupy a large part of our kingdom."

"Certainly, João, and why was that?"

"Entering the Order of the Knights Templar was the only way I could satisfy the wishes of my parents, who dreamt of an ecclesiastical career for me, and at the same time continue fighting against the Moslems. I did not do this in Portugal because the Master of the Order in my country was an enemy of my family."

They chatted a bit more, said their prayers and continued on their journey until the fortress of "Le Petit Gerin", where they spent the night. They departed the next day before dawn. The escort commander was worried and wanted to arrive in Nablus early. The stretch they would be covering that day was the most dangerous part of the trip. He called the knights together before their departure, and said, "Brothers, two groups of pilgrims that passed by here before us were attacked in this region. Most were killed before they could reach Nablus. We are going to be on the alert all the time. If we are attacked, all the knights, with the exception of the youngest and five sergeants, should close with the enemy and fight until victory or death. The knight who remains with the pilgrims shall guide them to Nablus. Two of the sergeants who are accompanying them are experienced and know the way to our fortress well. God help us!"

Jean was the youngest knight. Pierre remained with him and four more sergeants joined the group.

The sun was already high when they began to prepare for their meal and rest at the next stop. At that moment, the Saracens appeared suddenly, coming from a small hill not very far off. They were seventy men on horseback, armed with spears, curved swords—scimitars—, round shields, and some were carrying bows and arrows. Lagéry brought his men together and they galloped toward the Saracens. Jean shouted to the pilgrims, "Run as fast as you can and stay together."

He and his five subordinates seemed like shepherds leading their sheep. The comparison made him smile, despite the seriousness of the situation. He felt no fear. Since his misfortune, he had completely lost his appetite for life. He was calm and alert. On looking back, he saw the violent combat. The distance did not diminish the sound of the combatants' shouts, full of rage and pain, nor the confusing noise of the clashing swords. Little by little, the attackers' numerical superiority was beginning to prevail. The Templars were selling their lives dearly. In a short time, of the forty Christian fighters, only a group of eleven men were still fighting. The renegade chief gathered ten men together and went in pursuit of the pilgrims, who were running away with their small escort. He had left, however, thirty men to exterminate the knights and sergeants who were still resisting Jean shouted for them to run faster, and spied the enemy group which was approaching at a gallop. Then he recalled his squire's skill with the bow. Pierre had become famous in Anjou for his marksmanship. He was always the winner in the tournaments. He never failed to carry with him his bow and his famous arrows, made with special care and technique, wherever he went.

"Pierre, aim at the Saracen chief, and do not miss."

They were less than two hundred meters away, when the first arrow hit the enemy chief a little above his breastplate. The arrow went in at the neck level. The other Saracens pulled up their horses to help their chief. At that moment, a second arrow hit another man, this time in the face. It penetrated the Saracen's left eye. It was enough for all of them to wheel around and abandon the pursuit, returning with their wounded to the fight with the other Templars. At this time Jean had a bright idea. There was a group of ten young pilgrims, armed with wooden spears, willing to fight. Pierre's friend was among them. Jean shouted, "Sergeants, let's attack! You armed pilgrims, follow us and shout as loud as you can. Let's go!"

They set off at a gallop in pursuit of the group that had attacked them a few moments before. It all happened very fast. The Templars, who were fighting with their last remaining strength against a more numerous group of Saracens, on seeing their brothers from the Order coming to their assistance, took new heart and began to cut down the attackers. Jean and the sergeants reached the group of the wounded Saracen chief. Together, they were knocking down their opponents with deadly blows. At that moment, the group of pilgrims, running with the two sergeants who were taking care of the mules, began to shout loudly, intimidating the enemy, who fled, unsettled by their appearance. The Saracen chief, although wounded, was still fighting until then. He gave Jean a look full of hate, before turning his horse around and fleeing. The monk would never forget that face, so cruel and revengeful. The Templars and pilgrims shouted even more. But now their shouts were joyful, giving thanks to God for their victory. Lagéry, who was leading the small group that was still resisting, had been wounded twice but not seriously. He ordered Jean to call the rest of the pilgrims to help the wounded. Unfortunately, almost all those who were hit were dead. The final count wasn't very heartening. Of the 15 knights, ten were dead and one was seriously wounded. Of the sergeants and squires, 20 were dead and three were badly wounded. João was the seriously-wounded knight. He had an arrow in his right shoulder, a deep cut on his right arm and another one on his left thigh, which was bleeding copiously. They counted 41 dead Saracens. After treating the wounded and placing them on stretchers, Lagéry ordered them to bury the dead and pick up their weapons, leaving that place as fast as possible to avoid a second attack. They weren't able to go very far, due to their exhaustion. Then they stopped on the banks of a stream that was flowing into the Jordan River, where they rested and ate, and afterwards continued on their journey. Shortly before nightfall, they finally arrived in Nablus.

COPACABANA

R einaldo had awakened tired and sweating. He had the
vivid sensation of having taken part in the struggle
with the Saracens. He smiled and thought, "I must be
going completely crazy. The only thing lacking is for me to be
hit by an arrow during the dream!"

He looked at the clock; it was six in the morning. His habit
of awaking early still persisted. He woke up at the same time as
reveille in the barracks, despite his having gone to bed late the
night before. He arose, went to the bathroom, and put on a pair
of bermuda shorts that he had found in the dresser drawer. He
was surprised to see that they still fit him, which meant that he
hadn't put on hardly any weight in the last few years. He went
to the kitchen and discovered that his mother was still sleeping.
He decided to wait for her to have his breakfast. Leaning out
over the living room window, he noted that winter in Rio
seemed more like another phase of summer. The sun had already
risen, heralding a beautiful day. Memories of his childhood
returned with every passing moment. When his family moved
to Copacabana, he was six years old and Eduardo was nine. His
father had bought the apartment after many years of laboriously
saving money. Doctor Roberto Mendes Tavares, general
practitioner. He was a good family man, a good husband, loved
by his children. Very religious, he used to have long talks with

the boys, trying to explain to them the importance of spiritual life in the evolution of human nature.

Reinaldo's thoughts were interrupted by the presence of his mother, who gave him a good morning hug and kiss. While they were having their abundant breakfast, Reinaldo asked his mother about his cousin Luís, who was a psychiatrist. He told her everything that had happened, including the dream. She was very impressed. She urged him to seek out Luís, who was very competent, and would certainly help him to understand what had happened. She also commented that her son's decision to come to Rio in search of the answers had been the most correct one. They would phone Luís at his office and schedule a visit, after ten o'clock. Before that, they would walk together along the boardwalk.

An hour after their walk, now back at the apartment, they succeeded in phoning Luís and making an appointment for four o'clock that same afternoon. After an invigorating bath, he heard his mother call him, "Reinaldo, I'm going to take you to lunch at the restaurant on the corner facing the beach. You're going to eat some delicious fish."

"Yes, that's all I do in the Amazon region. We eat fish almost every day."

"Fresh water fish isn't the same thing . . . But no problem, I know you love shrimp and you're not going to have any reason to complain, you'll see."

Sitting at a table with a view of the beach, with Leme District to the left and Fort Copacabana to the right, they savored a tasty dish of shrimp and rice, accompanied by Chilean white wine. After escorting his mother to the door of her building, he walked along Avenida Atlântica until the corner of Miguel Lemos Street, where his cousin's office was located.

He arrived shortly before four. The building was an old one, probably dating back to the beginning of the nineteen fifties. The old-fashioned elevator with the sliding gate door took him up to the floor of his cousin's office, where he was received by a young receptionist. He sat down in a comfortable armchair in the waiting room and browsed through an old weekly magazine, while he waited. After twenty minutes had passed, Luís himself came to the door and called him. "Reinaldo, it's been such a long time!"

They conversed rapidly and recalled the happy times when they were youngsters on the beach in Copacabana. After a short pause, Luís asked, "What's happened to you? Tell me everything from the beginning."

Reinaldo then told his cousin everything that had happened since he had entered the army. When he reached the part of the combat on the border, he tried to furnish more details, and when he was describing his dreams, he noted that Luís had become more attentive.

"Have you ever heard about regression to previous lives?", Luís asked.

"I've read something about this, but I confess I didn't understand it very well."

"Well, therapy involving regression to previous lives can cure physical pain, relationship conflicts and depression due to the loss of dear ones, in addition to changing people's attitude with regard to death. It's not limited to the knowledge of previous lives, but allows people to pass through mystical and spiritual experiences. I want you to know that I'm not a specialist in this type of therapy, but I normally utilize hypnosis techniques with my patients. It's through hypnosis, applied by the therapist or even self-induced, that we can many times regress to the past and, possibly, to lives that we lived in other periods." At this point Reinaldo signaled to his cousin that he wanted to say something. "I'm sorry, Luís, but I can't help mentioning that my religion doesn't accept reincarnation. I can't accept that I was dreaming about my life as a Knight Templar in the Middle Ages."

"Take it easy, cousin, there are other explanations for this phenomenon. You could be also visiting the past and meeting a loved one, in this case, one of our ancestors!"

"But in France? I'm not aware that we had any French ancestors . . . In any case, João de Tovar is in my dreams. Who knows, could he be our ancestor?"

"All indications are that the message your dreams will bring you isn't finished yet. Let's wait and see where they'll lead us. Then, I believe, we'll have the answer to our questions, and you'll know which path to follow."

Reinaldo realized that his visit was over. His mother had commented that Luís wouldn't charge his cousin anything. Thus, they said good-bye and scheduled another visit for the end of the following week.

He returned on foot following the same route as before. The late afternoon was very clear and beautiful, displaying an absolutely cloudless sky. The blue of the sea mingled on the horizon with the blue of the sky.

Along the boardwalk, he had sat down on a stone bench near República do Peru Street. All alone, he was contemplating the sea, pensive, recalling all the fun he had had on the beach in the old days. On arising to continue on his walk, he spied a familiar face. It was Captain Souza e Silva, his father's faithful old friend. It was a friendship which had lasted since the time they had been students at the Pedro II High School. At first, the Captain hadn't recognized him.

"How are you, Captain, don't you remember me?"

The older man gazed at him, but without any sign of recognition.

"I'm Doctor Roberto's son, my name's Reinaldo."

The old seaman's face lit up with joy. He rose nimbly and embraced the young man warmly. "Reinaldo, it's been such a long time! How are you? I learned from your mother that you entered the army and were in the Amazon region. And what are you doing here?"

"That's right, Captain, I'm on leave."

Reinaldo told him, summarizing, about his entry into the army, about his religious and community activities on the border, but he left out the most recent events that had been upsetting his life. The Captain listened attentively to everything, without interrupting. At the end, he said, "I suppose your father, wherever he may be, must be very proud of you, my son. First of all, because you're preaching the word of Christ, since he was a very religious man. Secondly, because you're in the Brazilian Army, one of the last bastions of our nationality. Despite the crisis of credibility in our institutions that our country is experiencing, our military personnel still deserve credit with the Brazilian people. I'm certain you'll always honor your father's memory and will be in the front line of defense of our Christian, Brazilian values. Congratulations, my son, God be with you."

After embracing again his father's old companion, Reinaldo continued on his way and arrived home rapidly. On top of the table, right at the apartment entrance, he found the note from his mother. "Son, I've gone to the theater with a friend. I left a snack all ready in the pantry." It was already night. Reinaldo took a bath, watched the news on television and ate, with relish, the excellent snack prepared by his mother. The telephone rang, it was his brother Eduardo. They chatted for a while, but he didn't mention anything about his problems. They said good-bye, promising to spend Christmas together with their mother, which hadn't been the case for many years. After contemplating the sea for half an hour, Reinaldo went to bed. He prayed, relaxed his body and mind, and immediately encountered the light that opened the doors to that far-off mysterious place . . .

JERUSALEM

The sight of the fortress of Nablus and its high walls was a great relief for the group of Knights Templar and the pilgrims, already very tired. Sunset was nearing and all of them hurried to cross the drawbridge over the deep moat that encircled the castle. Lagéry made arrangements with the Knight Abbot for lodging, food and care for the wounded. At night, they all prayed fervently in the large chapel of the fortress, giving thanks to God for their victory, for their lives and for the souls of their companions who had died. Jean and Pierre went to say good-bye to João. "Dear friend, tomorrow we shall continue on to Jerusalem. We shall say many prayers for your recovery in the holy places that we shall visit. I am certain that you will recover and will be able, in the near future, to visit the holy city and pray in the Holy Sepulcher."

In a very weak voice, João could only murmur his thanks and wish his friends a safe journey.

The next day, leaving the wounded behind, they continued their trip. Ten sergeants from the Nablus garrison joined them to reinforce the escort. Jean and Pierre set out worried about João's condition. His wounds had stopped bleeding but he was very weak and feverish. The trip to Jerusalem was uneventful, without any incidents. At nightfall they sighted the walls of the Holy City. There was much excitement. Many pilgrims fell to their knees, crying and praying very contritely. Jean was impressed by the imposing walls. Destroyed by Tito, the Roman general, during the Diaspora in the year 70 AD, they had been rebuilt during the reign of the Emperor Hadrian, also during the period of Roman domination, and later strengthened by the Fatimid rulers of the Cairo Caliphate. The column of pilgrims and their escort entered the city through St. Stephen's Gate, and followed the narrow streets of the Syrian quarter. To the right was the Patriarch district, where the Church of the Holy Sepulcher and the headquarters of the Order of the Knights of St. John of Jerusalem were located. Further ahead, they turned to the left and continued on to the Splendid Gate, arriving at the ancient Temple of Solomon, now the headquarters of the Order of the Knights Templar. Before the capture of the city by the First Crusade, on July 14, 1099, the site of the Temple was occupied by the Al-Aqsa Mosque. The monks began to use the installations for lodging, and storage of weapons, clothing and food. On the ground floor of the building, immense stables were built, capable of sheltering thousands of horses. It is estimated that around 300 knights and 1,000 sergeants lived in the complex. There were also the turcopole templars, who were sergeants of Syrian origin, hired by the Order. The Temple also possessed a large number of staff members, such as grooms, blacksmiths, stone masons and others of various professions.

Exhausted from the journey, the pilgrims and their guardians had their evening meal, said their prayers and went to sleep in the enormous lodgings which existed in the Temple. The next morning, after their ritual obligations and breakfast, they were free to visit the holy places with the pilgrims. Initially they visited, on the southeastern side of the Temple, St. Simeon's house, where Virgin Mary's bed and the cradle and bathtub of the infant Jesus were located. Then they went on to Josaphat's Gate. A church was built in its vicinity where the home of Our Lady's parents, Joaquin and Anna, had been located. After that, they prayed in the Church of the Holy Sepulcher, which Saint Helen, the mother of Constantine, the first Roman emperor to be converted to Christianity, had built. Now tired, they returned to the Temple shortly before 6 p.m.

The next day, following the same routine, they left the city and arrived at the house of Zachariah, the birthplace of John the Baptist; they went to Mary's well and then headed for Bethlehem, where Jesus was born. The Church of the Nativity, also built at the request of Saint Helen, had been completely renovated by the Knights Templar. The pilgrims and their protectors went inside to pray, guided by a Cistercian monk. The image of the Virgin with the infant Jesus on Her lap made a great emotional impact on Jean. The suffering caused by the memory of his loved ones made him avoid thinking about the past. Every day he prayed fervently for the souls of his wife and son, before turning his attention to the Order's work and rituals. At that moment, however, the past came back abruptly to his thoughts. Then he recalled the first time they had met.

Melissande was the youngest daughter of the Marquis de Challons, whose lands neighbored those of his father. Relations between the two noblemen were the best possible. They always used to go together to the wars waged by the Duke of Anjou, of whom they were vassals. On a spring morning, when he was riding close to the lake which divided the two fiefs, he saw Melissande for the first time. She was running along the lake shore, with her long blonde braids tossed by the wind and a florid face. The surrounding field was a mantle of the most varied types of flowers, and the sun was lighting up the blue water of the lake. She was the prettiest girl that Jean had ever seen. At the age of eighteen, which she had reached two weeks before, she had already read all the classic Latin works in her father's valuable library. Her skin was very white and her eyes were deep green, going well with her angelic face. Horseback riding, one of her greatest pleasures, contributed to the graceful harmonious shape of her body. The girl was playing with her little dog and was accompanied by an elderly lady, her kind old nursemaid, Irene. Jean went closer, dismounted, left his horse grazing and walked toward the lake. His arrival went unnoticed by the ladies because the trees that lined the road blocked the view of anyone going along the lake shores. When he arrived nearer them, he saw the girl, who was still running along with the little dog, trip and fall down. He ran, knelt down and took her in his arms. Melissande, besides the fright caused by her fall, was surprised at the young man's sudden appearance. "Who are you?"

The dog barked continuously and tried to bite Jean, who didn't know whether to answer the question or flee from the brave little animal. The old nursemaid came to his assistance and held the dog. "I'm Jean, your neighbor, the son of the Marquis de Mont-Rémy."

She looked at him, intrigued. "But I know the son of the Marquis, his name is Gilbert."

"He's my younger brother."

"And why have I not met you before?"

"I have been in the court of the Duke of Anjou for some years, I'm one of his squires. I should be knighted next month, during the Spring Tournament."

They continued conversing, happily, enchanted with that chance encounter.

The nursemaid, who was watching them from the other side, cleared her throat loudly, calling the youths' attention to the fact that they were almost embracing each other, lying relaxed on the grass. They got up quickly, laughing at Irene's scandalized look.

Jean felt his heart pounding. His eyes seemed hypnotized by the girl's beauty. He could hardly speak or put his thoughts in order, until finally he stammered, "And what are you doing here?"

Melissande was looking admiringly at the young man with black hair and black eyes, tall and strong. She was feeling a sudden unavoidable attraction. "I'm Melissande, the daughter of the Marquis de Challons."

The little dog continued to bark, now jealous of its mistress, who was not paying any attention to it any more.

"Then your brother Robert is my companion at the court. He will also be knighted and will take part in the tournament. Will you be present?"

"Yes! My family will be there."

"Would you accept being my patroness?" Jean had already invited his sister, but he thought he would not have any problem with the sudden change of plans.

"Your unexpected invitation surprises me. After all, we have just met, have we not?"

He did not expect this reaction, which made him blush rapidly. Melissande could not resist smiling at the young man. "I am joking. I shall be honored to be your patroness in the tournament",

It was Jean's turn to show his happiness with a radiant smile. At this moment, Irene, who had the little dog on her lap, said, "Mistress, we need to return now."

The two youths looked at the nursemaid in such a way that she thought she had uttered a blasphemy. Jean came forward and took the girl's hand, kissing it with great emotion. "See you soon, Miss, I shall be anxiously counting the hours until I see you again."

Tears rolled down the knight's face on recalling the moment in which the beautiful young girl, who would later become his wife, responded to his gesture with a charming smile.

THE WARNING FROM
THE NORTH

Suddenly, it was as if he had dived into a deep dark crater. He was falling, but shortly afterward he seemed to be flying. Then he heard music, instead of a voice. He awoke abruptly when someone seemed to be calling him far away. It was his mother's voice. "I'm sorry, son, but I couldn't resist the desire to talk to you. I went to see a very good play and I'm feeling so good. I don't always have one of my sons here at home to talk to. Did I interrupt one of your fantastic dreams?"

Reinaldo couldn't help smiling at his mother's happiness. "To tell the truth, mother, yes, and by the way, it was one of the most beautiful dreams."

He told her in detail about the dream she had just interrupted. He had already told his mother about the visit to his cousin Luís and that, in the latter's opinion, it could be a case of regression to a previous life, in which some important event would influence his present behavior. She listened to it all very attentively, and remarked, "The first meeting of Jean and Melissande was so beautiful! It's like I was watching a movie. But what do you think of that hypothesis of regression?"

Reinaldo looked pensively at his mother, and after a few moments, replied, "Mother, you know very well that I've always had an open mind. I can accept new things that change my habits or established beliefs. However, reincarnation is a theory which isn't accepted by my religion and was already considered to be a heresy. I have to respect the rules of my church that I vowed to obey and carry out as long as I'm a priest."

His mother sighed, remained silent for a little while, and decided to change the subject. She began to tell about the pleasant evening she had spent in the company of her friends and commented, "Dear, we had a snack after the theater and I'm not hungry. But if you like, I can prepare a quick meal and bring it here for you to eat in bed."

Reinaldo smiled and shook his head.

She kissed her son, turned off the light and left the room. Reinaldo went back to sleep, but he didn't dream about the distant past. He had nightmares all night long, with scenes of combat in the jungle, in which he was shooting and killing several soldiers of an undefined enemy.

It was good to wake up late and be on vacation! It was already eight o'clock when his mother entered with his breakfast arranged on a tray.

His mother laughed at her son's appearance. "Did you sleep well? Did you dream about Melissande and Jean?"

"No, I only had nightmares last night, I dreamt about war all the time."

"What a pity! But now eat your breakfast and enjoy yourself."

A few minutes later, he was already preparing to take a walk along the boardwalk when his mother called him to answer the telephone.

"Chaplain? This is Colonel Peçanha. Reinaldo, how's your vacation?"

"Colonel, I'm having a good rest."

"Great! Look, Reinaldo, I've two important things to tell you. The first one is regarding the final report on the combat with the FARC guerrillas. The report made by Lieutenant Alves, who fortunately has almost recovered from his wound, shows that your intervention saved his life. One of the guerrillas that you shot was ready to shoot the lieutenant who, despite being wounded, was standing up, firing on the invaders. I added this fact to the recommendation for a medal that I forwarded to headquarters in Manáus. The second thing is with regard to a report I received from the intelligence people. One of the dead guerrillas was a Brazilian, the brother of one of the biggest drug dealers in Rio, named Serginho do Cirado. Since the case drew many comments in the media, including the mention of your participation in the combat and your trip to Rio, I want to warn you to be careful and avoid going out at night. We never know what those guys can be up to. Do you understand?"

After saying good-bye, Reinaldo remained for some time with the receiver in his hand, reflecting on the Colonel's words. Lieutenant Alves had reported to the Battalion, coming from the School for Jungle War, a little more than two months ago. He was born in the interior of São Paulo State, was married and lived in the officers' quarters, in São Gabriel da Cachoeira. He had conversed with him twice and was accustomed to seeing him with his wife at Sunday mass. He was a cheerful young man, very pleasant and well regarded by the troops. "Fortunately, he's recovering from his wound," he thought. And he put the telephone back on the table.

His mother had already left to take her walk. She had advised her son to go earlier, in order to avoid the hot sun from ten o'clock on. Reinaldo, who was already wearing his shorts,

T-shirt, sneakers and cap, then went for his walk. He left the building and walked to the sidewalk on Avenida Atlântica, stopping at the traffic light to cross the street. For a winter Friday, the weather was very pleasant. It was the famous Rio de Janeiro Indian summer, with a beautiful sunny day, crowds on the beach and a legion of elderly athletes on the boardwalk, which was characteristic of the Copacabana district. First he walked to the left, toward the Leme district. He took advantage of the opportunity to think back over all the recent events in his life. He thought it was funny, noting how his days used to follow a predictable routine and were monotonous. Now everything had changed suddenly. He laughed, thinking about the sermons he had preached on the strange designs of the Lord.

He arrived at the rock at the end of Leme and turned about face, now walking toward Lifeguard Station Six, at the other end of the beach, where Fort Copacabana was located. On passing by the corner of Siqueira Campos Street, he remembered the Copacabana Parish Church, which was a little further ahead. Two of his colleagues in the seminary were priests at that church. He'd certainly find them at the 6 p.m. mass. So he decided to surprise them, going to the church at that time. Who knows, maybe he could join them in celebrating mass together. He'd arrive at five thirty, in time to prepare himself. He turned around at the entrance to the Fort and returned to his starting point on the corner. "That's funny," he thought, "I didn't meet my mom." She must have stopped to chat with friends and decided to drink coconut water at one of the kiosks along the boardwalk. He took a cold shower, got dressed and waited for his mother to have lunch together.

After a light lunch and much conversation in a small restaurant, with delicious food sold by the kilogram, they

said good-bye. His mother had some matters to look after . . .
Reinaldo walked down Avenida Nossa Senhora de Copacabana,
He looked at the shop windows and observed the passers-by
with their accelerated pace. It was three o'clock when he passed
in front of the Roxy movie theater, a familiar place in the past,
since he had always been attracted to movies. He was just in
time to attend the three-to-five showing before going on to the
church. And that was what he did. He chose one of the movies
being shown in the three projection rooms and went inside.

It was an action movie, one of those that the American
film industry produces in abundance and are quickly forgotten.
Walking rapidly, he managed to arrive half an hour before mass
and to meet his former colleagues from the seminary, Father
Sílvio and Father Demétrio, who greeted him affectionately. It
was easy to find vestments in his size in the vestry and to jointly
celebrate the six o'clock mass, in the church completely filled
by the faithful. After mass, Reinaldo was invited for supper,
served in the large parochial hall, where they would attend a talk
given by a monk from the São Bento Monastery. The monk was
well-known to the priests, since for many years he had been a
teacher of Greek Philosophy at the seminary.

Seated between his two friends, Reinaldo savored his
supper while he tried to answer all their questions. They wanted
to know about the life of an army chaplain and why he had
chosen that career. They chatted until the time came for silence
requested for the talk by Brother Rodolfo, the monk. First,
the vicar of the Copacabana Parish welcomed the visitor, also
mentioning Reinaldo's presence. All told, there were twenty-five
religious figures present, including some monks that were
accompanying Brother Rodolfo.

For about thirty minutes, the latter discoursed on the eternal struggle between Good and Evil. He commented on the work of the Greek philosopher Aristotle, more specifically on his book *Ethics*, in which he deduced that most men are born with the natural tendency to do good, while some choose the path of "moral deficiency", that is, the path of Evil. The very history of the human race and its search for perfection in the relations between individuals and nations has been the battlefield for the struggle between Good and Evil. He showed the importance of the Church and its components in this endless struggle and called for all to unite zealously in this holy crusade. On hearing the word "crusade", the chaplain couldn't help smiling, recalling his dreams. After conclusion of the talk and the usual formalities of gratitude and congratulations, everyone could rise and converse informally.

At a certain moment, the monk came toward Reinaldo and said, "How are you, my son? We haven't seen each other for such a long time."

The priest was impressed by the memory of his former teacher. "Do you still remember me?"

"Of course, Reinaldo. But before that, I had help from the vicar, who told me of your presence and mentioned your name. That way it was easier, wasn't it?"

They all laughed and began to recall episodes which had happened with each one of them, during their time in the seminary. While they were talking, the chaplain had a sudden inspiration and decided to ask the question which was intriguing him so much. "*Mestre,* may I ask you a question about a matter which has been intriguing me?"

"Of course, Reinaldo, if I can answer it . . ."

"Do you think that it's heresy for a priest to believe in regression to previous lives, that is, in the existence of reincarnation?"

Brother Rodolfo thought for a while before answering. "Look, my son, many priests, holier than us, have already believed in reincarnation."

Reinaldo looked at the monk in amazement. "How do you mean?"

"During the Second Council of Constantinople, held in 553 AD, the concept of reincarnation was declared to be a heresy. It has been commented that the Emperor Constantine and his mother, Saint Helen, believed that the future of the Church would be threatened if men had too much time, during their lives, to seek salvation of their souls. Before this, they believed in reincarnation in a quite natural way. There were references to it in the Old and the New Testaments, and Christians accepted the idea. There are reports that the ancient Gnostics, Clement of Alexandria, Origen, Saint Jerome and various others commented on their previous lives and believed in future lives. In this way, Reinaldo, until a new proposal appears for belief in other lives, to be presented to our Holy Father in a future Council, we have available only the present one."

They all laughed, except the chaplain, who remained pensive. So the ancient Church accepted reincarnation. He had been swept up in a whirlwind of emotions. And if in the past he had been Jean? He tried to return to the conversation, for they were all looking curiously at his face. After some time and a cheerful exchange of ideas, the monk began to say good-bye individually to each one present, before returning to his beautiful monastery, on Mauá Plaza Hill. When it was Reinaldo's turn, he looked fixedly in his eyes and said, "If you believe in it, my son, go ahead and fight for your ideas. These days our Church is more open to changes, as long as they're coherent, sensible and authentic."

Reinaldo embraced his old teacher affectionately and said good-bye.

After another half hour of conversation, he thanked the vicar and went home, walking. His mother was waiting for him, seated in her favorite armchair, watching the evening news on television. She turned off the TV with the remote control, rose, hugged and kissed her son. "The news is always the same thing. Wars, economic crises, violence, breaking down of good behavior, etc., etc. But as long as I can remember, it's always been that way. I think its characteristic of human nature. Love, raising a family, building civilizations and progress in human relations are also characteristic of human nature but let's concentrate on what's important. I've prepared a nice little snack for us. Come to the pantry and I'll serve it to you."

The young man accompanied his mother in silence. It would be his second snack that night. He'd just have to put up with it, he wouldn't want to spoil his mother's happiness. He'd eat everything as though he were starving. The supper, it would be better to call it this, was excellent. It's enough to say that it was washed down with French wine, a very delicious Bordeaux. He told her about the mass and his conversation with the monk. "Can you imagine, mom, that I could have been Jean, and that I'm recalling now everything that happened to me in that life?"

She began to laugh at his expression of amazement. "Son, I'm astonished to see that after all these years, you haven't given up the habit of drinking wine from your former country!"

"That's right, after that one I guess we better go to bed, because that wine is going to your head faster than to mine."

They laughed a lot, tidied up the kitchen, said good night and went to sleep.

This time, possibly because of the wine, Reinaldo traveled more rapidly back to the past . . .

SALADIN

Jean emerged from his fond memories on hearing Pierre's call, "Sir, the pilgrims are ready to leave, it's time to return to the Temple."

The afternoon was drawing to a close. They all returned cheerfully to Jerusalem, where they arrived at nightfall. They ate a sumptuous meal in the enormous hall reserved for the pilgrims. Then they prayed, accompanied by the knights, sergeants and squires of the escort and retired to spend another night in the holy city.

A month later, the pilgrims decided to leave. Four of them decided to remain in Jerusalem, performing services in the Temple. Pierre's friend Gaston was among those that remained. With his friend's help he was accepted as a sergeant, and on his return to Acre, would take his vows.

Everything was prepared for the pilgrims' departure on Palm Sunday, after mass. The escort had been restructured with reinforcements coming from St. John of Acre. The number of its components was the same as on the previous journey, except for the missing knight João de Tovar, who, having recovered from his wounds, would join the group in Nablus. Lagéry left Jerusalem in the opposite direction from the one Jesus had followed many centuries earlier. There were no incidents during the journey to Nablus, where they arrived shortly after nightfall.

João was waiting for them at the entrance to the fortress. The two friends had a warm reencounter.

After being dismissed by Lagéry, they led their horses to the stables and then went to their lodgings to bathe. They met later in the mess hall, where they had supper and said their evening prayers. João called his friends and led them to a small room, near the storehouse, and said, "I need to tell you some things that I discovered that may affect our life here overseas. I have talked at length with the Abbot Commander of Nablus. He is Spanish, but his mother is Portuguese, which established a bond between us. She is still alive and is from the region where I was born. Her family possibly had ties of friendship with my family. Hernando, that is his name, has been here for almost six years, having arrived in 1181. The Grand Master of the Temple, at that time, was also a Spaniard, Arnoldo de Torroja, and Hernando came to Acre with a group of Spanish knights, at Arnoldo's request. Later, in 1184, Arnoldo died in Verona, and was succeeded by Gérard de Ridefort, the current Grand Master, a knight of Flemish origin."

Jean made a gesture with his hand for his friend to stop talking. "Wait, João, I brought you a present from Jerusalem. It was given to me by a French knight who came in a pilgrimage to fulfill a vow. I told him about your bravery in the fight near Nablus and he asked me to deliver this to you. He had been saving it for this special occasion."

Having said this, Jean took out from inside his mantle a sheepskin jug containing an excellent red wine.

João first poured himself some of the delicious French wine, and was followed by the two friends. Jean then said, "João, please continue your account."

"Young King Baldwin V, seven years of age, died a few months ago. His mother, Sybil, married a nobleman named Guido de Lusignan, who thus was crowned King of Jerusalem. Well then, I found out that the most powerful man in the Latin Kingdom is not King Guido. Power is concentrated in the hands of Reinaldo de Châtillon, a French knight, the son of the Count of Gien-sur-Loire, who came overseas in the crusade led by King Louis VII. A year after his arrival, Hernando was called upon to join the forces that Reinaldo de Châtillon had brought together, planning an attack against the Saracens. This would have very serious repercussions."

João paused to drink a little more wine and then continued, "Reinaldo had galleons built which were taken to the Gulf of Aqaba. There forces consisting of French knights, Knights Templar and a heterogeneous group of Latin soldiers embarked. They sailed southward, toward the Red Sea, attacking the ports along the coasts of Egypt and Arabia. The galleons also attacked the Saracen merchant ships which were sailing through that region. These forces arrived at the port of ar-Raghib, from where they set out, by land, to attack Mecca. Reinaldo intended to bring back the body of the Prophet Mohammed."

This time it was Pierre who interrupted, making a signal for João to stop. "Until today I have not been able to understand who the king of the Saracens is. Some time ago, in France, they commented that it was Nur ed-Din, but here I heard that there are three kings."

From his companions' look, João realized that they knew little or nothing at all of the Saracens' power structure. He explained, "Well, before conversing with Brother Hernando, I too was ignorant of the matter. It is true that there are three, but they are not kings. They are Caliphs, which is the title they adopt. The Caliphates' names come from the names of the families of their founders: the Abbasids in Baghdad, the Fatimids in Damascus and Cairo, and the Ommiads, in Cordoba, Spain. Another thing: Nur ed-Din died, and he was succeeded as Caliph of Damascus and Cairo by Salad ed-Din, or Saladin, the nephew of Nur ed-Din's leading general. In fact, Saladin is the most powerful Caliph and has proclaimed himself as the guardian of the holy places of Islam. As you know, Mecca is the most sacred city in their religion. Saladin is very powerful and beloved by his people, a great warrior and excellent ruler. Continuing Hernando's story, the Latin knights' forces were heading toward Mecca when, on the third day of their journey, they were intercepted by numerically superior Saracen troops that had been sent from Cairo by Malik, Saladin's brother. Surrounded and about to be annihilated, a small group, in which Hernando took part, succeeded in breaking out of the encirclement and fled to the coast, where they took ship to return to Aqaba. The survivors of the combat, who had been made prisoners, were taken to Mecca and executed there."

Pierre looked at the friends and commented, "What an insult to Saladin! I suppose they must be thirsty for vengeance."

"As you can see, the end of the truce must be near and great battles should be taking place soon. According to Hernando, if the Latin army has to face the Saracen forces from Damascus and Cairo together, it will be outnumbered, both with respect to knights as well as to foot soldiers."

Jean recalled that there was a truce between the Christians and the Saracens. "João, but are we not in a truce?"

"After the attack on Mecca, I believe it is very unlikely that the truce will be maintained. In fact, the action was an act of war by the Latins. And even more so since the initiative was taken by Reinaldo de Châtillon, who among all the noblemen, had the most influence with King Guido. Therefore, my friends, we must be prepared for days of much fighting and suffering, since according to Hernando, we are not likely to receive reinforcements from the Christian realms."

They fell silent for a few moments. Finally, Jean sighed and said, "Well, brothers, we entered the Order with the mission of fighting and dying for Christ. If that be His will, we shall humbly fulfill our mission, which is to defend the holy places."

Pierre's affirmative reply was accompanied also by João.

Jean rose. The other two accompanied him. "Let us go to the chapel and recite the complines and then go to bed, since tomorrow we shall set out on our return trip to Acre."

Then they headed for the chapel, where the other monks were gathered for the last prayers of the day.

The following morning, the column of pilgrims began their journey through the same region where they had been attacked previously. This time, however, they were accompanied by a force of twenty English knights who were returning from a pilgrimage to Jerusalem and had agreed to travel together with them to *Le Petit Gerin*. From that point, they would head toward the coast, where their ship was docked in the port of Haifa. Jean was riding with his gaze alert for any strange movement when he heard someone call him with an English accent. It was one of the English knights who was approaching, asking "Jean, how are you? Do you not remember me?"

He immediately recalled the time he was a squire at the court of the Duke d'Anjou. "Certainly, Thomas. How could I ever forget those training sessions with swords, lances and battle axes, which lasted all day?"

Thomas was the son of the Marquis of Norwich, who in addition to his English properties, possessed a castle in the Anjou region and, in that way, was a vassal of the Duke. "I see you are wearing the Knight Templar insignia. What happened? Our last meeting was on the occasion of your wedding with Melissande, it must be more than eight years ago."

Jean told his companion everything that had happened during those years and that he was seeking in religious work a little solace for his pain. After some words of condolence, the English knight moved away, visibly saddened by the bad news.

Jean began to think once more about Melissande and recalled their second meeting. It was in the Cathedral of Orléans, two days before the opening of the Spring Tournament. The knighting ceremony was held annually, always two days before the tournament. This was done to make it possible for the new knights to participate in the jousts and fights. The knights took their vows during the holy mass, in the presence of the Duke, who presided over the knighthood ritual. Numerous members of the knights' families were also present, and with the participants in the tournament, completely filled the large church. After the purification, confession and communion ceremony, the title of knight was bestowed on behalf of the Holy Trinity. The fifteen squires who were going to take their vows as knights entered through the central nave of the cathedral in three lines of five men each, wearing their coats of mail, white mantles with their families' coats of arms, leather belts with battle swords and their helmets, held in their left arms. They took their position on the right side of the main altar, where the Bishop of Orléans would celebrate mass. On glancing to the left, Jean spied Melissande in the third row. She was beautiful, in her pink brocade dress lined with squirrel skin, and her white cloak of Bruges cloth, fastened at the shoulders with a ruby clasp. Her blond hair arranged in an elaborate hairdo made her look less youthful than her actual age of eighteen. They exchanged glances. He smiled at the girl, who nodded her head slightly and reacted to his gesture with an unforgettable smile. Duke Robert d'Anjou, dressed splendidly, was seated on the left side of the altar, alongside Duchess Marguerite. Soon afterwards, the Bishop and his entourage, pompously clothed in their vestments, emerged from behind the altar, on the right, to begin the ceremony. After communion, the squires were called one at a time by the herald to take their oath of knighthood. Then they kneeled in front of the Duke, who touched each one's shoulder with his sword and declared them knighted. Jean felt his heart skip a beat when his turn came, and feeling strong emotions, looked at his parents, who were near Melissande. Finally, he fixed his gaze on the latter, now certain that she would be his eternally beloved companion. His father, Marquis Guy de Saumur, came up and placed golden spurs on him. Then Jean made his vow: "I promise to believe in the teachings of the Church and respect its commandments. I promise to protect it from all dangers. I shall respect the weak and shall be their defender. I shall love the country where I was born. I shall not retreat in the face of the enemy. I shall fight against heretics without respite and without mercy. I shall fulfill loyally my knightly duties. I shall not lie and shall be true to my word. I shall be friendly and generous to my companions. I shall be forever a champion of Justice and of Good against Injustice and Evil."

After saying these words, he knelt down. Duke Robert then touched him on the right shoulder with his sword, saying, "On behalf of God, Saint Michael and Saint George, I declare you a knight!"

The knight arose and returned to his place in the group. At the end of the ceremony, everybody went to the archbishop's hall, in the rear of the cathedral, where an exquisite meal awaited them. The early spring weather was still cold, but the sun was shining in the blue cloudless sky. The master of ceremony directed Duke Robert's guests to their tables, already occupied by the families of the newly-anointed knights. At Jean's table his parents and relatives were seated, as well as the family of Melissande, whose brother Robert had also been knighted along with Jean. At the main table of the Duke and Duchess, the Bishop, the representative of King Louis VII and various noblemen who were vassals of Anjou were seated. Announced by the heralds, the Duke d'Anjou entered. The Bishop blessed the guests. Finally, at the Duke's order, dinner was served. First, servants appeared and headed for the tables with basins of warm water for everyone to wash their hands. Then, as if in a parade, the dishes of game were presented: pheasants decorated with beautiful plumage, roast kid dressed with sauces, wild boars roasted whole, redolent with spices. Then came the poultry dishes—ducks, chickens and quail—and fish dishes—salmon, trout and carp. The banquet closed with desserts: creams, sweets and fruit. Various types of wine were served uninterruptedly. The hall was transformed into a cheerful environment. At the end of the festivity, the Duke rose, greeted the new knights, thanked all the guests for their attendance, and left with his wife, closing the event. The young sweethearts, seated on opposite sides of the table, were unable to talk to each other, but exchanged passionate glances during the entire meal. The two marchionesses quickly perceived what was happening with the two young people. They tried to call their husbands' attention to this fact, which brought on laughter and jests at the table. Jean and Melissande ate little of the marvelous dishes which were served. They anxiously awaited the end of the feast so that they could finally approach each other. As soon as the guests rose to depart, the two young people met. Jean was the first to speak, "Miss, since our encounter at the lake, I have not thought about anything but you."

Melissande looked at him affectionately, pleased by his demonstration of love. "I have also thought much about you" "The day after tomorrow, in the tournament, you shall be my patroness and I shall display all my courage in your honor."

"I only ask the Holy Virgin to safeguard you from any wounds."

Her worried look made the young man smile with pleasure. "Do not fear for me but rather for the knights that oppose me."

They said good-bye soon after, with the arrival of the carriages that would take them to their rooms in the palaces of Orléans, where they were lodged.

Jean came out of his memory trance on hearing Lagéry's command for the escort to stop and dismount, for a rest and a meal. They had arrived at a well close to a small wood where they could provide themselves with water and eat. Pierre helped João to dismount, since he noticed that his friend was still weak from the wounds he had suffered in the battle. In a moment of greater reticence, Pierre went up to Jean and asked, "What is the matter with you, sir? Your face is so sad."

"It is nothing, dear Pierre, just memories from the past that always come back to wound my heart."

Pierre looked in a distressed way at his master, whom he had come to cherish as a son for a long time now, and said, "Come, let us have our meal together with João."

They ate, rested, cared for their horses and took water from the well to fill their canteens. At Lagéry's command, they mounted their horses and continued on their journey. Night was already falling when they spied the walls of *Le Petit Gerin*. They spent the night in the Templars' castle and the following morning took leave of the English knights, who would be going toward the coast, and then took the road to Saffran. It was a pleasant morning, with a clear blue sky. The large group of pilgrims on foot and the mounted escort were advancing slowly along the dusty road, opened thousands of years earlier by the Jews, the oldest inhabitants of those lands. The three Templar friends were riding together, behind the pilgrims, and a little way in front of the donkeys that were carrying provisions. Jean broke the silence that had endured since the beginning of the journey. "Today we shall spend the night in Saffran and tomorrow we shall arrive in Acre. I shall write a letter to the Duke d'Anjou, imploring him to send reinforcements to King Guido. I shall send it with the first Venetian galleon that leaves the port."

The friends looked at him with interest. João asked, "Do you think the Duke will heed the request?"

"I do not know, my dear friend, I do not know. All I know is that I need to try something that will help us to avoid the unequal struggle which, by all indications, should occur."

They remained silent for some time, until Pierre said, "I suppose the king himself must have asked the Catholic kings for reinforcements. Who knows, they may be already en route!"

"I hope God will help us and it will take time for the Saracens to gather their forces together, so that the reinforcements will arrive in time."

The pilgrims began to sing a religious hymn, terminating the companions' conversation. The journey was once more interrupted for a meal and a rest. The afternoon went by without anything special happening. At nightfall, they arrived in Saffran, the last stage before their arrival in Acre. They spent a calm night, and the next morning found the group cheered by the prospects of arriving at their trip's final destination. They left early, right after dawn. All day long they encountered caravans of Saracens and their camels, carrying merchandise to be sold in Acre. Jean could not help thinking how good it would be, for Saracens and Christians, if they could live in peace, with each group professing their faith and respecting that of the other group. They made the customary stop and, at the end of the afternoon, they saw in the distance the imposing walls of St. John of Acre.

THE SUSPECT

Reinaldo awoke in a very good mood that Saturday morning. It had been a cool night, with the temperature around 60° F, exceptionally low for the Rio de Janeiro winter. The alarm clock showed it was eight o'clock. His mother must have already been awake, getting breakfast together. He rose, went to the bathroom, and on his return opened the curtains. He gazed at the beach through the windowpane; the sky was cloudy and there was some wind. The sea was leaden gray, flecked with white foam on the surface whipped up by the wind. The scenery aroused in him an immense desire to travel, cross the endless ocean, get to know other lands, other peoples. He recalled his dreams, Jean, and suddenly he had the feeling that he had already known those faraway places. "That's crazy", he thought, "it must be the result of those dreams I've had." However, the richness of the details of the places he was seeing couldn't have been only the product of his imagination. He was visualizing clearly the streets of Orléans and the Templars' monastery. He was seeing clearly the walls of Jerusalem, the dome of Solomon's Temple and the Church of the Holy Sepulcher. The port of St. John of Acre, busy streets, strong walls and the Templars' castle couldn't be just the result of his imagination. Even stronger was the scintillating image of young Melissande, whose memory brought tears to his eyes. He felt a sudden strong tightening in his breast, and immediately tried to divert his thoughts to present-day matters. He dressed for his walk on the boardwalk and headed for the pantry, where his mother had just finished preparing breakfast.

She smiled with pleasure and ran to hug her son. "Did you have a good night's sleep? I was worried, thinking that you were going to feel cold and I hadn't left the blanket on the head of the bed so you could cover yourself."

"Yes, it was a little cool, but I slept in my pajamas and covered myself with the sheet. Besides, yesterday's red wine warmed me up a lot."

They sat down to have breakfast. His mother took much pleasure in her son's company, but immediately afterwards Reinaldo went to take his walk without his mother, who feared the early morning cold. "I'm not going to risk getting caught by the rain."

Well, I'm going, I have to keep in shape, mainly after eating the way I've been doing these last few days."

His mother, laughing, recalled she had planned a barbecue.

On the boardwalk, despite the cold, there were many people walking along, and there were a reasonable number of surfers taking advantage of the high waves. He walked as fast as he could, thinking of his mother's plans and repeating some psalms. Around an hour later, he was already home taking a bath. He got dressed and looked at the clock, it was ten after twelve. He was reading in the living room the newspaper his mother subscribed to when she appeared, all ready, a few minutes later.

They left and took a taxi to the Leme district, where his mother's favorite barbecue restaurant was located. After a pleasant lunch, they returned walking along Avenida Atlântica, conversing in a lively manner. In the middle of their walk, they decided to take Avenida Nossa Senhora de Copacabana. Reinaldo pointed to a bookstore and they entered. "I'm going to look for a book which deals with regression and previous lives."

With the help of a clerk he discovered "My Lives", written by the American movie actress Shirley MacLaine. He browsed through the book and decided to buy it. They returned home and his mother went to her bedroom to rest. Reinaldo sat down in the living room and began to read the book. He read uninterruptedly until 5 p.m., when he remembered he had agreed to celebrate the six o'clock mass in the Copacabana Parish Church. He walked to the square where the modern church building was located. Father Demétrio came over to greet him, as soon as he saw him in the vestry. "Reinaldo, it's a good thing you came. Sílvio has a bad case of the flu with fever, and will have to rest at least until tomorrow. Today we'll have the mass of the charismatic movement and we'll need a larger number of priests. You'll see the enormous number of faithful worshippers that attend this celebration."

They began to prepare for the mass, which began punctually at six o'clock with the large church completely full. What most impressed the visiting priest was the people's happiness and everyone's intense participation. "It's not without reason that this movement is growing in all the parishes, "he thought. The work in the parish continued until after eight o'clock and supper was served at nine. Seated alongside each other, while they ate the two friends conversed cheerfully about matters involving religious work. At a certain moment Demétrio asked, "And what about your thoughts about regression?"

The chaplain was surprised by his friend's question, since he didn't think that Demétrio had paid much attention to his conversation with Brother Rodolfo. "Do you know anything about this subject?"

Demétrio laughed at Reinaldo's reaction. "Answering my question with another question isn't fair. Take it easy, we're no longer in the time of the Inquisition, you can tell me about your other lives."

His friend ended up laughing also at the joke and was amazed at Demétrio's insight. "Yes, I've been going through an experience involving regression, brought on possibly by a traumatic event that happened to me on the border."

Then he recounted all the events that had occurred since that Sunday morning on the Colombian border. Demétrio listened very attentively, interrupting once in a while to ask for more details about one point or another of the account. At the close, he commented, "Look, Reinaldo, I know a little bit about the matter. I began to discover it on researching a little more after a parishioner came to talk to me about this subject and asked for advice. For many years she had been feeling sharp pain in her right forearm, and no doctor had been able to discover the cause and cure it. She was taking extremely strong pain-killers constantly. Until one day she visited a psychotherapist who was a specialist in regression. On her very first visit, she regressed to a previous life, in which she was working in a grain mill and had suffered an accident, losing her forearm. The accident occurred at the end of the XIX century, in southern Mexico. The wound became gangrenous and she died, suffering a great deal of pain. Surprisingly, understanding what had happened made her pain stop completely. She was and continues to be a very devout Catholic. On discovering that the Church doesn't recognize reincarnation, she became very confused and came to talk with us."

The chaplain couldn't help interrupting. "So what's happening to me isn't so exceptional. Many people must have already experienced the same phenomenon. What did you say to her?"

"I told her it was a very complex matter and that I'd study it and consult some of my brothers who are specialists in theology, and then I'd be able to offer her better guidance.

Well, the fact is that I've been able to discover very little or nothing. I found out that the Church doesn't discuss this matter very much. The opinions are very vague and inconclusive. I decided to maintain my own opinion on this issue."

"And what's your opinion?"

The priest looked at his brother and gave him a big smile. "Personally, I don't believe in reincarnation, until I have any evidence to the contrary, that is, until I experience some type of return to previous lives. I believe that we live only once. However, I respect the belief of others who have passed through this experience. I tried to transmit my point of view to that lady as if it were the position of the Church. I told her that we didn't believe in reincarnation, but we respected personal belief in this matter, and that such belief didn't interfere with the believer's faith. Reinaldo, your case seems very complex. If you allow me, I'd like to follow it closely. Perhaps in this way I might even change my opinion. If during the course of your dreams, or better still, your regressions, you discover the cause of your behavior during the combat on the border, I'll re-evaluate my position in this matter."

They remained silent for some time, finishing their snack and drinking iced tea with lemon, a present from the charitable parishioners.

It was already growing late and Reinaldo began to take leave of his brothers, assuring Demétrio that he'd keep him posted on everything that happened. It was more than 10 p.m., the night was cold and the sky full of stars. He walked unhurriedly along Avenida Atlântica, amazed at the heavy automobile traffic in both directions. There were also many pedestrians that Saturday night. The bars, with their open-air tables, were full. It was a different sight for him, unaccustomed to all that activity. "That's right", he thought, "I'm becoming a small-town priest, unaccustomed to the bustle of the big city."

He stopped on the corner of República do Peru Street and waited for a car to pass, in order to cross safely. At that moment he sensed a strange presence. He was being followed. He recalled precisely having seen the man standing at the church door, staring in his direction. He was a youth of around twenty, with light brown skin, wearing sneakers, khaki pants and a black leather jacket. His face was partially hidden by a black cap on his head. The chaplain crossed the street, and to test his supposed pursuer, turned to the left along República do Peru Street, detouring from his original itinerary.

The young man continued following him, at a distance of approximately ten meters. Colonel Peçanhas's words immediately came back to him. Was there any relation to what had happened on the border or was it all just a mere chance occurrence? He stopped on the corner of Avenida Nossa Senhora de Copacabana and pretended to be looking at a store window display. The youth passed by him and continued walking calmly down the avenue. Reinaldo breathed more easily, it had been just a coincidence. His mistrust must have been due to his weariness and to his commander's words. Now calmed down, he continued walking toward his street, which already was nearby. Finally he arrived at the building where his mother lived. He paused to await the arrival of the night doorman and looked to the left, toward the beach. His blood froze. Standing on the corner, there was the young man, looking at him calmly. At first, Reinaldo felt an impulse to approach him and ask him what he wanted. But instead, he waited for the night doorman to open the heavy iron entrance door and went in rapidly, after greeting him. On arriving home he went to the window and looked out at the street corner. The youth wasn't there any longer, he had disappeared. His mother came out of her room, hugged him and asked if he was hungry, and was disappointed at his negative reply.

Reinaldo decided not to make any comment to his mother about the mysterious young man. He said good night to her and retired to his room. After lying down, he began to reflect on what had happened. It's true that it could have all been a coincidence, but after the colonel's warning, he should be careful.

He'd phone his brother the following day, to ask his advice. As a policeman, he'd be able to give him good guidance. He turned off the light, closed his eyes and went to sleep. It wasn't long before the dream came. He was once more in the Holy Land . . .

THE SPRING TOURNAMENT

Night was beginning to fall when they finished taking care of the horses and left the stable. Lagéry dismissed the escort, after having thanked the brothers, sergeants and squires for their devotion and courage in the face of the great difficulties they had encountered. Then they headed for the large chapel, where they recited their vespers. Afterwards the evening meal was served. They were in Lent, on the eve of Good Friday. It was a period for fasting, but the Templars, because of their responsibilities as warriors, were allowed to have normal meals, only abstaining from eating meat. The next day, all the Church rituals relating to the death of Christ would be performed. The Stations of the Cross would be repeated, one by one, and the fasting would be complete. Jean took leave of João and Pierre and went to bed. Good Friday mobilized the whole community with the rituals of the Crucifixion and Death of Our Lord Jesus Christ, which had occurred so near that place, 1,154 years earlier. It had rained a lot all day long and was cold. The entire Catholic population of Acre took part in the rituals in the churches. The military orders of the Templars and the Hospitallers held great ceremonies, each in its own headquarters. At the end of another day, Jean went to bed, certain of his faith in Christ, ever more resolved to defend his Church, its holy places and its faithful worshippers, even at the sacrifice of his own life. Next Saturday afternoon, a small tournament was organized by order of the Grand Master, Gérard de Ridefort. Only those knights who had been overseas for less than a year could participate. Apparently, the Grand Master wanted to evaluate the level of weapons training of the newest group of warrior monks. Jean was included in this group. João would not participate because he was still convalescing from the wounds he suffered in Nablus. The combats would occur in individual jousts, *à plaisance*, that is, using weapons with blunted points, and the competitors would be chosen by lot. Armed with lances and shields, the knights would ride toward each other, at a signal by the tournament judge. At the point of encounter, the one that knocked the other off his horse would be the winner. Up to three trials would be held. If there was no winner at the end of the trials, both would be eliminated.

The winners would then face each other until only two combatants were left at the end. Since each individual combat lasted only a few minutes, a large number of knights could participate in the tournament. The number of candidates exceeded eighty, but only forty knights were called. The choice was made by lot and five knights were designated as reserves for any eventuality. The truce with Caliph Saladin provided a certain tranquillity, which made it possible to hold the tournament in an area located around a kilometer outside the walls, to the south of the city. It was held on a flat ground, near the sea, covered with low grass, approximately nine hundred meters long and four hundred meters wide. Several tents were erected where squires and sergeants, assisted by Syrian serfs, took care of the equipment and served water to the contestants. A tent in front of the central part of the lists was occupied by the Grand Master and his main assistants. The sun was on high and it wasn't very cold when Ridefort gave orders for the bugles to be blown, so that the Tournament Master, an elderly knight of Spanish origin, could announce the rules of combat:

FIRST: the knights should take their position, one half of them at each end of the lists, awaiting the call to combat. Two heralds, one at each end, shall announce the names of the combatants, to be chosen by lot. The lances to be used must have small spheres on their points, to avoid wounding the opponent.

SECOND: the order to attack shall be given by the Grand Master, by means of a bugle call.

THIRD: should the combatants continue mounted on their horses after the first clash in the lists, another order to attack shall be given, immediately after replacing the damaged lances. Three trials shall be held. If at the end of these trials, there is no winner, both participants shall be considered to be losers.

FOURTH: the combats shall continue so that, at the end, only two knights are left. If there are an odd number of participants, a reserve knight shall be called to participate in the combat.

FIFTH: no award or penalty shall be given to the winner or losers.

Right after that, the first two combatants were announced. They were two French knights who took their positions at the ends of the lists. They used helmets with visors and the Templars' coat of arms, not those of their families. Their mounts were large warhorses belonging to the Order. The Grand Master gave the order for the bugle call, and the knights galloped toward each other. The clash of the lances against the shields echoed noisily and the two fell off their horses. With the help of squires, they were taken to the ends of the lists and prepared again for another attack. After another bugle call, they galloped with their lances aimed at each other. The knight on the right succeeded in hitting his opponent's helmet and, at the same time, in warding off the blow of the other's lance with his shield, without falling off his horse. The knight on the left was thrown to the ground by the blow on his head, which fortunately didn't cause any serious wound. Declared the winner, the winning knight returned to the tent, where he awaited another combat with another winning knight. Jean was called after a dozen knights had already been eliminated. He wasn't feeling any kind of emotion, concentrating only on making use of his knowledge of chivalry to the maximum possible extent. His opponent was a German knight whom he knew slightly. The first two trials occurred without any result—their lances hit the shields, but the two knights remained mounted on their respective horses. In the third trial, Jean broke his lance, but he knocked down the other knight. Some time later, he was called to combat for the second time. This time his opponent was an English knight. In the first trial, Jean aimed at his helmet and succeeded in hitting it. On realizing that he would be hit in the head, the Englishman lost his concentration and missed his adversary's shield with his lance. He was unconscious for a while, but was able to recover before the end of the tournament. The sun was already beginning to set and only four knights were left in the lists, with Jean among them. The bugle sounded once more and he was called to combat. His opponent now was one of the French knights who were knighted together with him in Orléans. He was from Brittany and appeared to have long military experience. The bugle call sounded and Jean spurred his horse. The clash at the center of the lists seemed undefined, but this time Jean felt the Breton's lance lift him up and throw him far from his horse.

With slight wounds, he was taken to the tent. He learned then from Pierre that the Breton knight had won the tournament, defeating in the last combat the Marquis de Sedan, a Templar of noble origin. Night was falling and they all waited only for the Grand Master to close the tournament, after congratulating the Breton knight. João, who had come to watch the event, commented to Jean, "I miss the complete tournaments and the beauty of the feminine participation. A tournament without the "Queen of Beauty and Love" and the knights' patronesses is so incomplete!"

His friend's words brought back memories that awakened Jean's emotions.

The day after the knighting ceremony, held in the Orléans cathedral, was devoted to the preparations for the tournament. Around two kilometers from the Paris Gate, outside the city walls, was a flat grassy area, in the form of a rectangle 1,800 meters long and 800 meters wide, bordered by a woods of oak trees and a small stream with very clear water. Surrounding the entire rectangle was a wooden palisade with gates at the two ends. One of the ends was closer to the walls and the other faced a small hill covered by vegetation. At the beginning of spring, the whole area of the hillside was covered by wild flowers, giving that region especially beautiful scenery. At the center of the lists a large covered wooden platform was built, where the Duke and his guests would stay, including the "Queen of Love and Beauty", who would be chosen by the Duke from among various candidates. Normally the young patronesses of the knights competing in the tournament, who belonged to noble families, would be candidates. Near the entrance at the side of the walls another pavilion had been set up, which would house the challenger knights. Their shields, displaying their coats of arms, would be placed on a pedestal, and their squires would be posted at their sides. There were eight challengers: Charles, Marquis d'Artois; Robert de Bouville, a Breton knight; Enguerrand, Marquis de Trye; Jean de Brest, a Norman knight; Henri Zacour, Guillaume Lefranc and Honoré d'Avenel, all knights from the court of the Duke and, lastly, an English knight, James of Kirkland. The first three were veterans of several wars and had participated in the famous battle of Montgisard, in the Holy Land, in November 1177, in which Saladin was defeated by the Christian army of King Baldwin IV. The fourth was a young knight who had won two tournaments in Normandy, and the rest were knights with long combat experience. At the other end of the lists, the pavilion of the knights who would face the challengers would be erected. A fourth pavilion would accommodate the guests of lower hierarchy. On that day, Jean didn't meet Melissande. The preparations for the tournament took all his time and energy. He was sure that he'd be successful in combat and that his patroness would be proud of him. At night, he went to bed very early, anxious with regard to the expectations of such an important day for his future as a knight and a man in love. In a similar manner, Melissande wasn't able to stop thinking about the young knight and about his sincerity in demonstrating his love for her. At first, she thought it was just a game without consequences, but with the passage of time and Jean's displays of affection, she had allowed herself to be taken up completely by the young knight. That night she went to sleep thinking with special tenderness about the knight who would become the only love in her life.

The sunrise, with a blue cloudless sky, announced a beautiful spring day, completely favorable for the opening of the Spring Tournament of the Duchy of Anjou. Starting early, a large number of people with the most varied origins were arriving from the villages and castles in the neighborhood. High up on the walls, hundreds of inhabitants of Orléans snuggled together to watch the tournament. Soon afterwards, the bugles and trumpets announced the arrival of the Duke and his entourage. Then the heralds announced to all present that Duchess Marguerite had been elected "Queen of Beauty and Love". It was an obvious display of affection on the part of her husband, who couldn't contain his happiness since the announcement, a few days earlier, of his wife's long-awaited pregnancy. The Duchess would award the winner of the tournament with a small gold crown, in the shape of laurels, the symbol of victory since the time of ancient Rome of the Caesars. After the inaugural parade, the knights' patronesses would deliver to their protégés colored ribbons which would be tied to the hilts of their lances. At the Duke's command, the trumpets would sound again, announcing the start of the parade. At the head came the eight challenger knights, mounted on their warhorses, equipped with silver-colored harnesses and reins.

The knights were carrying their shields with their families' coat of arms, were wearing coats of mail and helmets with visors and colored plumes. The lances, five meters long, were held vertically. They conveyed a strong impression of strength and power. Around ten meters behind them came the knights who would take part in all the combats in the tournament. There were 96 participants all told, including the challengers, coming from the most varied corners of the Christian realms. They were riding on beautiful chargers and were arranged in rows of five knights. Six of the new knights were going to participate in the tournament. Jean was in the tenth row and his heart was beating fast, since it was his first participation as a knight in a tournament. When they passed the Duke's pavilion, they all lowered their lances to salute the tournament chairman. The parade finally arrived at the other end of the lists and the knights that had patronesses trotted over to the pavilions to receive their ribbons. Jean spied Melissande in the main pavilion, accompanied by her parents. Beautiful in her light blue brocade dress with gold embroidery, she waved to him happily with the green ribbon that he should tie on the hilt of his lance. He rode up to his beloved and extended his lance for her to tie the ribbon with a simple knot on the hilt. Then all the knights went to their respective tents.

The herald announced the start of the individual jousts. The knights that accepted the challenges would ride up to the front of the tent of the knights being challenged and touch with their lance the shield of the knight they wished to face. If they touched it with their hilt, the combat would be *à plaisance*, that is, with blunted weapons. If the touch was performed with the lance point, it would be *à outrance*, without limits, until death or a serious wound. Each knight being challenged could only receive one challenge at a time, up to a total of five. Only after having fought and won, could he receive the next challenge. The defeated knight lost to the winner his warhorse and weapons, which nevertheless could be resold to the loser. On the first day of the tournament, the combats would be with lance and shield. Those who succeeded in knocking their opponents off their horses would be considered the winners. Should neither knight be knocked down after five trials, the Duke, as tournament chairman, would declare one of the knights to be the winner. And thus various combats took place, all won by the challenger knights. If one of the latter were defeated, the winner would take his place and fight as a challenger knight. In his third combat,

Henri Zacour was defeated by a knight from Burgundy, Juvenal de Harsigny, who took his place. Honoré d`Avenel, also in his third combat, had also been defeated and had died on breaking his neck in the fall from his horse. His executioner had been an Italian knight, named Andrea Petrazzi.

During the morning Jean was called to combat by a herald. His heart skipped a beat, and only after a few seconds' hesitation, he remembered that he had to ride up to the challenger knights' tent and touch the shield of one of them. Beside the shield was a number indicating how many combats the knight had already won. Without thinking very long, he touched with the hilt of his lance the shield of the challenger knight with the least number of victories, the Italian knight. Andrea Petrazzi was called to combat with Jean a little after learning of the death of his previous opponent and was very shaken. He rode to the encounter with Jean almost blinded by despair, since that was his first death in combat. On meeting at the center of the lists, the Italian's lance was too high, possibly due to nervousness, and didn't hit his opponent. Jean's lance, however, hit his shield squarely, breaking in two.

The impact was very violent and Andrea was thrown off his horse. It was Jean's first victory. He could hardly believe that he had won. He was completely dazed. He returned to the tent and learned from the herald that he would receive the Italian's horse and weapons, and that he could only be challenged to one more combat. Each challenger knight could fight only five times, and he was accumulating the combats of his predecessor, d`Avenel, and the combat with Petrazzi, with only one more lacking to reach a total of five. Forty-eight knights would participate in the first day of the tournament. In the morning of the second day, a combat between two groups of knights would be held, with each group made up of twenty knights who would fight with swords, until the victory of one of the groups. In the afternoon there would be a combat between eight knights on foot, armed with battle axes. The third day would be a day of rest, and the fourth would be devoted to competitions with bows and arrows and ax handling, in which squires and peasants could take part. At the end of the day, the tournament would be closed and the Duke would choose the grand winner, who would receive his crown from the "Queen of Beauty and Love."

After an intermission for a meal, the tournament began again. A herald came to tell Jean that he had been challenged. Pierre, who had been accompanying him from the beginning, helped him mount and take his position for the gallop. On hearing the herald announce the names of the rivals, Jean's blood froze. His challenger was Robert, Melissande's brother. The idea of having to hurt the mistress of his heart, even though unwillingly, pained him. He had hardly formulated these unfortunate thoughts when the bugles gave the signal to gallop. The knights charged each other. Their lances hit the shields violently. Jean's lance broke in two, but Robert's remained intact. The two knights momentarily lost their balance, but succeeded in staying on their horses. At the ends of the lists, they received new lances and awaited another signal to attack. For the second time they charged each other. Jean was no longer thinking about his opponent's identity. At that moment only the concentration and technique learned during years of training counted. In a fraction of a second, he noticed that Robert was aiming at his helmet and succeeded in turning his head aside to avoid the lance point, which passed only a few centimeters from his visor. Because of this, he lost his balance and was unable to hit his adversary with his lance. Once more they awaited the signal to attack, and for the third time, they charged. The maneuver required great concentration on Jean's part. When he galloped toward Robert, he had decided that he wouldn't hit Melissande's brother. When only a few meters remained before their encounter, he aimed at his friend's head and purposely diverted his lance a little upward, almost repeating what had happened to the Italian knight. Robert in turn hit Jean's shield very violently, throwing him off his horse. The fall left the young man momentarily unconscious. Aided by Pierre and two more men, he was taken to the tent where he recovered rapidly. A herald came to tell him that he should deliver his weapons and charger to the victorious knight. Then Robert arrived, very worried. Seeing his companion in good shape, he commented, "My good friend, I am happy to see that you are all right. My dear sister would never forgive me if I had wounded you in any way. I must return and tell her that you are not wounded. Regarding your weapons and warhorse, I shall not accept them and I beg you to keep them."

The two young men smiled and embraced each other, and Robert left. Jean then asked Pierre to take a message to the Italian knight, saluting him and returning his weapons and warhorse, which had been brought by the defeated knight's squire. The first day of the tournament ended and the Duke announced the name of the knight who had won the first stage: Jean de Brest, the Norman knight, who had triumphed in all his combats, knocking down his opponents with his first attack. He was announced by the heralds and paraded at the sound of the bugles and trumpets, accompanied by his two squires, one of whom carrying the flag of his fief on the cold coast of Normandy. Trotting past on his gorgeous white warhorse, acclaimed by the quite numerous audience, framed by a lovely spring sunset, Jean de Brest was the very image of victory, bringing to a close in an extremely beautiful way that first day of the tournament.

Jean de Saumur went to his lodgings in the Duke's palace, accompanied by faithful Pierre. Still dazed by the fall, he had a meal in the company of his friend and then, being tired, took leave of him and went to sleep. Lying on his bed, he was thinking of his beloved Melissande. She had been worried about his fall and had sent her brother to find out about his condition. He fell asleep smiling with pleasure at the display of love by the beautiful young lady and satisfied that he had acted in accordance with his knighthood vow. Offending a damsel by wounding her brother would be deed unworthy of a knight.

The second day of the tournament followed with the combats between two groups of twenty knights each. The first group was commanded by Geoffroi de Troyes, commander of the Duke's guard, and most of the knights belonged to the court of Anjou. The other group was composed of Breton knights, commanded by Guy de Vannes. The combat began on horseback, with blunted swords and shields. It continued on foot, and after two hours of fierce fighting, the Duke's group won the combat. Twelve Breton knights had already withdrawn from the struggle with slight wounds and the remaining eight surrendered to the fifteen knights led by Geoffroi, who had lost five of his men. In the afternoon, the combat with battle axes and shields occurred. It was unlikely that this type of weapon, a sharpened piece of iron tied on a handle, would be used without causing wounds. The rules of the combat provided that four pairs of knights would fight each other, and the winners would then fight each other until only one victorious knight was left. A judge, appointed by the Duke, would accompany the combats and would interrupt them if one of the knights were seriously wounded. Of the eight knights, five were wounded and lost much blood, and one was in a serious condition and died the following morning. Jean, already recovered, and Pierre worked all day long in the organization and supervision of the combats. At the end of the day, Robert came to join them and said, "Dear friends, I bring good news. My father invited you, Jean, for a hunt tomorrow morning. My sister will be present. She loves hunts!"

Jean was so happy with the invitation and the prospect of being with his beloved that he didn't stop embracing his friend. Pierre and Robert burst into laughter at the impassioned young man's reaction. At that point, a knight approached, and Jean recognized him immediately. It was Andrea Petrazzi, the Italian, who declared, "Noble knight, I've come to express my gratitude for your gallant gesture, returning my weapons and horse. It is a relief to learn that I was defeated by a knight with great skill at arms and with even greater magnitude of heart."

"I am the one to feel honored by your kind words, sir. Let me introduce my friend, knight Robert de Challons, who also took part in the tournament, and my faithful squire and friend, Pierre Gabin."

The three young men soon began a lively conversation regarding the episodes of the tournament combats. The Italian was received very affectionately and Robert invited him also for the hunt on the following day. Petrazzi accepted the invitation, touched by the display of esteem and companionship. The next day would be the day of rest in the tournament. They heard the bugle call and the herald announce the two winners that day, Geoffroi de Troyes and an English knight who had been victorious in the struggle with battle axes. The winners withdrew after being acclaimed by the public and the Duke, who then ordered the closing of that day's activities. Tired, they went inside the walls of Orléans at the sight of a glorious sunset.

His companion's voice brought Jean back to the shadows of the walls of Saint John of Acre. "Jean! Where were you? You were pensive for such a long time and with such a serene look that I did not dare to interrupt you."

"It was nothing, my dear friend. I was just recalling another tournament which took place a long time ago back in Anjou. Let us return to Acre, since night is falling and everyone is leaving."

While the serfs carried all the tents, weapons and equipment, the squires led the horses and weapons back to the entrance gate to Acre. The large group of Knights Templars, with the Grand Master at the head, walked solemnly, recognizable at a distance by the Cross of Christ on their mantles and their beards, since cutting them off was prohibited by the Order. Night was falling on that Easter Saturday in 1187 AD . . .

THE WARNING

Reinaldo was awakened by the daylight that entered through the window. He had forgotten to draw the curtains. He looked at his watch, it was eight o'clock. He was getting lazy. When he returned to the barracks, he'd find reveille at daybreak very strange. He rose, took a bath and went to have breakfast with his mother, who had just prepared the meal in the pantry. She said, "I slept marvelously well. And you? You've a rather worried look on your face. Did everything go all right at mass yesterday?"

"The charismatic movement is different. Have you ever attended their mass?"

"I went once. It's cheerful and spiritual, but I confess that I prefer the traditional mass, perhaps because of my age. I think I'm very conservative. Sit down, let's have breakfast."

His mother told him that she was leaving for Petrópolis, where she was going to stay until the afternoon of the following day. One of her friends was celebrating her sixtieth birthday and she couldn't miss the party. Nevertheless, she said she had left him a surprise which she had prepared for his lunch. "I'll attend the six o'clock mass there in Petrópolis, with the girls," she added. "And you, what are you going to do this Sunday?"

"I'm going to read a little, have lunch and afterwards participate in the six o'clock mass at the Copacabana Parish Church."

They said good-bye affectionately. His mother went downstairs with a small suitcase to take a cab to the bus station, where she'd take the bus to Petrópolis, a city in the mountains approximately an hour's ride from Rio.

The chaplain, comfortably seated in the living-room armchair, was reading the Sunday newspaper when he remembered to phone his brother and tell him what had happened the night before. He looked in his agenda for Eduardo's phone number in the city of Foz de Iguaçu . . . The phone rang four times and then he heard the voice of his sister-in-law, Silvia. After a few friendly words with her, he inquired about the children and then asked to talk to Eduardo. Silvia explained, "He's on duty at the Brazil-Paraguay Bridge. I'll do the following: I'll call him there and on his first break, Eduardo will get in contact with you in Rio Is that OK?"

Reinaldo returned to his armchair and his newspaper. It was almost eleven o'clock when the telephone rang. It was Eduardo. "How are you doing, my brother? So you decided to take some leave?"

Reinaldo went directly to the point. He recounted everything that had happened, from the combat on the border to the strange occurrence the night before. His brother listened attentively, without interrupting. At the end he said, "Well, it could be somebody linked to the drug dealer or it could have been just a coincidence. Let's suppose the worst. I'm going to call today a friend of mine who's a detective chief there in Rio, and ask him to get in contact with you. I'm also going to ask him to give you his mobile phone number, so that he could take immediate action in case of any request by you. Avoid exposing yourself. Try not to go out at night and pay close attention to any suspicious person who approaches you. Call me back if anything happens."

The chaplain thanked his brother and took down the name of the detective chief, and after a few more minutes of conversation, hung up the phone . . . He had very little information to give his brother regarding the youth who had followed him. However, there was one sure thing: the malevolent look, foretelling misfortune. He tried to turn his thoughts away and went over to the window to look out at the sea. It was a beautiful day, with the deep blue cloudless sky mingling with the turquoise water on the horizon. The white foam of the waves was whipped up by the cold wind, reminding him that it was winter. He amused himself by watching the bustle down below and when it was ten minutes to twelve noon, he went to the kitchen to look for his mother's surprise. There was a note on the refrigerator door with instructions. Shrimp cocktail, his favorite dish when he was an adolescent. There was also a lettuce and tomato salad, codfish hot pie, white rice, guava jelly and cheese for dessert and a half bottle of white wine. He smiled with pleasure and thought, "What a mother God has given me! Later I'm going to call her on the mobile phone to thank her for the banquet." He prepared the table for lunch and before sitting down to enjoy it, he went to the living room and placed a CD with *The Four Seasons* by Vivaldi on the record player. Good food, good wine, good baroque music—they made a perfect combination. He prayed, thanking the Lord for this evidence of His generosity, and began to eat very slowly. After the repast, he felt like going out and walking a little, but recalled his brother's advice and decided to stay home, reading. He went over to the bookcase to choose a book. He happened to notice *Dom Casmurro*. He'd read the work when he was fifteen, as a school assignment. He recalled Capitu's interesting enigma and became curious. "I'm going to read this book by Machado de Assis again", he decided. He sat down in the armchair and began to read. Hours passed and the intriguing story absorbed all of Reynaldo's attention. "It's good to change my type of reading from time to time," he thought.

At five o'clock he remembered the mass and closed the book. He began to get ready to go out.

He went walking along the boardwalk, very attentive to what was happening around him. Nothing unexpected occurred. He arrived at the church twenty minutes before mass. He was already feeling "at home". All the priests were already greeting him familiarly. Father Silvio came over to talk to him as soon as he entered the vestry to put on his vestments. "My dear Reinaldo, I haven't recovered completely from the flu, but I'm much better and I thought I couldn't deny myself the company of my brothers at the six o'clock mass."

The chaplain noticed that Demétrio was missing. "And Demétrio, is he in the confessional?"

"Yes he is, and after mass he'll come to join us."

After greeting the vicar, who replied welcoming him and thanking him for his help, the chaplain began to prepare for the mass. That type of encounter with Christ had the power of renovating Reynaldo's faith. It was a moment in which his sentiments were intensely felt.

Later, at supper, he sat between Demétrio and Silvio. After a few moments of silence, Demétrio asked, "Reinaldo, I've been reading about the epoch in which your dream took place and I discovered something interesting. Do you know what was going to happen in the Holy Land in the year you mentioned?"

Reinaldo confessed that he hadn't had enough time yet to research the matter more deeply.

"In the middle of 1187, a great misfortune happened to the Christians of that epoch. The Latin army was destroyed by the Saracens in the battle of Hattin and few Christians survived the catastrophe. Jerusalem was lost forever by the Christians, except for the period from the First World War until 1948, when it was in the hands of the English. Most of the Knights Templar died in the battle or during the days that followed it. I'm very sorry, brother, but I believe your life in the Holy Land won't last much longer. And by the looks of things, your dreams will come to an end."

The chaplain didn't know what to say in reply. He hadn't thought of that possibility. If Jean were to die, that would be the end of the regression. And everything else would lose its meaning. He wouldn't find any replies or explanations for the recent happenings. Silvio's voice brought him back to reality. "Take it easy, Reinaldo. If he dies, we'll celebrate a mass in his memory and your life will continue as before, right?"

"That's true, brothers. But I was surprised by this revelation and by the fact that I hadn't thought of this possibility."

Father Demétrio smiled and added, "There's also the possibility that Jean may have survived. It's known that a few Templars succeeded in escaping from Acre with the Order's treasure, sent by the Grand Master to Cyprus."

"The future belongs to God, as the wise saying goes. I trust God that I'll find some sense in all this and the answers I seek. I've prayed for Jean every day, asking the Lord to help him find comfort and peace in the faith of Christ, and that the pain over the loss of his loved ones be alleviated by the comforting certainty of re-encountering them in the eternal life."

They finished their supper in silence and said good-bye to each other. Reinaldo returned home, again walking along the boardwalk. The fear of encountering the young man from the night before made him look attentively at everybody within his range of sight. The night was cold and there weren't many people on the streets, as on the night before. After making sure that he wasn't being followed, he calmed down, began to walk more slowly, enjoying the view of the South Atlantic. He was still confused by the information offered by Demétrio. Every time he dreamt of Jean, an inner, intimate voice said it was he who was living through those extraordinary experiences. He no longer had any doubts about his regression. But he needed to know the reason for all that. It must have some meaning. But he needed to be patient and wait. He'd pray a lot, asking God to help him find the answers to all his doubts.

He was already approaching the street where his mother lived. Everything seemed calm. He turned to the left and after walking a few more steps, arrived at the building. On entering the apartment, he missed his mother. He had been getting accustomed to his mother's warm reception whenever he arrived home. He looked at the clock—it was ten o'clock sharp. There was still time to call and thank his mother for the lunch. She answered the mobile phone rapidly and they exchanged some fond words.

He settled back comfortably in the armchair and again took up reading *Dom Casmurro*. He read until eleven thirty at night. He recalled his mother's advice, "Don't go to sleep with an empty stomach, OK?" But he had had a snack at the church and wasn't hungry. He went to his room and lay down. Sleep came rapidly, and with it, once more, the dream . . .

ISLAM

Several days after the Grand Master's tournament, Jean was called by the Abbot, who said, "Brother Jean, you have been chosen to accompany an ambassador from the Saracens who will stay with us for four days. His name is Usamah Ibn-Munqidh and he is from Damascus, in Syria. The Grand Master, who came from Jerusalem yesterday, shall receive him, in the afternoon, tomorrow and the day after tomorrow. He speaks our language well, he is a man of great culture. He shall come accompanied by a small escort. You should take him, whenever he requests, to the room that was prepared especially for his five daily prayers. His meals shall be prepared by the Egyptian cook who accompanies him, and if by any chance you are invited to dine in his company, you are authorized to do so. Every day, after the complines, you shall come and tell me how the day went and what they did and said, in every detail. You shall be released from all your tasks and religious services, given the importance of your mission. You may answer any question asked by the ambassador and take him to any place within the city walls. It is unlikely that there is anything about us that the Saracens do not already know. I think he probably will not ask any questions about our defenses. This would be totally out of line with his diplomatic duties. Should he do so, however, tell him that you know nothing about it."

"When is the ambassador arriving, Brother Abbot?"

"He should arrive today, a little before sunset. You should wait for him at the Antioch Gate."

That afternoon, accompanied by Pierre, Jean headed for the Gate, where he would await the Saracen and his escort. After a wait of some time, he spied a group of four Saracen horsemen, accompanied by four animals carrying their luggage. When they approached, Jean ran to meet them and welcome them on behalf of the Grand Master, The ambassador from Damascus seemed to be around fifty years old, was richly dressed in oriental clothes and had polite manners, besides speaking French well. He was bringing with him a younger individual and two servants. Jean and Pierre went in front, leading them to the south end of the city, where the Templars' installations were located. Night was already beginning to fall when they left the foreigners in their lodgings, each one compatible with their respective hierarchical positions. A little later, on offering the foreigners a meal, Jean received polite thanks and the explanation that one of the servants, the Egyptian cook, was bringing all the material necessary for serving complete meals for his master and the other members of the group. After checking to see that they were all properly installed, the knight took his leave and sought out the Abbot to make his first report.

The following morning, after breakfast, the knight presented himself to the ambassador, who was already expecting him. "Sir, I hope you had a good rest in our humble home."

"Young knight, I thank you for your hospitality and attention. I learned from a letter sent by your Grand Master that you would have a place prepared for my prayers, am I right?"

"Yes, I shall take you to a room where you may pray in complete privacy. In this room the direction of your holy city is duly indicated."

"My son Omar, who is accompanying me, shall always be in my company. And my servants shall say their prayers in the accommodations which you placed at our disposal. I would like to pray now and afterwards walk a little through the city to become familiar with it."

The young Templar complied with the ambassador's request, guiding the guests to the place for their prayers. From a distance, he waited for them to finish. Without thinking what he was doing, he knelt and also began to recite Ave Maria and Our Father, very fervently and contritely. When he noticed that Usamah and his son had finished their prayers, he went to them and led them toward the main exit from the Templars' installations. On encountering the brothers who were passing by, Jean observed their curious glances directed at those Saracens who, with their rich garments, showed that they belonged to their people's nobility. They walked through the bustling streets of Acre, full of Christian and Saracen merchants. They differed very little from the streets of the other Arab or Christian cities in that region. Usamah stopped a few times to ask the price of merchandise and observe articles coming from Europe. Then he asked to return, since he wished to dine. On arriving in his lodgings, the ambassador said to the knight, smiling, "Have you ever tried Syrian food, young knight?"

Jean had had the chance several times to eat Saracen food. However, out of respect for the rules of his Order, he had refrained from eating it. He was very curious, since he knew that the spices and condiments utilized made Saracen food tastier than European delicacies, which were cooked or roasted only with salt. Whenever he passed nearby Saracen residences, he could smell the exotic, very appetizing aroma which came from their kitchens. It was unavoidable that one day he'd want to savor those meals. Now, with due authorization, that day had arrived.

"I would be much honored to accept your invitation, sir", he replied.

One of the servants took his belt, sword and helmet. All took off their sandals and sat down on a beautiful large carpet, spread out on the stone floor and surrounded by various cushions, which served as backrests for the diners. In the middle of the carpet, a folding platform made of fine wood with colored geometric designs had been placed. At a sign from Usamah, the servant brought a finger bowl, a small silver basin with rose petals in perfumed water, and a towel, made from a fabric that Jean was unable to identify. The Templar, being the guest, was the first to wash his hands, followed by the ambassador and his son Omar. Then came the platters with the delicacies, which were placed on the platform. They were copper platters with designs in thin golden layers. The strikingly beautiful designs represented inscriptions in Arabic or leaves and flowers. A very light silver plate and a small skewer with two points, also made of silver, were placed before each diner, so they could serve themselves. The glasses were made of copper, with golden designs, and would be filled with cold tea, sweetened with sugar, another product almost unknown to most Europeans. A very appetizing aroma arose from the food, carefully arranged on the platters, in a great variety of colors and shapes. Omar politely began to guide the guest, who knew very little about that food. "Knight, here we have chickpea paste, surrounded by green olives, that should be eaten with the thin round bread from the plate alongside; rice, prepared with condiments brought from Damascus and dressed with boiled figs and bananas; pieces of peeled oranges, adorned with pomegranates, two fruits which are very popular in Syria; on the larger platter, roast lamb, purchased this morning in the Arabian market of Acre, and prepared by our cook. It is well seasoned and adorned with peaches. Finally, to be eaten at the end of the meal, Damascene sweets, made from wheat, honey and sesame, and adorned with dried dates. You should start with the chickpeas."

Jean was amazed at those delicacies. On several occasions he had had meals at the court of the Duke of Anjou. The dishes were richly decorated and seasoned. The condiments cost small fortunes. Venetian merchants used to bring them from Saracen ports. However, they were also served in small quantities and improperly prepared by the French cooks. There was no comparison with the banquet now being served. He already was familiar with oranges and peaches and had eaten dates in Jerusalem. Jean had never seen or tasted the other fruits. He replied, "Thank you, noble Omar, I shall follow your advice and shall taste each one of the delicious dishes from your land."

In silence, Jean asked God's blessing for the food he was going to eat, served by enemies of his faith.

The dishes were delicious, the knight had never savored anything so tasty. The Saracens ate slowly with harmonious movements, as if that act were a ritual. They all kept a respectful silence, perhaps because they knew the monks' rules, which forbade them from conversing during meals. When they finished eating, the ambassador addressed his guest, "Noble knight, your company has honored us greatly, and I hope you have enjoyed the frugal meal."

"It has been a long time since I last had such an exquisite meal. Your food is splendid. Our religious calling and our vow of poverty prevents us, unfortunately, from repaying you by inviting you to eat such tasty delicacies with us."

Usamah smiled and recalled the several times he had tasted French food. With a few exceptions, he had been disappointed and had ascertained that their ignorance of condiments and spices greatly limited the good taste of the infidels' kitchen. On the other hand, the growing trade in this type of merchandise, carried out by Venetians and Pisanos, was beginning to provide great wealth for the Damascus Caliphate. The ambassador commented, "I believe that your stay in Acre is being useful, in the sense of getting to know better the life and customs of our people."

Knowledge, for Jean, during almost his entire life, was limited to the arts of war. Until his marriage, he didn't know how to read or write. Melissande, in long, pleasant conversations with her husband, was the one who showed him the richness of knowledge that reading could offer. She loved to read. She possessed six books, presents from her father and an uncle who was a Cardinal, and displayed her treasure with great pride. She spoke Latin fluently, and was able to read and write it as well as she could in french. As most of the books were written in the former language, she began, patiently, to teach her husband to read and write in the two languages. Her premature death interrupted the learning process, but since he had entered the Order, Jean had resumed his studies with much interest. With the copies of the books centralized in monasteries and religious orders, it wasn't difficult to find good teachers. But he knew little about the Saracens' country and the origins of their religion. He confessed, "Ambassador, sir, unfortunately I know almost nothing about your people or about your religion."

"I suppose not, noble knight. I had the good fortune to study the religions of the Peoples of the Book. Thus, I can say that I know the similarities and the differences, that is, the things that unite us and those that divide us. Would you like to hear a little about the fundamental points of the Islamic religion?"

"Yes, I would be very grateful if you could tell me, I am very curious to learn about it. In the first place, I would appreciate your telling me the meaning of the word 'Islam'."

"Islam means 'resignation to the word of God'. That word was transmitted by the prophet Mohammed, by means of the holy book, the Koran. Mohammed was born in Mecca, in Arabia, 617 years ago. On reaching the age of 40, he went into a cave on the outskirts of Mecca to meditate. There he had a vision of the Angel Gabriel, who transmitted the word of God to him. 'There is no God but Allah, and Mohammed is His Prophet'. This revelation and many others were written down right after the death of the Prophet and became the Koran, which contains 114 *suras*, or sections. Based on this revelation, Mohammed began to preach in Mecca and ended up by entering into conflict with the important families in the city, who believed in the ancient divinities. The persecution of the Prophet grew so much that he was forced to leave for Medina, where he already possessed many followers. This immigration is known in Arabic as the 'Hegira', which means 'departure' or 'onset'. Our people began to count time starting from the year 622 AD, when the Prophet was 52. Therefore, we are in the year 565 of our calendar. Years later, at the head of an army of ten thousand men, Mohammed occupied Mecca, and subsequently, with ever larger armies, unified all the tribes of Arabia, reaching the borders of Syria, at the gates of the Byzantine Empire. He died at the age of 62, after a pilgrimage to Mecca, bequeathing to our people the word of God and a glorious and prosperous destiny."

Jean listened to it all, taken simultaneously by admiration and fear. Admiration for the unshakable faith which he observed in the words of the Saracen nobleman. Fear of that people's power and determination, threatening to destroy his faith and his civilization. He realized, at this moment, that his compatriots were not evaluating accurately their opponents' strength, the real danger which the latter represented to the army of Christ.

They paused briefly for tea. The beverage, made by brewing herbs and also unknown to the knight, was strong and pleasant. When sweetened with the white powder they called sugar, it became even better. On tasting the brew, he noticed that the visitors were looking at him, waiting for some comments on his part. He asked, "What happened after the Prophet's death?"

"After his death, God bless him, leadership began to be exercised by the caliphs, a word which means successor. At that time, Islam was divided between the Sunni, followers of Abu Bakr, the father of Aixa, Mohammed's youngest wife, and the Shiites, followers of Ali, the husband of Fatima, Mohammed's daughter. Initially, the Shiites accepted Abu Bakr as caliph. He died two years later and was succeeded by Omar, another son-in-law of the Prophet. Omar began a period of conquest, considerably expanding the Arabs' territory. In 636 AD, Byzantine Syria and Iraq were occupied. In 641, Egypt came under Arab domination, and in the following year, Omar conquered Persia. Omar was very wise to take advantage of the opportunity presented by the weakening of the two great empires, the Byzantine and the Persian, which were exhausted by a long war between them."

Usamah poured himself a little more tea and continued his narrative. "Islam's expansion continued down through the centuries. At the beginning of the VIII century, our armies reached Central Asia, in northern India, and after occupying North Africa, crossed the Strait of Gibraltar, occupying a large part of the Iberian Peninsula. In 732 AD, they reached southern France, where they were contained at Poitiers by Charles Martel. The Arabian language became the official language of all the conquered lands, replacing the local languages. And thus, noble Christian, the religion of the Prophet has spread to the most diverse corners of the world."

At this moment, a Knight Templar asked permission to interrupt the conversation between Jean and the Saracens to announce that the Grand Master was awaiting the Syrian ambassador's presence. Usamah excused himself and accompanied the knight to conference room in the Templars' castle. Jean thanked Omar for the meal. He had to wait for the end of the meeting between the two chiefs. His thoughts were seething: "How would the Christians be able to resist the crushing expansion of these Saracens?" In Spain, they were struggling bravely against them. In a certain way, they were being contained, with great sacrifice, by the Spaniards and the Portuguese. In the other regions, the efforts were lesser.

Constantinople and the Byzantine Empire were also still resisting, and, God willing, the holy places would be successfully defended, if Saladin were to attack. Time passed and it was already night when the Saracen nobleman returned to his lodgings and took leave of Jean. The latter, very tired, sought out the Abbot to make his daily report, and after reciting the complines, went to bed. On the second day of his stay, the ambassador received in the morning an envoy of King Guido, who came from Jerusalem. Jean wasn't present during the visit, nor was he invited to the luncheon that the ambassador offered the envoy. During the afternoon, he accompanied Usamah to the place reserved for prayer and afterwards took him to the audience with the Grand Master. At night, after making the customary report to the Abbott with regard to the day's events, the knight went to the chapel to pray. Then he'd have his last meal of the day and went to his lodgings to sleep. Lying on his bed, he was thinking about the difficult task facing the Order, to defend the holy places from an enemy whose people were so well prepared, both in the military as well as in the cultural fields—people whose faith in God was as strong as that of his own people. It would be a great challenge for all the Christians in the Latin Kingdom. He recalled the deadly combat which he had engaged in with the Saracen renegades in Nablus and the difficulty that they had in successfully protecting the pilgrims they were escorting. He also recalled that the truce with the caliph would probably not be maintained after the frustrated attack against Mecca. He prayed, pleading for Our Lady to help them accomplish such a difficult task, and fell asleep with his thoughts turned to his beloved Melissande and André.

The third day of the ambassador's stay was quite calm. All his commitments had already been fulfilled, and he asked the knight to accompany him, together with his son Omar, on a walk through the city. Pierre went with them and provided company for Omar. First they visited the port. Several galleons were docked and the activity involving the loading and unloading of merchandise was intense. Usamah observed everything with great interest.

"Ambassador, sir, have you already visited Europe?"

"Yes, Sir Jean. I was in Spain visiting the caliph of Cordoba. I am familiar also with your beautiful country, I have traveled through it, from the port of Marseilles to Paris, the capital. Finally, I have visited Venice, Genoa and Rome. I would like very much for our peoples to live in peace so that we could travel freely, exchanging not only merchandise but also living experiences and cultural riches. I dream of a time in which all this shall be possible."

Jean looked at the Saracen with admiration. He had never thought about a world in peace. Since he was a small boy, he had always been preparing to fight. Every knight yearned for combats, and a state of war was for him much more natural that a state of peace. Usamah seemed to have perceived his thoughts, when he asked, "Have you already been in combat against us, knight?"

The Templar replied in an embarrassed way, "Yes, ambassador, I have. And it was while the truce was in full effect." He told him briefly about the combat with the renegades in Nablus.

Usamah listened attentively to the narrative until the end, when he commented, "I am very sorry for your suffering. The renegade who caused this violation of our truce was punished by the caliph. His group of bandits was disbanded, and the chief, who was wounded by your squire during the combat, is a prisoner in Damascus. His name is Al-Ashfar and it seems that he has recovered from the wounds he suffered in the combat. Al-Ashfar made a request for clemency to the caliph, who should pardon him."

The knight and the ambassador remained silent for the rest of their walk through the port. The sun was on high when they returned to the castle. The ambassador told Jean that he would remain in his lodgings for the rest of the afternoon, since in the morning of the following day he would depart for Damascus. After taking leave of the Saracens, Jean joined his congregation for prayers and a meal, realizing that he had learned a great deal. Then he made his report to the Abbot, as usual. The next day, he and Pierre should accompany the ambassador and his entourage up to the city gates and transmit the Grand Master's farewell.

Next morning Jean and Pierre accompanied the visitors to the Antioch Gate. Usamah thanked him for his services and bade him farewell, saying, "Noble knight, I have had the opportunity to get to know you and admire your character and the firmness of your faith. Always remember that we are imperfect human beings. We follow the word of God, but sometimes we wrongly interpret His intentions. I sincerely wish that your destiny be that which your heart came to seek in this distant land."

Jean thanked him and wished the group a good trip, and the Saracens rapidly left the walls of Acre behind as they headed for the road to Damascus.

THE DETECTIVE CHIEF

Reinaldo woke up around eight o'clock with the noise of the traffic on Avenida Atlântica. He recalled that it was Monday. It wasn't bad being on leave and able to stay in bed. He also recalled his dream. It was as if he had two lives. He was trying to separate one from the other, at a considerable sacrifice, but he was succeeding. He had faith in God, that everything would become clear in the very near future. He arose and prepared his breakfast, since his mother was still in Petrópolis. After cleaning up the kitchen, he went over to the window to have a look at the weather: it was a sunny day. The temperature had dropped, but this wouldn't prevent his walk. He began heading toward the Leme district, perspiring after half an hour of walking at a rapid pace. In fifty minutes he covered the distance from Leme to Lifeguard Station Six at the other end of the beach, back and forth.

He returned to the apartment, took a bath, and while he was dressing, the telephone rang. He answered right away, full of doubts and apprehension.

"Please, I'd like to speak to Chaplain Reinaldo. I'm Dr. Brito, Assistant Chief of Detectives here at the 12th Precinct in Copacabana. Your brother Eduardo, my friend, asked me to get in contact with you and help you, in case you happen to receive any threat on the part of the drug dealers."

"Dr. Brito, he told me about you, I'd like you to give me some guidance, if anything happens to me."

"Look, Chaplain, the ideal thing would be for you to have two bodyguards, twenty-four hours a day, but that's not possible. So I'm going to give you my mobile phone number for you to call me, at the slightest sign of any abnormality."

After making a note of the mobile phone number, Reinaldo thanked him for his help and told the detective chief that he had been followed by that strange individual. He also told him about the warning his commander had given him, and mentioned the relative of the guerrilla he had killed on the border. Dr. Brito asked about the possibility of their meeting personally, since he wanted to give him some instructions regarding security. Reinaldo invited him then to lunch and they made an appointment for twelve noon at the 12th Precinct headquarters. After hanging up the phone, the chaplain remained still for a few minutes. He was thinking about this new problem that had unexpectedly arisen in his life. It was still early to get ready for the meeting. The Precinct headquarters was close by, around ten minutes away on foot. He took advantage of the wait to read a few more pages of *Dom Casmurro*. At eleven thirty he closed the book, got ready and left for the meeting.

He arrived before the scheduled time. The police station was a two-story house, with simple architecture, seeming more like a residence than a police station. He was taken to Dr. Brito's office by a detective, and was received very kindly. The detective chief, a man around forty or so, tall, thin, bald and with very light skin, seemed like he'd never been exposed to the sun. They greeted each other and exchanged amenities. Then they went to a small restaurant very near the police station, at the chief's suggestion.

Dr. Brito ate rapidly and, in less than fifteen minutes, had already finished his lunch. While he waited for Reinaldo to finish eating, he told him that he had met Eduardo at a technical police congress in Brasília, at the beginning of the previous year.

They were maintaining frequent contacts because of their duties, since they exchanged information regarding the cases they were working on. When the lunch was finished, the priest paid the bill and they left, walking back to the police station. It was then that Brito touched upon the matter. "Chaplain, I'm very familiar with the police record of that Serginho do Cirado. The bandit is a psychopath. You must take maximum care. The best advice I could give you is to return as soon as possible to the Amazon region. You'll be safer there."

"I can't return before I resolve a serious problem, Dr. Brito. I have faith in God that nothing will happen to me."

"Excuse me, Chaplain, but from my own experience, I know that God doesn't usually get involved in these police problems."

"In any case, it's not possible to return before my leave is over."

The detective chief shrugged his shoulders and didn't say anything more until they arrived at the police station. They went to Brito's room, where they had a small black coffee. The chief sat down and motioned for him to sit down also, pointing to the chair alongside his desk. He opened a folder, took out a photograph and said, "This is Serginho." Reinaldo looked attentively at the photo. There was something that was vaguely familiar in that face with hard features. "It's just my impression," he thought. He hadn't seen the face of the man's brother that he had shot down on the border. He hadn't wanted to look at his body. It was impossible to recognize him in the photo. He gave it back, without commenting anything. He rose, thanked the detective chief for his company at lunch and said good-bye, promising to keep him posted regarding any abnormality. He left the police station and walked back to the apartment.

Being close to the Copacabana Parish Church, he entered and took a seat in the rear. Many faithful churchgoers were praying and he went unnoticed. He saw that one of the confessionals was occupied. Perhaps one of his brothers was there, hearing the parishioners' confessions. He prayed for a few minutes. Prayer was an effective means of bringing peace to his mind. At that moment, he was feeling a kind of energy that was difficult to define. On these occasions, the Holy Spirit revealed itself to him more intensely. He felt reinvigorated and serene. No fear or concern tormented him. Past and future happenings reflected God's will. They were simply to be experienced and accepted tranquilly.

He rose, left the church and walked to the beach, turning in the direction of the apartment. He'd wait for his mother to arrive. He was already missing her. On arriving home, he made himself comfortable in his favorite armchair and resumed his reading. He read rapidly, having already arrived at chapter 147, "You know now that my soul, no matter how lacerated it may have been, didn't stay in a corner like a pale solitary flower." Soon he had reached the end of the book. He had no doubt that Machado de Assis was the greatest Brazilian writer of all time and undoubtedly one of the best in the world. "It's a pity our people read so little, thus missing the chance to get to know other worlds", he thought. He was reading *Dom Casmurro* for the second time and he still was unable to discover Capitu's secret. The doubt persisted in his mind, "How to know the truth?" Whenever he finished reading a book, he felt a tug at his heart, a farewell. It was like saying goodbye to a friend who would travel far away.

His wandering thoughts were interrupted by the arrival of his mother, who, feeling a longing for her son, left her suitcase at the door, on entering, and went to greet Reinaldo affectionately, talking about how she had yearned to see her friends again, and the fun they had together.

Reinaldo summarized his activities for her, omitting the lunch with the detective chief, since he didn't want to worry her unnecessarily.

After a lengthy bath, his mother appeared in the living room with some small packages, full of delicious sweets and snacks from Petrópolis. She set the table and told him in detail all the events of the birthday party. Reinaldo listened to the stories, enchanted by the way his mother spoke of the happenings. He hadn't inherited that gift from her. He had studied Public Speaking and had trained a lot to master this art and present narratives, but he could only do it with a great effort.

Night was already falling when they finished their snack and put everything in order. They went to the living room and sat down on the sofa. His mother took his hands in hers and they remained silent for a few moments. She looked at her son tenderly and broke the silence by saying, "You know, Reinaldo, one of the girls that was at the party was a psychologist. She has a lot of experience and has even published some books. I talked to her about you. Regression isn't her specialty, but she knows a good deal about the matter. In that psychologist's opinion, you must have suffered a trauma during the combat on the border, which provoked the regression to a previous life. She also said that the process should bring some form of revelation, which will result in comprehension and relief for your psyche. Yes, she used this term. I believe it means the same as soul."

He remained silent, reflecting on his mother's words. He recalled Father Demétrio's research, and replied, "That's true, I also believe things are pointing in that direction. Yesterday, at church, I talked with Father Demétrio. He researched the year I visit in my dreams and discovered something important. Almost all the Knights Templar that were in the Holy Land died in a battle that same year. And if Jean also died? Wouldn't it all seem senseless?"

"Well, in the first place, you said almost all and not all. Thus it's possible he was one of the survivors and the story continues. In the second place, you're alive and healthy, and that, for me, is the most important thing of all."

The incisive manner in which she pronounced the last sentence made the chaplain smile. Nevertheless, his mother's conclusion was the most logical one.

"Let's wait and see what happens."

They decided to watch the evening news on television. When it ended, his mother went to bed, saying she was tired from the trip. Reinaldo turned off the TV, remembered the book he had bought and began to read, *My Lives*. He needed to know more about the phenomenon of regression. Shirley MacLaine's experiences could be of great value at this point. He plunged into the reading. Shortly after midnight, he felt sleepy. He closed the book, turned off the lights and went to his room to sleep. He prayed, and when he closed his eyes, he already knew he'd soon travel to that distant world . . .

JAFFA

Two weeks after the ambassador's departure, Jean received a letter from the Duke d'Anjou, brought by a French knight who was coming on a pilgrimage. The Duke had received his request for help, asking him to send a force of knights to face Saladin. In the letter, he said it was impossible to help them, because he had gone to war against the Duke of Armagnac two months before, and all his subjects were mobilized for this combat. King Guido had already been informed that Saladin was preparing a large army, which would include forces from the Damascus and Cairo caliphates. Several envoys had left for the Christian kingdoms seeking reinforcements, but up to then no help had arrived. They were already in the middle of the month of May and life in Acre, in the Templars' community, was following the same routine: prayers and sacrifices. João had completely recovered from his wounds, and whenever it was possible for him, would join Pierre in conversing with Jean. They were very satisfying moments for Jean. He esteemed the two of them greatly, and his friends' company now meant the only joy for his suffering heart. Time was passing, but the pain of his loss seemed to increase. In his countless daily prayers, he always asked God to take him as soon as possible to join his family.

Regarding the danger to the Holy Land, the Abbott, that same morning during prayers, had recalled the letter that the monk Bernardo de Clairvaux had written to the King of England, requesting help for the Second Crusade.

"Our Lord in heaven is losing his land, the land in which he appeared to men, the land in which he lived among men for more than thirty years. It is well known that your country has many young vigorous men. The world is full of praise for them, and the fame of their courage is on everyone's lips.

"You now have a cause for which you can fight without endangering your souls, a cause in which winning is glorious and for which dying also represents victory. Do not lose this opportunity. Follow the sign of the cross. You shall immediately be pardoned for all the sins you confess with a contrite heart. It shall not cost you very much, and if you use it with humility, you shall see that it is the kingdom of heaven."

The Abbott also told the warrior monks about the serious loss the Order had suffered on the first of May. On that day, a force made up of Templars, Hospitallers, and Turkopoles (sergeants of Syrian origin) was heading from Jerusalem to Tiberiades, under the command of the Grand Masters of the Templars and the Hospitallers. The detachment, which totaled 130 knights, a few dozen Turcopoles and 400 infantrymen, was attacked close to the Cresson fountains by Saracen troops numbering approximately 1,000 soldiers, commanded by Muzaffar al Din Gökböri. The Christian cavalry attacked in an untimely manner, without waiting for the infantry, and was completely annihilated. Only the Templar Grand Master and a small group of knights escaped alive.

Also during the morning of that same day, Jean was summoned by the Abbott. He was to travel to Jaffa, a city in the French kingdom of Jerusalem, which was on the coast, to the south of Acre. He and Pierre were to leave the next day at dawn, and should arrive at their destination by mid-afternoon. They would be taking a message for Grand Master Gérard de Ridefort, who was passing through Jaffa on his way to Jerusalem. They received the document and made preparations for the trip. They awoke early, prayed and had their breakfast. The weather was clear and the day was a little hot. Despite their youth, the two men—the knight was then twenty-nine and his squire was thirty-nine—looked much older due to their long beards. They were impressive figures, their bodies completely covered by their coats of mail, mantles of small linked steel rings which took a year to make and were very expensive. On top of the coats of mail, they wore white linen mantles with a red cross on the chest, and on their heads, steel helmets with visors. On their waists, belts held the heavy battle swords. They also carried shields, decorated with the cross, and lances. While they were traveling, the lances and shields were strapped to their backs. The only difference with relation to Pierre was that he, as a squire, wore a brown mantle, besides also carrying his bow and quiver of arrows tied behind his back. Since the trip would be for a short distance and wouldn't take long, they didn't carry any luggage. They only carried their water canteens and a bag with food. Pierre used to be very pleased with these trips. He commented to Jean that it was a unique opportunity to get to know the sumptuous, famous places that had lived in his imagination since he was a boy and heard, in church, readings from the Gospel.

They rode toward the south, near the coast. The blue sea, extending to the right, delighted the travelers' eyes with its gleaming beauty. A soft sea breeze was blowing, which greatly relieved the sensation of heat, aggravated by their heavy garments and the weapons they were carrying. They were constantly passing through rural properties, mostly belonging to the Syrian population. Large olive tree plantations extended out as far as the eye could see. They also frequently encountered flocks of sheep. When the sun was already on high, they decided to stop near a fountain, alongside a large white house. Some children were playing under the olive trees, bordering the path which led to the house. They dismounted, tied their horses to the nearest tree and sat down on a large stone, in the shade of the trees. They greeted the children in French, but they laughed and didn't answer, seeming not to have understood. Apparently, they weren't surprised at the knights' presence. Many French knights had probably passed by there, traveling between the several Latin castles and fortresses in the vicinity, which made them familiar figures for the local inhabitants. They took out of their bags bread with pieces of cooked salted lamb to eat, drank water from their canteens and rested for a few minutes. A woman in Syrian dress with a veil covering her face was surprised by their presence. But quickly noticing their peaceful attitude, she continued on her way to the fountain, where she filled the jug she was carrying with water. She said something in her language to the children and returned to the house.

Jean smiled, pleased by that moment of peace, wishing that the world were always like that, just children playing joyously, mothers taking care of their homes and nature surrounding them with harmony and protection. They resumed their journey. The knight was now riding silently and pensively, since the stop for a rest. The children made him recall the image of his little son André, in the bloom of his joyful, enchanting boyhood. He remembered his golden hair, the same color as that of his mother, his small brown expressive eyes, his features which they said resembled very much those of his father, making him very proud. He was suddenly brought back to reality by Pierre's voice, "Sir, on that small hill up ahead, we shall be able to see the walls of Jaffa and its port."

"Yes, Pierre, Brother Charles, who gave me guidance regarding our path, said we would encounter that small hill from which we would be able to see the city."

They began to climb the hill and soon saw, in the distance, the walls of Jaffa and the port, with three galleons at the dock. They weren't tired, so they could ride faster and approached the first dwellings, located outside the city walls. The houses were occupied by Syrian families; some buildings must have belonged to rich people, since they were well maintained, with inner gardens visible from the arches at their entrances, and with glass windows. They began to encounter groups of people that were going about on foot, carrying baskets full of merchandise which would possibly be sold in the city market. Few Europeans were to be seen. They met two men on horseback, possibly French knights, armed with swords, dressed in coats of mail and carrying shields with coats of arms. They saluted each other and Jean noticed their admiring look when they realized that Jean and Pierre were Templars. Finally they arrived at the main city gate, where they inquired as to the direction they should take to reach the Order's castle. They went around a small hill located close to the port and continued their journey. Then they passed through several very narrow streets and reached the southern end of the city, where they recognized the Order's flag, with its red cross on a white background, waving at the at the entrance to a large stone fortress. The castle walls extended down to the sea. It could be easily seen that its location had been chosen so as to entrust the defense of that important sector of the city to the Knights Templar, in case of attack.

They were immediately taken to the Abbot. He welcomed them and received the message to be delivered to the Grand Master, who was in the castle. With their mission accomplished, they were told they could remain in Jaffa for the rest of the day and return to Acre the following morning. After a brief rest, they were again summoned to the presence of the Abbot, who told them, "The Grand Master wishes you to be present at the meeting of the lords of the Latin kingdoms, which is being held in the castle."

They got ready quickly and followed the monk through several corridors and stairways. They arrived at an antechamber, where they awaited Grand Master Gérard de Ridefort. The knight seemed to be a little older than Pierre and had a very vigorous manner, which irradiated authority. He said, "You brought very serious news. I shall take you to the meeting so that King Guido will become aware of it."

Jean looked at Pierre in astonishment, which was immediately perceived by the squire. They didn't have the slightest idea of what was contained in the message they had brought. On the other hand, they didn't know that the King of Jerusalem was in Jaffa, nor who were the other authorities present. They just stammered a "Yes, sir" and followed Gérard to the next room. It was a very large hall, with an enormous table, where a large number of knights of noble blood, richly dressed, were gathered. At the head of the table was a blond man, tall, appearing to be about forty years old, whose garments showed his noble rank. They deduced that he was King Guido. The Grand Master addressed him in a loud, firm voice, "By your leave, Majesty. I bring news received now, by means of these two Templar messengers, sent by the Master Abbot of Acre, that I consider to be of the utmost urgency and seriousness; I ask Your Majesty's permission to read the message, so that all of you shall be familiar with it."

A great silence came over the hall and they all turned toward the Templar, anxiously awaiting the news to be announced.

"Dear Brother Grand Master, I am sending knight Jean de Saumur and his squire Pierre Gabin to deliver to you this urgent message that I believe to be of the greatest importance for the overseas Latin peoples: I have just received from one of our spies at the court of the Sultan, in Damascus, information that the principality of Mosul has become a vassal of Saladin, and that the latter is sending southward an army of ten thousand men, including six thousand horsemen, to join the armies that shall attack us. We all know the military importance of the Seljukian Turks and their archer cavalry. These reinforcements for the Saracen army make the force ratio very unfavorable for our Latin kingdoms. The information was confirmed by another Syrian authority in whom we confide, who certified that it was true. The document is signed by our brother, Master Abbot of Acre."

There was a series of murmurs and King Guido invited the Grand Master to sit on his left. Jean and Pierre remained among the several knights who were standing around the table. A knight near Jean placed his hand on Jean's shoulder and said, "Knight Jean, what a surprise to find you here!"

The Templar immediately recognized the firm voice and the Italian accent, and replied, "Noble Petrazzi, what are you doing here in Jaffa?"

The last time they were together was at the funeral of Melissande and André, but they spoke to each other very little, under the circumstances and due to the Templar's state of deep sorrow. Petrazzi explained, "I came here last year, accompanying a cousin of King Guido who was making a pilgrimage, and I ended up in the court of Jerusalem, where I am Captain of the Guard."

The Italian turned and greeted Pierre, who was behind Jean. The Templar, who understood nothing of what was happening, heard the King discuss something with a knight with a strong personality who was sitting at his right. Jean asked, "Petrazzi, could you tell us what is happening and who are the noblemen that are together with the King?"

The Italian knight took them by the arm to a corner of the room and began to give an account of what was happening. "In the first place, I shall identify for you who are the main barons seated at that table. Obviously, you already identified King Guido and the Grand Master of your Order. The knight on the right of the King is Reinaldo de Châtillon, the lord of Karak or Krak, in Transjordan. He wields great influence over the King. They say that His Majesty agrees with everything that Reinaldo suggests. The strong knight seated beside the Grand Master is Count Raymond of Tripoli, rival of Reinaldo, and is considered to be the most intelligent and capable Christian leader. Alongside Reinaldo is the Grand Master of the Hospitallers. The last nobleman is the Count of Harenc, Gotardo de Mogúncia, representative of Prince Beomundo of Antioch. The King came to inspect the defenses of Jaffa and called an emergency meeting, on learning that Saladin is gathering a large army to attack us."

Petrazzi was speaking in a low voice, in order not to disturb the meeting, which continued heatedly. Jean took advantage of an interval of silence to comment, "But the truce? What happened to it?"

Petrazzi replied, "Knight Reinaldo has been repeatedly breaking the truce, since his attack on Mecca in 1182. The Sultan never forgave such a serious offense. Well then, at the end of March this year, Saladin's brother left Cairo with an enormous rich caravan transporting merchandise bound for Damascus. Knight Reinaldo gathered together a force of French knights which attacked and plundered the caravan. That made Saladin forget the truce once and for all. The army that he is gathering together in Damascus shall be the largest army ever organized by the Saracens until now. The meeting called by the King should, as His Majesty has already told us, decree the mobilization of the Christian forces from all the cities in the Holy Land."

They became silent, hearing the King close the meeting, "Noble barons! The Saracen leader is gathering together his armies to attack us and try to take over the holy places guarded by us! I order all the Christian knights in the Holy Land to gather together as soon as possible, in Acre, so that we can together march against the enemies of Christ and destroy them!"

The meeting was closed and everyone awaited the departure of the most important noblemen. Jean, Petrazzi and Pierre walked out of the meeting room together.

THE TEMPTATION

All of a sudden, there was a dazzling light. It was the sun that was entering through the gap in the curtains, hitting him right in the face. He no longer was in that stone corridor of the Templars' castle in Jaffa, but rather in his bed, in his mother's apartment in Copacabana. He was impressed by the speed with which he went from his dream to his awakening. He looked at the clock—it was 8 a.m. "Tomorrow will be a week since I arrived in Rio," he thought.

The day began with a sunny morning bringing pleasant warmth. As usual, he got ready and headed for the kitchen, where his mother was preparing the breakfast table. She looked very well, dressed sportingly in Bermuda shorts and T-shirt, ready for her walk, and asked, "And you, then? Did you enjoy your trip around Palestine?"

He told her about the dream he had had that night. His mother listened to it all attentively, and commented, "I'm impressed by the number of different people you see in your dreams; I don't understand how you remember all of them and everything else as if you were really living among them."

"The sensation that I have, mother, is that I'm really living two lives."

"Well, judging by what you've told me about regression, what's happening is that the memories of your previous life are coming back to you, night after night, through your dreams. Look, let's have our breakfast before it gets cold. Sit down right away, and then we'll take our walk, our daily exercise."

After cleaning up, they went to the boardwalk. The sea displayed few waves and a mild breeze was blowing. They joined a large number of people walking along the shore. They arrived home tired, and after taking a bath, his mother took leave of him, to go to the bank and do some shopping. Reinaldo offered to go along with her, but she refused decidedly.

He picked up the newspaper, took a look at the main news items and then returned to reading Shirley MacLaine's book. The book left some unanswered questions in his mind: "My God, why doesn't the Church explore this matter? The Old Testament of the Bible, with its kings, saints and prophets, contains a great deal of spiritual information. It doesn't seem to condemn reincarnation." It was then that the telephone rang. It was Josephine. She wanted to confirm the concert they had scheduled for the following night, in the Municipal Theater. Reinaldo replied that he'd be happy to go. Then came a sudden invitation: "Would you like to have lunch with me today? As my guest, of course!"

He remained silent for a few seconds. His thoughts raced through his mind at high speed. He sensed that this type of relationship might not work, due to his religious calling. On the other hand, he didn't see any harm in meeting again a friend from his adolescent years.

Reinaldo accepted the invitation and they arranged the meeting. He put away the book he was reading and got dressed. When he was ready, he left a note for his mother, telling her he was going to have lunch with Josephine, and went downstairs. There were still a few minutes to go until the scheduled time, when he arrived at the corner. He looked in the direction that the vehicles were coming from. After some time, he noticed a silver gray Vectra with a brand-new look that had slowed down and stopped in front of him. Jô made a sign for him to get in the car. He got in and fastened the seat belt. She leaned over and kissed him on the cheek. She was very pretty, dressed in a black suit, which highlighted her beautiful blond hair. She had such a youthful appearance that she didn't seem to be three years older than him.

"How've you been, Reinaldo?"

"I'm fine, Jô. I was really needing a vacation, after all that time in the Amazon region. I was very pleased with your invitation, it was very kind of you."

"I'm the one to thank you for having accepted accompanying me. I can't stand it any more, going out to lunch with my colleagues from the office and talking about our work all the time."

She was driving along Avenida Atlântica toward Lifeguard Station Six and the chaplain was trying to guess which restaurant they'd have lunch in. It seems that Jô read his thoughts, and she explained, "I'm taking you to lunch at a restaurant I'm very fond of. It's at the end of the avenue, and I hope you enjoy French cooking."

He smiled on hearing her mention the word French. She couldn't have the slightest idea of how he'd been living, at least at night, involved with everything that was French.

"I like it very much, Jô. But I'm only familiar with the very old dishes that were served during the Middle Ages."

She smiled, without understanding what he meant. They arrived at the last building on the avenue, left the car with the parking attendant and went inside. It was a luxury hotel, an environment which the chaplain wasn't accustomed to. They crossed the spacious lobby and took the elevator, getting off at a middle floor. In the exquisitely decorated foyer there was a large picture with the image of Virgin Mary being crowned by three kings. Reinaldo wasn't a fine arts connoisseur, but the picture seemed to him to be a work painted in Cuzco, in Peru, where a school had flourished that specialized in that type of art. The three kings must have represented the Magi, or perhaps the Holy Trinity. After walking through an enormous hall, they arrived at the luxurious restaurant. In the cozy atmosphere, there was an enormous grand piano in the center, under a beautiful dome. The name *Le Pré Catelan* sounded very French to him. There were few people present, since that time was considered early for lunch according to the Rio tradition. They chose a table near the window, with a view of the sea. On reading the menu, brought by the *maître*, he was confused, since he wasn't familiar with any of those dishes. Jô immediately came to his rescue, "May I order for you? I guarantee you'll like it."

"Thanks very much, I'm sure I will. I'm not used to the luxury, as you can well imagine, but I'm enjoying the experience very much."

Then she ordered: *shrimp salad in basil oil with "baroa" potatoes, grouper scallops in "vongole" and saffron sauce with mashed peas and tomatoes "confit". For dessert, cashew napoleon with whisky-flavored ice cream.* She chose a good vintage French white wine to drink.

Reinaldo was thinking how high the check would be, and deducing that Jô must earn a lot of money as a lawyer. He recalled some people he knew in the same profession who weren't so lucky. The waiter left them and Jô turned to the chaplain, saying, "So, are you enjoying your vacation?"

"It's been good to be with my mother again—I hadn't seen her for a long time. Seeing my city again, some friends like you, it's an indescribable joy."

She looked at him pensively with her big brown eyes and said, "I was thinking, Reinaldo, what would a priest's life plans be like? What would he expect in the future? Would he have the ambition to become a bishop, cardinal, that sort of thing?"

He smiled and thought a little before replying, "In my case, I can tell you that my plans are for the very short term. I try to live each day seeking to achieve the goal I set for myself on devoting my life to the Lord. This goal, basically, is to bring the word of Christ to the believers, through the Gospel, its values and rituals; I believe I've achieved it. I don't think at all of rising through the Church hierarchy. If this happens, it'll be something natural that I'll accept, more as a task to perform than as a reward."

He knew he was omitting the main point that his immediate goal was to find the answers to the question that was leading him toward the greatest decision in his life: whether his religious calling was genuine or not. However, this would be too complex a revelation for such a superficial relationship, like the one he had with Josephine.

"Your life seems to flow very calmly, my friend. Besides your religious work with the troops, do you participate in any civilian activity there in your city?"

"Yes, I do, Jô, I help the parish priest close to the barracks, who in turn also helps me, when I need it. We perform social work, collecting donations that are invested in assisting needy children, very poor families, guidance for adolescents, and we maintain a small home for the aged, with the help of volunteers from the parish and of military personnel from the Border

Battalion. As you can see, there's no lack of work. Remembering this, my conscience is bothering me, being here enjoying all this luxury, while the poor parishioners are missing me. That is, if they really miss me!"

"Of course they miss you, Reinaldo, and I'm sure they'd be very happy to know that their priest is having a little rest and receiving a small retribution for the alms he distributes in his daily work."

At that moment their waiter arrived with a cart carrying their lunch, which gave out a delicious aroma. He was surprised at the artistic arrangement of the food on the plate and its quantity, which he found diminutive. Now he turned his attention to tasting the delicious food. He smiled, recalling the same sensation that Jean had felt, on having the meal with Usamah in Acre. At least, from the gastronomic viewpoint, his life had improved considerably, in comparison. The waiter brought the second dish, removing the empty plate. The chaplain was observing that ritual attentively.

"Did you like my choice?"

"Jô, I'm grateful to God for having the opportunity, thanks to you, to enjoy this marvelous meal."

"Amen, father! I'm very happy you're enjoying the lunch. It was good meeting you again. Recently my life has been limited to my work. It's going to be a year since I terminated a love affair, and since then I haven't wanted to get involved with anyone else. In all due modesty, I know I'm an attractive woman. Men are always trying to pick me up, but I refuse to have passing affairs. So I've been very lonely. Sometimes I regret that I avoided having children during my marriage. My parents live in Teresópolis in the mountains, and at least once a month I spend a weekend with them. As I mentioned before, I have several friends at work, but they're people I only want to meet during my professional activities. And this is my life. Let's drink a toast, in the hope that our meeting is the beginning of a great lasting friendship."

Reinaldo raised his glass and inwardly felt sorry for that beautiful thirty-seven-year-old woman, who seemed to feel so lonely. "Perhaps it's the price women pay for their independence, both sentimentally as well as financially," he mused. He was thinking how the large cities' hostile environment also made it difficult for a woman to become involved in a loving relationship and to form a new family nucleus.

"You were so pensive after what I said," she observed.

"That's true. I was thinking about how a woman's life these days has become complex! On the other hand, she's won access to places that were denied to her for centuries."

At this point, many of the tables in the restaurant were already occupied. The waiter brought dessert, just as delicious as the rest of the meal. They ate silently in the pleasant atmosphere which promoted a feeling of well-being. They ordered small coffees and soon afterwards Jô asked for the check, which she tactfully paid with her credit card. He asked, "Are you still going back to the office, Jô?"

"No, I'll drop you at the door of your building and then go on to the courthouse downtown, where I have a hearing scheduled. And you, what are you going to do?"

"I'm going home, chat with my mother a little, if she's there. Then I'm going to the Copacabana Parish Church, where I intend to participate in the celebration of the six o'clock mass. I've two classmates from the seminary who are priests there."

They left the restaurant, went down to the lobby and waited at the door for the parking attendant to bring Jô's car. They returned along Avenida Atlântica, and in a few minutes, arrived in front of his building. She said, "I'll phone you at nine p.m. to make arrangements to go to the concert tomorrow, OK?"

When he began to turn around in order to get out of the car, Jô took his hand, bent over and kissed his cheek. He returned the kiss naturally and got out.

He crossed the avenue and entered his building. He greeted the doorman, who told him that his mother was already in the apartment. On arriving there, he found her seated on the living room sofa, reading the newspaper. "Hi, mom, I was already missing you."

"I don't believe you. Having lunch in a swell place in very good company . . ."

"We went to a restaurant called *Le Pré Catelan*. Do you know it?"

"No, but a friend of mine was there and liked it very much. What did you think of it?"

Reinaldo sat down beside her, leaned over and gave her a kiss on the cheek before replying, "I'm not a connoisseur of good restaurants, for obvious reasons, but I could see that it must be one of the best in the city. It was very kind of Jô to invite me."

"Nonsense! When you're a cardinal you'll get to know better places."

He laughed at his mother's joke, realizing that at the moment his chances of becoming a cardinal were almost nil.

"You told me she's divorced, didn't you? Doesn't she have a boyfriend?"

"No, mother, she said she doesn't want any boyfriends, after terminating a long relationship."

"Don't forget to tell her you already have a girlfriend, in case she has some crazy idea."

"And may I ask who my girlfriend is?"

"Of course! Our Mother Church, my son. Or isn't she?"

"Let's say that in reality we're married, and at the moment we're going through a period of marital turbulence."

"I know, but I have the impression your dreams will end up by providing a happy ending for that turbulence."

The chaplain wasn't very certain of that and thought it better to change the subject. He tried to guide the conversation to a different path, asking her where she had had lunch.

"Nearby here, in a restaurant that charges by the kilo. What are you going to do now? Do you intend to go out? Surely you'll rest a little before going to the parish church to participate in the celebration of the six o'clock mass, won't you?"

As it was still early, he asked his mother to excuse him, went to his room to change clothes and returned to the living room, looking for his book to continue reading. His mother was no longer there, having retired to her room. On reaching out his hand to pick up the book, he happened to notice an old edition of poetry by Guilherme de Almeida. He immediately recalled his father. That writer was one of Dr. Roberto's favorites. He opened the book at the page someone had marked with a flap—probably his father—and was moved. The poem on the marked page was entitled *The Guest:*

> *You don't need to knock when you arrive*
> *Take the iron key that you'll find*
> *Under the pillar, beside the gate,*
> *And open with it*
> *The silent old low door.*
> *Enter. Here is the armchair, the book, the rose,*
> *The clay jug and the wheat bread.*

The friendly dog
Will rest its head on your knees.
Let night fall, slowly.
The chest and room's smell of grass and the sun,
The linens are abundant,
And the home smells of oil lamps.
Sleep. Dream. Wake up. From the beehive
The honey morning dawns against the window.
Close the gate
And go. There's sun in the orchard fruit.
Don't look back when you take
The sleepwalking path that goes down.
Walk—and forget.

He remained motionless for a few seconds, without thinking about anything; he just felt an old and senseless melancholy. He closed the book, put it back on the shelf, as if he were safeguarding a treasure in the safe, and picked up the book which interested him momentarily.

He snuggled up in the armchair and began to read. His mother passed through the room, saying she was going to visit a sick friend. The afternoon was chilly, despite the good weather. He stopped reading a little before five thirty, got dressed and went to the church. This time he decided to take a different route, so he went along Avenida Nossa Senhora de Copacabana. At that time of day the traffic was heavy, both vehicles and pedestrians, which made him a little dizzy. On arriving at the church, he went directly to the vestry. Father Sílvio came over to greet him when he saw him. "Reinaldo, have you been enjoying your vacation?"

"Sílvio, I've been resting a lot and even enjoying some luxuries. Today's lunch, for example, in a luxurious restaurant paid by a charitable friend."

"Gosh, man. Couldn't you arrange to take me along on one of those events, huh?"

Sílvio's way of talking made the chaplain laugh a lot before replying, "Next time I promise to pass by here and take you along, OK? Where's Demétrio?

"He went to a meeting in the Archdiocese and he hasn't returned until now. It's just as well you came to celebrate the six o'clock mass with us."

They began to put on their vestments and a little later started the holy mass ritual. Once again that group of faithful worshippers came together to remember the sacrifice of Christ, that completely changed the course of humanity but is still so little known.

After mass, the small group went to the parish hall for the traditional evening supper. The friends, now joined by Father Demétrio who had returned, sat down together.

"So, Reinaldo, how are your dreams coming along?"

Demétrio's way of asking made the chaplain smile, as he answered, "They've been coming every night, punctually."

"Have you any idea of what month they're in?"

"I think they're in May, Demétrio. Why?"

"I went back to researching that epoch and now I've found the exact date of the battle that resulted in the death of most of the Knights Templar that were in the Holy Land. It was on July 4th. It seems that in a month and a half it will all be over."

The chaplain became apprehensive as he reflected on the information furnished by his brother priest. In his dreams, time was not continuous, that is, it made jumps, sometimes of several weeks. According to Demétrio, these dreams could end very shortly. He tried to turn away his thoughts, in order not to go crazy, and said, "That's true, Demétrio, but I have faith that before that, everything will be clarified."

"Yes, let's hope that happens, since I'd also like to know the end of this enigma."

Then they began to converse about other things, to Reinaldo's relief. When they finished supper, the chaplain said good-bye to everyone and returned home. It was a little after eight and the night was chilly. The digital clock in the center of Avenida Atlântica showed the temperature was around 57° F. Reinaldo was wearing a woolen jacket over his shirt and even so felt cold. There were few passersby on the sidewalk under the cloudless starry sky. He arrived quickly at the apartment. His mother was watching the eight o-clock soap opera on TV and already knew about the customary supper in the parish church. Even so she offered her son a snack, which he politely refused. Reinaldo went back to his book, sat down in the armchair and began to read. At nine o'clock sharp the telephone rang.

It was Jô. They arranged to meet at eight p.m. the next day, at the same place where she had picked him up today. She said good-bye and good night, with a hug for his mother. The latter knew about the invitation for the concert, but she was so taken up with the soap opera that she didn't even ask about the phone call. Soon afterward, she gave her son a good night kiss and went to bed. Reinaldo read until eleven, when he became sleepy. He turned out the living room lights, went to his room, put on his pajamas and turned out the light. He took his time reciting Our Father. He fell asleep almost immediately after his prayers. And the dream came, as always . . .

THE HUNT

After they left the meeting with the barons, Jean, Petrazzi and Pierre walked to an outside patio located near the wall that went along the seacoast, with a beautiful view of the turquoise Mediterranean Sea. Petrazzi showed the Templars the main points of the large construction: the main tower, also called the citadel or *donjon*, separated from the rest of the castle by a moat and a drawbridge which, in case of an attack and the occupation of the castle, would be its last bastion of defense. The Master Abbot of Jaffa also had his quarters in the citadel. They visited the chapel, the stables, the secondary lodgings and the guardhouse, located close to the main gate, which looked out on the drawbridge.

It was sunset, and the approaching night would paint the sky with the most exotic colors from nature's palette. Jean asked his Italian friend for permission to go to the chapel to recite the vespers with his brother Templars and then participate in the community meal. So they broke up, arranging to meet again in the morning of the following day. The young Templar was lodged in a large dormitory reserved for the knights. The cot was clean and the place very cold. Several oil lamps lighted the surroundings during the whole night, in accordance with the Order's rules. He wasn't sleepy. He was thinking about the day's happenings and the meeting with Petrazzi. His Italian friend's image brought to mind memories of the hunt during the Spring Tournament. The memory of the occurrences on that radiant morning made him smile. How much time had passed! It seemed like it had all occurred in another world, a world of joy and happiness that he thought would never end. Sometimes he wondered why God had given him such a heavy burden to bear. He anxiously awaited the moment in which the Lord would grant him relief. Suddenly, the sad thoughts were pushed aside by remote images in his memory.

It was the third day of the Spring Tournament—a day of rest. All the guests invited to participate in the hunt organized by the Marquis de Challons, the father of Melissande and Robert, were gathering in front of King Pepin's Gate. The scene was one of perfect harmony: the clear morning, the air redolent with the perfume of the wild flowers, the blue spring sky. The hunt master blew his horn from time to time, calling on the participants to gather in groups around the banner of the Marquis. Jean had been one of the first to arrive, always accompanied by faithful Pierre. He was an excellent hunter, a master of falconry. During his training as a squire, at the court of the Duke, he had stood out among the best. Hunting with falcons was a very sophisticated art and a sure way to fill the feudal lords' larders with lots of poultry. This day's hunt, however, would be performed with the help of bloodhounds, another way of filling the larders with other types of meat. Robert, and then Petrazzi, arrived and joined Jean and Pierre. They wore light clothing, shorts, leather boots, embroidered shirts and hats. Jean's heart beat faster on seeing Melissande. The young girl was riding with a small group of ladies, all richly dressed, and on glimpsing Jean, she gave him a big smile, which he returned charmingly. Then the Marquis arrived and ordered the hunt master to blow his horn, to mark the start of the hunt. The beaters said they had seen a large wild boar in the woods, a few leagues distant. The hounds were let loose, and at the sound of the horn, everyone rode toward the woods. Jean drew away from his friends and rode near the group of ladies, within sight of Melissande. He intended to be alone with his beloved, who, guessing his intention, began to move away tactfully from her group, so as not to let the other ladies notice it. On arriving in the woods, the couple rode through the trees, drawing further and further away from the hunt. They reached a small clearing and dismounted. Without saying a single word, they ran toward each other and engaged in their first anxiously-awaited hugs and kisses. It was a magic moment of love. The earth stopped spinning, time stopped for the couple of sweethearts, who felt they were the only ones in the world. They had kissed in their thoughts, since they had seen each other for the first time, and now gave vent to their desires. They laid down in the grass, near the roots of an old leafy birch tree. They didn't know how much time had passed—perhaps half an hour, perhaps more. The discovery of their soft touches, of the warmth of their skins, was an indescribable sensation. The first words Jean succeeded in uttering came from the depths of his heart: "I love you very much, Melissande!"

The young girl, still embracing the knight, looked tenderly in his eyes, and replied, "I love you too, Jean. I was dreaming all the time of this moment."

"It seems like a dream from which I do not want to awaken."

"I do not want to wait any longer. I am going to talk to my father this very day and ask him to seek out your father, the Marquis, to arrange for our marriage. God was good to us and everything should go smoothly, on behalf of the friendship which unites our families."

At that moment, they heard the sound of an approaching horse, followed by an exclamation, "Sir Jean! Do you need any help? Is the lady hurt?"

Jean immediately recognized Petrazzi's voice and understood what he had imagined. It was obvious that the Italian knight had encountered them by chance and had concluded that Melissande, having fallen off her horse, was at that moment being rescued by Jean. The Italian's face showed such concern that the pair of lovers could not help bursting into laughter. Petrazzi soon realized what had happened and became really confused, which increased even further the couple's laughter. After a big effort to contain his laughter, Jean replied, "My noble friend, we are hiding from the others because we love each other and you shall be the first to learn that we are going to get married."

The Italian gave a big smile, pulled the reins of his horse to the side and said before leaving, "I would never forgive myself for interrupting such a beautiful romance."

The lovers went back to kissing each other, and during a long time remained in a close embrace, having completely forgotten the rest of the world. It was then that they heard the hunt master's horn blow twice, announcing that the bloodhounds had found the game. At this point in the hunt, all the participants would converge on the place where the animal was held at bay by the master's assistants, accompanied by their valiant canine friends.

"I think we had better go back now," Melissande ventured. "My lady companion must be nervous already at my disappearance and perhaps she has even sent word to my father."

With a sigh of suffering, Jean agreed and helped her to rise from the grass. Then, approaching the horses that were grazing nearby, he helped her mount and they left for the place from which the sound of the horn was coming. They rode until they succeeded in locating the group of participants in the hunt, surrounding the wild boar.

The animal was very wounded by the hounds' attack, and the master waited for the command by the Marquis to give it the coup de grace, with a stroke of his lance. Melissande's father, already made aware of her disappearance by her lady companion, was relieved to see his daughter arrive, accompanied by young Jean. Finally, then, he ordered the master to end the prey's suffering. As was the custom, they began to sing a song in praise of the game:

We give thanks. Lord,
For giving us this splendid animal.
It shall feed us,
And shall live again in us.
Its pain shall be transformed and shall bubble over
Into sweet happiness.
We shall honor its memory and
This memory shall endure.
Powerful animal, juicy meat.
Energy and health, joy and feast.
Your struggle to get away reinforced our friendship.
Let us all sing joyously,
For the hours of riding through the fields
And for this gift from the Lord.

The couple separated, Melissande rejoined the group of ladies and Jean that of the men. The master of the hunt prepared the animal for carrying and the Marquis terminated the hunt. Three long notes of the horn ended those enjoyable hours. They all rode back to the palace, where the host would offer dinner. Wild boar meat would be the main dish. On arriving at the castle, they dismounted and delivered their mounts to the servants. The participants then went to the rooms reserved for changing clothes. Around two hours later, the sound of a bell announced the start of the dinner. The guests headed for a large tent raised in the garden, where several tables had been set up. Jean's satisfaction was overflowing. The hours he had passed in the company of his beloved were the happiest hours in his whole life. He still felt the freshness of her sweet lips and he would remember during his entire life the magic of this first contact with Melissande's soft delicate body. He ardently desired to be with her again. Even more so, he wanted to live forever at her side. He never thought love could be such an overwhelming sentiment that it made everything else seem senseless and unimportant. He prepared for dinner with great care and headed for the garden, also accompanied by Pierre, who gazed at him pensively, with an astute smile. They spied the table reserved for the Saumur family. His parents and relatives were arriving, a little ahead of him. He greeted his father, the Marquis, who stared at him laughingly, and said, "My brave son, I heard that you got lost during the hunt. Is that true?"

The young man blushed and looked at Pierre reproachfully, supposing that he had been the informer of his flight with Melissande. "Yes, father. I moved away a little to converse with the young lady, Melissande, and before I realized it, the group was already far away."

The cheerful Marquis burst out in loud laughter, as if he had been hearing the biggest joke. "And what is this conversation that you could have with the young lady, Melissande?"

The youth felt the time had come to reveal his love and ask his father's help to make his dream come true. "Father, we are in love with each other, we want your blessing and your permission, and that of the Marquis de Challons, for our engagement."

The Marquis looked with pleasure at his young son. Everyone in the two families had already noticed the young couple's romance. They were only waiting for Jean's request to formalize the engagement, which pleased the two noblemen. Jean's father replied, "Yes, my son. You and the young lady, Melissande, have my blessing and my permission. Right after dinner, I shall request the approval of the Marquis, and as I am certain he looks favorably on this union, we shall arrange the date of the engagement."

Jean was so pleased with his father's reaction that he couldn't contain himself, and moved by a vigorous impulse, gave his father a strong embrace. The Marquis de Saumur laughed at his son's reaction. He was happy with that union that would benefit the two families so much. His wife, who was conversing with their daughter a little further away, approached jubilantly, and exclaimed, "I heard the whole conversation and I also am very happy about your choice, my son. We were always dreaming of this union, but we wanted a marriage, uniting our two families, that would come about naturally, and not by means of an arrangement of convenience."

The Marchioness hugged her son affectionately. Then they went to the table, where they all settled themselves. Jean received congratulations from his relatives and from Pierre, who declared, "Sir, I did not say anything to your father. It was not necessary. For a long time now, everyone in the two families has been following your steps, hoping for this outcome."

"Forgive me, my good friend. Today is the happiest day of my life and I would like everyone to toast my happiness."

At that moment, the members of the Challons family entered the tent and headed toward the table reserved for them, beside the Saumur family table. The two marquis met and embraced. Everyone noticed when Jean's father spoke at length with his friend, who at the end embraced him euphorically. Returning to the table, the two marquises told their families they had arranged for the marriage of their children on Saint John's Day. The cheerful atmosphere came over the two tables. At that moment, the Marquis de Challons, who was the host, ordered wine served to everyone and offered a toast to the marriage of Melissande and Jean. The young man was invited to sit at his future father-in-law's table, alongside his fiancée. Then the order was given to serve dinner, and the servants began to parade in with delicacies and beverages.

It had all happened so fast. It seemed the fiancés were living in a dream of magic and love. They gazed at each other tenderly all the time, as if magnetized. The other guests shared that moment of good cheer and all laughed happily, surrounded by the abundance of food and drink. Petrazzi was invited to sit at the Marquis de Saumur's table, occupying the place that was Jean's, alongside Pierre. He told everyone, proudly and happily, that he had been the first to learn of the romance. And the dinner became a party. The Marquis ordered wine to be served continuously and everybody stayed there until nightfall. Torches were lit in the garden, and some time afterward, the already tired guests began to take leave and depart. Jean and Melissande conversed happily about their plans for the future. They wanted to have many children. She was hoping for two pairs of boys and girls, while he wanted three boys and two girls. When the fiancée's parents called their children and said good-bye, this ended for the young couple a day which would be remembered as the happiest in their lives. Both had difficulty falling asleep, recalling every moment they had spent together on that blessed spring day.

On the following day, the fourth day of the Spring Tournament, the archery and battle ax competitions were held. Jean, Robert and Petrazzi, aided by other knights and squires, served as supervisors. Pierre competed in both contests. He was the great winner of the archery contest, leading the other competitors by a wide margin. And so he became one of the greatest archers in the realm. Later, in the presence of all the competitors, the Duke proclaimed the grand winner of the tournament: the Norman knight Jean de Brest. After the horns blew and his name was announced, Jean de Brest paraded past, accompanied by his two squires, in front of the winners of the other contests. He received the laurel crown from the hands of the Duchess, the "Queen of Beauty and Love", and right afterward, returned to the parade, now applauded by the crowd of noblemen and plebeians who attended the event. When the parade ended, the Duke formally closed the tournament. The Tournament Master ordered a call by the horns and bugles which ended the ceremony. The beautiful sunset which was taking shape on the horizon provided the backdrop for the departure of the spectators, who were noisily commenting the day's exciting happenings.

Sleep finally came to the knight. A smile lit up his face, the result of so many pleasant memories.

In the morning of the next day, they said good-bye to Petrazzi and left to return to Acre, as the Abbot had ordered.

THE KIDNAPPING

The day dawned chilly that Wednesday. It was winter. Reinaldo, not in a hurry to get up, stayed in bed a little later, thinking about the great struggle which was approaching in the life of Jean and his brother Templars. A wave of dizzy thoughts invaded his mind: "Would Jean be able to survive the hecatomb announced by Father Demétrio? What could be the meaning of his dreams?" Shirley MacLaine's book revealed a new universe, in which the spirit took on much larger proportions than those shown by his Church. The discovery of certain fundamental aspects of the oriental religions, older than their western counterparts, greatly increased the scope of his spiritual horizons. These concepts, described very well in the book, had already been the subject of reflection for countless Christian thinkers, and it wouldn't be Reinaldo, a simple country priest, not very erudite, who'd venture into philosophical incursions regarding human spirituality. He got up, followed his daily routine and headed for the kitchen, practically guided by the good aroma arising from the coffee prepared by his mother.

At the table he told her about his dream of Jean that night, even venturing to hum a part of the hunters' song. His mother laughed a lot at that off key voice that was solemnly trying to imitate the medieval singers. Together, they cleaned up the kitchen.

He noticed that his mother was not wearing her customary walking dress that morning, and asked, "Aren't you going to walk today?"

"I have to visit the doctor, but don't worry, it's my semi-annual visit, just to check that everything is in order, that famous preventive medicine, you know. Take your walk alone, OK?"

Already dressed for his walk, Reinaldo left the apartment and headed for the boardwalk. He was suitably dressed, but even so felt cold. A southwest wind was blowing, lowering the temperature below that shown by the thermometers, around 57° F. The sky was cloudy and gray, announcing rain later in the day. He recalled he'd be going to the Municipal Theater that night with Jô, to attend a concert by the Brazilian Symphonic Orchestra.

When he returned to the apartment, his mother had already left. He took a bath and, as it was still early, picked up Shirley MacLaine's book. He gazed for a few moments at the photo of the actress on the cover. She had written her story courageously, and he was reading it very moved. It recalled other religious revelations that had awakened his doubts.

He thought of his study of philosophy, Pythagoras, Plato, and of literature, Ralph Waldo Emerson, Walt Whitman, Goethe and Voltaire, where all of them believed in reincarnation and wrote about it.

Shortly before noon, his mother arrived, carrying some shopping bags. He hurried to help her. They set the table and sat down to eat the meal already prepared that his mother had brought. She talked about her visit to the doctor and said she'd only learn the results after having blood tests which the doctor requests whenever she appears there.

"You look extremely well," he said. She smiled and thanked him. After finishing lunch, they cheerfully shared the task of cleaning up the kitchen. They conversed a little bit, and his mother went to her room to rest. Reinaldo returned to the absorbing reading of Shirley Maclaine's story. She had traveled to Peru. She had gone to see the frozen peaks of the Andes, ancient territory of the Incas, a people with great mystical experiences. Suddenly there came to his memory a book he had read while he was still an adolescent, *Pumasonco*, written by the couple Ofélia and Narbal Fontes. The story also involved the ancient Inca civilization. He returned to his reading and hours later, when he had reached the last page, it was already getting dark. He had finally finished reading the book. He had been very impressed by the experiences of the actress, who shared with the readers in a moving way her discoveries in the spiritual realm. He put away the book and went to the kitchen, where he found his mother already preparing a snack. "Mother, do you think life exists outside of the earth?"

She looked at him enigmatically and answered, "Look, my son, judging by what I've already experienced in this life, and despite the fact that my scientific knowledge is very limited, I'd say yes. It's possible that it exists, but I'm not the best person to make this affirmation. Was it about this that you were reading all day long?"

"Yes, it was, among other surprising revelations. For a long time now, scientists have been seeking contact with extra-terrestrials, but until now, as far as I know, they haven't been successful."

They ate almost in silence. Apparently, the subject didn't interest her very much, since she changed it quickly. After the snack, Reinaldo went to his room to get ready.

When it was a quarter to eight, he took leave of his mother and went downstairs to await Jô's arrival. He was standing on the corner of Avenida Atlântica at the place they had arranged. The weather had improved a lot and it didn't look like it was going to rain. He was elegantly dressed: gray pants, black shoes, a light blue blouse with a polo neck and a navy blue blazer. At five after eight, Jô's car stopped in front of him. He got in the car and they exchanged compliments. She was wearing a black dress with thin shoulder straps, which contrasted with her pearl necklace and the vaporous blue scarf covering her shoulders.

The sight of Rio at night was a novelty for him. They went through the New Tunnel, past Botafogo beach with its picturesque view of Sugar Loaf hill and continued along Flamengo beach, surrounded by the verdant beauty of the landfill park. Finally they arrived at Avenida Rio Branco, in downtown Rio. Jô parked the car close to the theater. It was still early, the concert would begin at nine. They walked calmly to the stairway leading to the main entrance. The theater's architecture, highlighted by the sophisticated lighting, was fascinating. It imitated the style of the famous *l'Opéra de Paris*, despite the building's smaller size. Jô presented the invitations at the entrance and they went to look for their seats in the dress circle, which they found easily, since the theater was still empty. Reinaldo had bought a copy of the program at the entrance.

"Do you like baroque music, Reinaldo?"

"Very much, Jô, it's my favorite type of music. The liturgical music from that epoch, I believe, is the most beautiful music of all the periods."

"Then read the program, I think you'll have a wonderful surprise!"

The priest opened the program and liked what he read.

1st Part: Cello Concertos by Joseph Haydn, Antonio Vivaldi and Luigi Boccherini.

2nd Part: Violin Concerto: *The Four Seasons* by Vivaldi.

Reinaldo smiled with satisfaction. He felt very grateful to Jô for having invited him. In silence, they were enjoying the theater's interior beauty and observing the arrival of hundreds of people, who began to occupy all the seats. A few minutes later, the lights went off and the curtain rose. The spotlights focused on the large orchestra and its conductor. There was warm applause. The first chords began to be heard. The priest closed his eyes. He let the music penetrate his soul and felt God's nearness, as never before.

During the intermission at the end of the first part of the concert, Reinaldo invited Jô to go with him to the *foyer* of the theater. She ordered a glass of champagne and he ordered a soft drink. "Reinaldo, the soloist is excellent, isn't he?"

"My soul was floating on those cello chords, Jô. It's an incredible instrument, when played by a virtuose on that level."

The *foyer* was full of people, of the most varied types and ages. The conversations were animated and the hullabaloo seemed like the noise of a mad swarm of bees. The buzzer announced the start of the second part of the concert. They finishing drinking and returned to their seats, just before the lights went off. Vivaldi's *The Four Seasons* was Reinaldo's favorite composition. At the end, the audience broke into delirious applause. The Brazilian Symphonic Orchestra deserved the acclamation.

On leaving the theater, they walked slowly toward the parked car. The night was chilly, but a beautiful new moon lit up the sky. They got into the car and Jô drove unhurriedly back to the south zone of the city. For some time they remained silent, each one absorbed in his thoughts. When they were passing by Botafogo beach, she broke the silence, "Would you like to go to my apartment? A good *ravioli* with red *Chianti* wine is awaiting me for dinner. If you'd like to accompany me, I'm sure you'll enjoy it."

The chaplain had difficulty replying. He didn't want, in any way at all, to fall into temptation. Jô was an attractive woman and the situation would surely put him at an increasingly dangerous crossroads. The serious problem he had been facing was enough. On the other hand, however, he enjoyed his friend's company, and didn't want to hurt her. "Reinaldo, please feel at ease. If you don't want to go, you don't have to be embarrassed, I'll let you off at your home."

"No, Jô, it's not that! It's my turn now to invite you and you jumped the gun. I'd like you to be my guest for dinner at an Italian restaurant which is located alongside my mother's building. They say the pasta there is one of the best in Rio. Maybe you already know it."

She laughed and thanked him for the invitation, accepting it immediately. "I know it, yes, it's an excellent restaurant. I was there a few times with an Italian girlfriend who's a journalist and works as the correspondent in Rio for a Roman newspaper. You know I lived in Rome for a few years, remember?"

"Yes, I remember you accompanied your parents when they left for the Embassy in Italy."

They were already in Copacabana and Jô was driving along Avenida Atlântica. She kept in the right lane, since she would enter his street two blocks ahead. And it all happened very rapidly.

A car braked to a stop in front of Jô and another stopped alongside. She also braked her car, so as not to hit the car in front. Two men jumped out, one from each car. One of them came over to Jô's window and the other one to Reinaldo's side of the car. Jô looked in the rearview mirror thinking of fleeing in reverse, but there already was another car stopped behind her. The windows were closed and the doors were locked, but the man on her side made a gesture displaying a 9mm pistol, threatening to shoot if she didn't open the window. Reinaldo told Jô, in a surprising calm voice, "Jô, open the window and stay as calm as possible."

They opened the windows and heard the man who was at the priest's side of the car say, "Father, get out of the car calmly and come with me; if you make a wrong move, the girl gets a bullet in her head."

The one that was on Jô's side of the car ordered, "Give me your purse, cell phone and car keys. Only get out when we've disappeared. If the police chase us, the priest dies."

They obeyed promptly. It was when Reinaldo recognized the man who was on his side of the car: the same youth who had followed him a few days before. The priest got out and accompanied him, sitting in the back seat of the car that had stopped in front. He noticed there were two more men inside the car. The car that had stopped alongside Jô left quickly, continuing along Avenida Atlântica. The other vehicle turned right, entered a cross street and then turned onto Avenida Nossa Senhora de Copacabana. The men were completely silent. The youth alongside Reinaldo placed a blindfold on his eyes and handcuffed him. Then they forced him to lie down on the seat, in a fetal position. They drove for a long time, perhaps an hour. Inside the vehicle, only the noise of the air conditioner was heard. Suddenly the car stopped. Someone pulled the chaplain by the arm, making him get up and get out of the car. They went along a sidewalk which seemed to be on a hill, and then entered a house. The place smelled bad. They walked a few meters and Reinaldo heard a door close. They took off his clothes, leaving him only in his drawers and the blue blouse. They forced him then to sit down on what seemed to be a mattress and chained his right leg. His tormenter then removed the handcuffs from his wrists and the blindfold from his eyes. Without saying a word, the kidnappers left the cubicle, locking the door on the outside. Only then was Reinaldo able to think somewhat clearly. He looked around him. The room must have been around twelve square meters in area. There weren't any windows, just a single door. The walls were of unpainted plaster, and besides the mattress, the only visible objects were an empty can with an eighteen liter marking and a bottle of mineral water. The can seemed to be for his physiological needs. On the ceiling there was a single light bulb. It seemed impossible to break through the wooden door. He noticed that there was a peephole through which he could be observed from the outside. He thought about Jô and prayed that nothing had happened to her. He thought about his mother, and imagined how she'd worried about his disappearance. He wasn't afraid. He was resigned to it all. Certainly, what Colonel Peçanha was fearing had happened. The brother of the guerrilla fighter he had killed was carrying out his revenge. He entrusted his fate to God. He felt great fatigue. He laid down on the mattress and closed his eyes. He had no idea of how long he stayed this way, lying down, motionless and with his eyes closed. He opened his eyes and saw the light. It was the light from the sun in the Holy Land and he was on the Jaffa road, heading for Saint John of Acre . . .

THE CASTLE CHAPEL

I t was a clear day and the sun shone in a blue cloudless sky. Jean and Pierre were on the road back to Acre. They were riding northward along the same coastal road. They stopped for a meal at the same place where they had stopped on their way south, near the fountain and the white house, in the shade of the trees. This time the children weren't in sight. They sat down and ate the bread with lamb they brought from Jaffa, and drank some water from their canteens. They rested a little, before taking care of their horses and continuing on their journey. On closing his eyes, Jean's thoughts returned to Melissande. The meeting with Petrazzi made him recall his wedding.

After having been knighted and having participated in the Spring Tournament, in Orléans, Jean returned with his family to Mont-Remy. Melissande and her family also returned to their castle in Challons. The two Marquises had arranged to schedule their children's wedding for Saint John's Day, in June. The families would have little more that a month to prepare for the wedding. The reason for such haste was the engaged couple's insistent request; they wanted to get married as soon as possible. Since Saint John was Melissande's family's patron saint, the date was chosen with general approval. Another request by the bride was to be married in the chapel of her parents' castle, where she had been baptized and had made her first communion.

She wanted Father Gilles, the castle chaplain, to officiate over the ceremony, the same priest of her baptism and communion.

The month of May passed by and June was already passing quickly while the two families labored so that the festive event would be as beautiful as possible. Knights were sent to the most varied regions of France, distributing invitations to friends and relatives. The two Marquises went personally to deliver the invitation to the Duke d'Anjou and his wife, Duchess Margaret. The Duke, who was very fond of his two vassals, was very happy at the good news and assured them of his presence. The best men and the maids of honor had already been chosen: for the bridegroom his sister Marie and his brother Gilbert; for the bride, her brother Robert and her cousin and best friend, Arlette. The bridal gown was being made in Orléans by the best seamstresses in the Duchy. The Challons castle went through a general sprucing up for the wedding. The chapel received tapestries to decorate the walls. Two of them, the main ones, displayed the coats of arms of the Saumur and Challons families. On the wedding day, wild flowers were placed on the altar and the sides of the chapel. A large tent was erected in the main patio, where the banquet would take place, after the ceremony. Lodgings for the guests, that would come from distant places, were carefully prepared.

The bridal gown had been ready two days before the wedding date, and was brought by two knights from the Marquis' palace guard. Melissande was in a hurry to try it on. She looked beautiful in it. The ladies who were helping to dress her gave little screams of admiration. It was a dark red dress, with green and silver silk ribbons, all embroidered with precious stones. A long white veil, held by a flower wreath, covered her blond hair, braided with green and red ribbons.

The guests arrived on the eve of the wedding, many of them coming from the farthest places in the realm. The last to arrive, when it was already night, was the Duke and his wife. They came accompanied by an escort of five knights and five squires. After a meal offered by the Marquis, they all retired for the night.

A beautiful summer day dawned. The bright blue cloudless sky and the pleasant temperature combined to make Jean's and Melissande's great day unforgettable. At eleven o'clock all the guests were already in the chapel. The bride and groom had only invited their closest relatives and friends. Accordingly, the chapel, while full, had enough room for everyone. The Duke and Duchess, pompously dressed, occupied the place of honor. In the front rows were the best men and the maids of honor, the parents of the bride and groom and the other relatives, followed by the other guests and friends. Among the latter were some knights who had been squires along with Jean at the Duke's court. Petrazzi, the Italian knight, was also among the bridal couple's guests. Jean was richly dressed, wearing a conical-shaped leather hat with silver trimming, a navy blue velvet tunic with the Saumur coat of arms embroidered in gold, a belt and sword, and white silk pants. He stood close to the altar, beside the old chaplain. Shortly afterwards, the bride entered, led by her father, the Marquis. Melissande was strikingly beautiful. Going up to the alter, she took Jean's hand and together, they waited for Father Gilles to begin the ceremony. With the celebration of mass, the bride and groom made their vows of eternal love, before God and the Church. After the exchange of wedding rings, the chaplain blessed the couple, declaring them husband and wife.

At the end of the ceremony, the married couple received the congratulations of the Duke and Duchess, and following that, of their relatives and guests. A banquet consisting of the most delicious dishes was served at the tables placed under the big tent. The minstrel hired to liven up the party sang and played on his golden harp joyous and romantic songs. Jean and Melissande were seated at the head table, flanked by the Duke and his wife and by their parents. They hardly paid any attention to the conversation and were exchanging passionate glances all the time. The young couple's excitement was so great that they barely were able to answer the questions put every so often by the others at their table. The couple's anxiety was clearly noticed by all the people at their table who whispered to each other, gazing amusingly at the newlyweds. The married couple was to depart, right after the banquet, for the castle of Mont-Rémy, which Jean had received from his father as his wedding present. The Marquis, with his wife and his other two children, was going to live on the beautiful property he had inside the walls of Orléans, next to the Duke's castle. Jean's father had been appointed Master of Arms of the Duchy, a position which forced him to live in Orléans. The newlyweds, after saying good-bye to everyone, left on horseback for their new home.

That specific moment was restored now, in all its details, to Jean's memory. The castle battlements were full of happy people—the parents of the bride and groom, relatives, friends, servants, soldiers of the guard—all cheering the couple. The newlyweds crossed the drawbridge and headed for Mont-Rémy, waving and looking back, as if they wished to record those beloved scenes forever. They went on, crossing fields and woods, passing through towns, until they arrived at Mont-Rémy castle after an hour's ride. The day would still dawdle by, in that radiant summer of 1178. The young couple was received by the captain of the castle guard, who welcomed them and expressed his congratulations on their wedding. They went to the tower, where their rooms were located. They embraced and kissed each other. The bride went to the adjoining room, where her luggage had been placed. When she returned, a few minutes later, she was wearing only a white linen nightgown. Her blond hair, cascading around her shoulders, made her look even more beautiful. Her heart was beating rapidly. The long-awaited and fearful moment, when the man she loved would make a woman of her, had finally arrived. Jean was also trembling from excitement. He undressed her delicately and carried her to the nuptial bed, elegantly made up by the Saumur family's ladies-in-waiting. Then they lived out the dream which had so happily come true. Time ceased to exist at that moment, and the lovers seemed to be in paradise.

"Should we continue on our trip, my lord?"

Pierre's voice brought the knight back from the happiest memories of his life. He answered, "Yes, Pierre, we've already rested enough and our horses also, let us continue."

He looked at the white house, wondering where the children and their young mother would be, since they hadn't appeared until then. That sight had provided him a moment of peace in his heart, when they stopped for a rest during their journey south. They continued their trip northward. Nothing would have led them to believe that the Latin territories were in danger. The appearance of the travelers, both European as well as Syrian, whom the Templars encountered from time to time, was completely normal At the end of the afternoon, they spied the walls of Acre. At last arriving at the Templars' castle, they reported to the Abbot. They gave him a complete account of the trip, answered a few questions, and were finally dismissed by their superior. João de Tovar was waiting for them in the large mess hall, and when he saw them, he greeted them with a fraternal embrace, exclaiming, "I am very happy to see you again, my brothers!"

The Portuguese knight was already completely recovered from his wounds and was once more displaying the energy and vitality that were peculiar to him. They recited vespers together with the entire brotherhood and had supper in complete silence. Tired from the trip, they fell asleep as soon as they laid down on their cots.

THE REVENGE

The chaplain awoke and instinctively glanced at his wrist to see what time it was. Then he remembered that they had taken all his belongings, including his watch. He didn't have the slightest idea of how long he had slept. He recalled the dream and smiled, thinking about the excitement of Jean's and Melissande's wedding. Besides his belongings and clothes, they had also taken his belt and shoes. There was total silence, the light stayed on all the time, which made it difficult to know whether it was day or night. At that point, Reinaldo placed his fate in God's hands and prayed. He felt a great inner peace. Everything led him to believe that he had been kidnapped by the gang of the brother of the guerrilla fighter he had killed on the border. The purpose would surely be revenge. Suffering and death were in store for him. He noticed a small opening near the ceiling through which the air he was breathing entered. At least it seemed they didn't want to kill him by suffocation. He discovered, behind the bucket, a roll of toilet paper and a package of cookies. He felt hot, although it was winter, and took off his socks. He stood up and tried to do a little exercise, bending his arms and left leg, since the right one was chained down. He laid down again on the mattress and remained motionless. A lot of time had gone by and everything continued in the same way. There was total silence. Suddenly, he heard the door being unlocked. Two men entered; one of them was the youth that had brought him there. They were armed with 9mm pistols and moved slowly, in a seemingly careless way. The chaplain recognized the second man immediately. He was Serginho, the drug dealer in the photo shown him by Detective Chief Brito. The criminal said, "Chaplain, I'm going to tell why you were kidnapped and what's going to happen to you. You killed my brother Pedrinho, there on the border. Since it was in combat, and there wasn't any cowardice, there won't be any torture. Sunday would be his birthday. My present is going to be your death, by rifle shot, to avenge his death."

Reinaldo remained silent while the drug dealer was talking. He was observing and listening to everything, as if he were watching a film in which he was only a spectator and not the main character. The two men didn't say anything else. They left the cubicle, locking the door. It wasn't a surprise that he was going to die, he thought. He wasn't afraid, just sad and frustrated due to the interruption of his search for his life's meaning and the true strength of his priestly vocation. He was hungry. He grabbed the package of cookies, opened it and began to eat. It seemed that God was testing him. He was sure that his faith would be tested in a definitive way during the next few days. He ate half of the package of cookies and drank some water from the bottle. He got up to urinate in the bucket, and then laid down again. He remained still, with his eyes closed. He began to pray in his thoughts, "Lord, enlighten me."

But Reinaldo didn't know that the night before, a little after 11 p.m., Captain Souza e Silva was leaving his apartment on Domingos Ferreira Street to walk along Avenida Atlântica, which he used to do almost every night. When he was on his way home, near the Lido Square, an extraordinary scene attracted his attention. A car braked to a halt, making the vehicle behind it stop. Another car stopped alongside the second vehicle, completely blocking any escape route. Suddenly, a man jumped out of each one of the cars that were blocking the other car. They went to the side windows of the other car and after threatening gestures displaying a pistol, they made the occupants roll down the windows. Everything happened very fast. A man got out and was taken to the car that was in front. The other man took the purse and mobile phone of the woman who was behind the wheel and returned to the car that was stopped alongside. The two cars drove away at a normal speed. The captain's heart beat more rapidly when he noticed that the man who had been taken from the car was Reinaldo, the son of his deceased friend Roberto. He didn't stop to think twice, ran to the street and hailed a taxi that was passing at the time. He got in, sat beside the driver and ordered, "Follow that car."

Souza e Silva had noticed, shortly before getting in the taxi, that the car carrying Reinaldo had turned right a little further ahead. The other car had disappeared, but he was almost sure it had continued along Avenida Atlântica. When they entered the street in which Reinaldo was living, which wasn't very long, the first car was no longer in sight. It didn't matter very much. Avenida Copacabana was a one-way street, so the car ahead had to turn right. The car they were following was a navy blue jeep station wagon, whose license plate, RDR6562, the captain had carefully memorized. Luckily, the traffic light on the corner of Rodolfo Dantas Street was red, and they approached the kidnappers' car in a normal manner. The captain was sure it was a kidnapping. He thought it best not to tell his driver right away, He didn't know how the driver would react. In case the latter found out, which was very probable, he'd see then how to handle the situation. He ordered the driver to continue. The driver was already looking at him mistrustfully. They left Copacabana, went through Botafogo district and entered the Flamengo fill-in park. The driver couldn't hide his curiosity, "Where are you heading?"

The captain didn't reply at first. He couldn't take his eyes off the jeep that was moving at a normal speed not very far in front of them. Then the driver observed, "It seems we're following that jeep station wagon you're not taking your eyes off."

The captain ended up telling the driver everything he had witnessed and his friendship with the family of the kidnapped man. The driver suggested, "We can call the police, I have my mobile phone here."

"No, they're being covered by another car, and I don't know where it is, and everything leads me to believe my friend could be killed if the police appear. They don't know they're being followed, which gives us a big advantage. We need to know where they're taking him. It's very important."

The driver shrugged and continued on the chase. At this point, they were already going along Avenida Presidente Vargas and thanks to the still heavy traffic, they were unnoticed by the kidnappers. A few minutes later they arrived at Bandeira Plaza, and then headed for the Andaraí district. The number of cars on the street began to diminish and they had to increase the distance that separated them from the station wagon, fearing discovery. They arrived in Andaraí and entered Pedra Street. At this point the driver commented, "This here is a rough neighborhood! Those guys are heading for the Cirado slum. It's drug dealers' territory. We can't go any further."

"You're right, turn right at the next corner and we'll return to Copacabana. Now we know where they're taking my friend."

"Yeah, and be prepared for the worst, because it's not going to be very easy for the police to go in there and find your friend."

Souza e Silva didn't say anything, but at heart he agreed with the driver. Reinaldo was just a priest. He didn't even live in Rio. His family was middle class.

Such a well-planned kidnapping didn't make sense. Could they have grabbed the wrong man? No, they seemed to be very sure about what they wanted. There must be something behind all this! It was already after 1 a.m. when they arrived at the street in front of the captain's building. He went upstairs to get some money, since he didn't have a cent in his pocket. After paying the taxi fare and noting down the driver's name, address and telephone number, the captain said good-bye and thanked him for his cooperation. At home, he searched in his agenda for Reinaldo's mother's telephone number. She answered the call promptly, noticing a great concern in the caller's voice. The captain went straight to the point, "This is Souza e Silva. You already know what happened, don't you?"

"Yes. They kidnapped my son! Jô, his friend, is in the Kidnapping Investigation Department reporting the occurrence. I've called Eduardo, in Foz de Iguaçu, and he should arrive tomorrow in Rio to follow up on the case. Why would they want to do this to a priest?"

"I saw it all when I was walking along Avenida Atlântica and I followed the car that was taking him. I'm going to call the police right away, and if need be, I'll go there immediately."

"And where did they take Reinaldo?"

"To the Cirado slum, in Andaraí district."

"Oh, my God!"

"I'm going to hang up now. Keep calm, everything will turn out OK."

In the Cirado slum, Reinaldo didn't have any idea of how long he was praying, maybe half an hour, maybe less, nor did he know that he had a Guardian Angel looking out for him. Prayer always brought peace to his heart. Comforted, he ended up by falling asleep. This time the dream took a little longer to arrive . . .

MEETING IN SEFORIA

May 29 dawned on the city of Saint John of Acre the same way as it did in all the other cities of the Latin kingdom, with a great bustle of knights gathering together their vassals for the war. In the morning, alarming news arrived from Jerusalem. Saracen troops coming from Cairo had attacked several fortresses in the southern part of the kingdom, and except for the Krak and Montreal castles, all had fallen into enemy hands.

The Templars of Acre were feverishly preparing for the campaign. Wagons with food, stacks of arrows, battle shields, spears, swords and all kinds of equipment for the use of the combatants, on foot or on horseback, were being readied under the direct supervision of the older knights. The Abbot was only awaiting the Grand Master's order to march, alongside almost all the knights, toward the meeting point of the Christian army, which had not yet been decided. Only the elderly knights and a few who were convalescing from wounds or diseases would remain in Acre. They would be responsible for the defense of the fortress, together with a few sergeants. The monks' concern was very visible. All of them knew that the battle they were going to fight would be decisive for the Latin kingdoms' survival. If the Christian army were destroyed, nothing could prevent Saladin from occupying, one by one, the unguarded Latin cities and forts. It would be the end for them all. The women and children would be made slaves, and the men who were unable to pay ransom would be killed. All the combatants associated with the religious orders who didn't die in combat would be killed by the Saracens. The holy places would be lost and the Christian religion's survival would be threatened. They had to defeat, at all costs, an army that was far superior in numbers to theirs.

Jean, João de Tovar, Pierre and Gaston were called right after reciting the sexte by Lagéry. The veteran Templar would be in command of a company of the Order composed of cavalry and infantry, totaling 180 combatants, one fifth of the entire Templar forces from Acre and Haifa, a fortress which was located on the southern side of the bay. He called upon all the survivors of the trip with the pilgrims to serve under his command. He explained that during all the army's maneuvers, they, together with the other brothers from the Templars' and Hospitalers' Orders, would remain in the rearguard square, under the command of Balion of Ibelin, the Lord of Ramala. The center square would be led by King Guido and the knight named Reinaldo de Châtillon, and the vanguard square would be headed by Count Raimundo of Tripoli, the best Christian commander. The squares were formed by infantry troops and served as protection for the cavalry, which remained in the center of the squares. This was a traditional tactic of the Frankish armies at that time. The knights, with their steel coats of mail and shields, were less exposed than their horses. In this way, the horses would be protected from the clouds of arrows which would normally be shot, at the start of the battles, and then the knights could destroy the enemy forces in rapid incursions. After being dismissed by the Templar commander, the friends met in the stable, where they were caring for their horses. Jean was the first to speak, followed by

João, "I asked God, in my prayers, to keep us together during the coming battle. In this way we shall be able to protect one another during the combat. It seems that the Lord heard my request."

"I was also very glad, my brothers, that we can stay together."

João had already completely recovered from his wounds, and seemed to be in his best physical shape. Pierre and Gaston had become inseparable friends. The fact that they were both born in the same village favored this great comradeship, solidifying their bonds. Jean had the impression at times that Gaston had undergone great suffering, since on several occasions he had encountered him in the castle chapel and observed him praying fervently and crying. In reality, almost all of them had reasons to cry because of past sadness, he thought. João made a sign for the friends and told them that he had received a recommendation from the Abbot for all the Templars to conduct a general inspection of their armament on that day and report immediately any need for repair or replacement. The armament was composed of the horses, including the war horses, the harnesses, the horses' armor which unfortunately only the more experienced knights possessed, the coats of mail, the breastplates which were also scarce, the cloaks with the emblazoned cross, the helmets, the swords, the spears, the battle axes, the maces, in addition to the bows and arrows, which had already been distributed to the archers. The Order's flags and banners would also be inspected by the Abbot himself. They were all told that the Bishop of Acre would accompany the army and would take with him Christianity's most precious relic, the Holy Rood, a piece of the cross on which Jesus Christ had been crucified and which was kept on the altar of the

Church of the Holy Sepulcher. Then they left for their lodgings, where they would begin the inspection. Later, after vespers had been recited, the Abbot told the Brotherhood that the meeting point of the Latin army would be in that region, close to the city of Seforia, a place of abundant grazing lands, much shade and a lot of water. Seforia was around 25 kilometers from Acre, a little more than a three-hour march. Christian combatants, from all corners of the overseas kingdoms, were converging on that place.

The days passed rapidly. They worked hard, readying their arms and luggage for the day of departure. During the meeting of the War Council, held in Acre on June 15, the King had ordered the army to come together by June 22. On June 20, the Latin forces from Acre and Haifa left in the morning for Seforia.

They moved forward in three columns—the cavalry in the center and the infantry on the flanks. In the rearguard were the wagons with the luggage, protected by a troop of archers. The Templars and the Hospitalers were at the head of the cavalry column, followed by Frankish, Italian, German and some English secular knights. Jean was calm, feeling neither fear nor anxiety. He was taking care that his group of combatants, that included João, Pierre, Gaston and another six sergeants, were always well equipped and correctly positioned in the formation of the column. The region they were passing through was almost a desert, without water. The inclement sun didn't permit the water in their canteens to last very long. Luckily, the distance to Seforia would be covered in around four hours and their camping place was forested and full of springs. Pierre approached Jean with a worried expression, saying, "Sir, I am concerned about Gaston. With every day that goes by, he becomes sadder and more taciturn. I try to converse with him, to cheer him up, I try to learn the reason for his affliction, but I am unable to make him open up. I asked him whether he regretted having entered the Order and his reply was negative. That is not the reason for his suffering. What should I do to help him?"

The knight thought for a few minutes and answered, "You should continue being his friend and remaining at his side as you have been doing. At the right moment, he will share his grief with you, who is his closest companion."

Pierre returned to his position, which was behind the Knights Templar, alongside his friend Gaston.

When the sun was on high and the heat became unbearable, the Christian force spied the Seforia woods. Like a salutary phenomenon, the temperature then became more agreeable. Minutes later, they came upon a stream of clear water, to which the most thirsty among them ran impatiently, alleviating the uncomfortable sensation of the heat. The camp was already being occupied by various Christian soldiers, coming from the most distant cities of the Latin kingdoms, who had headed there when called upon by King Guido. A sea of tents stretched out, nearing the walls of Seforia. The Templars from Acre finally found the sector reserved for them and began to set up their tents.

THE DRUG DEALER FROM
CIRADO HILL

While Reinaldo was dreaming, Serginho was looking through the window of the shack always in the direction of the square. Although he was high up on the hill, he was only able to distinguish the square through a gap between two buildings. He was recalling the time when he used to sell peanuts roasted on a small portable coal stove. "Roasted peanuts", he used to shout in the middle of the square. The AK-47 rifle on the table made him recall Baby Devil, the drug dealer who had been his boss, who also used to work with a gun there on the table, except that it was a Brazilian INA sub-machinegun. He and his brother had been born in the hillside slum. He was eight when his father had died, and Pedrinho was four. His old man used to sell marijuana on the street; he was one of Baby Devil's lieutenants. He died in a shootout with the police, in 1978. His mother had arrived from the northeastern state of Maranhão with her parents, when she was still a little girl. She had been run over and killed five years after his father's death, when she was on her way to work. She used to work as a maid in an apartment in the Tijuca district. At the age of twelve, Serginho began to work for Baby Devil. He rose through all the ranks in the drug traffic hierarchy, from lookout man to lieutenant, finally becoming the boss of the traffic on Cirado Hill. He killed Baby Devil personally, with a bullet in the head, during an argument three years ago. He always tried to protect his brother. He himself had only gone as far as the third grade in school. For this very reason, he had forced Pedrinho to study and finish high school. Later, he needed his brother's help in his drug dealings, which had increased a lot and the competition from rival gangs was very strong. It was then that the war began for control of the points of sale of the drugs in the neighboring zones of the district. The attacks were becoming more and more sophisticated, and heavy weapons and battle tactics were constantly utilized. The police themselves didn't cause many problems. There were several spies inside the police force who were handsomely paid and provided warning in advance of the police raids. When a confrontation with the police occurred for any reason, the drug dealers were usually in an advantageous position, since they possessed arms with much superior firepower. It was at that time when that Colombian appeared, representing the drug suppliers, offering training in his country for one of them. There they would learn the battle tactics used by the guerrillas in that region. Serginho regretted the unfortunate moment in which he had sent Pedrinho to Colombia. So much sacrifice, only to be killed by that damned chaplain. He had succeeded in learning from the men that the guy was here in Rio, very close—"He's going to pay for what he did!" This would be Pedrinho's birthday present; the death of his assassin, in the same way that he'd been killed. He wouldn't have the chaplain tortured because he had killed Pedrinho in a fair fight, without any cowardice. The priest was going to have a quick death, at noon on Sunday.

The kidnapping was mobilizing Reinaldo's whole family. Eduardo, his brother, traveled in the morning to Curitiba on a regional flight. From there, he took the plane for Rio, arriving at the airport at 1:00 p.m. He phoned his mother, telling her he was already in Rio and would go directly to the police station. His mother was very shaken, but confident that it would all work out well and Reinaldo would be freed soon. Eduardo tried to calm his mother down on the phone, but he feared that his brother's situation was more serious than she imagined—All that could be said was, "May God help His servant!"

The Kidnapping Investigation Department of the Rio police was located in the distant Barra da Tijuca district. He needed to take a taxi to get there. It was almost 3:00 p.m. when he entered the building. He identified himself and was immediately taken to the Chief Detective's office. The latter explained, "It was wonderful of you to come, Eduardo. Fortunately, we had two witnesses to your brother's kidnapping, and one of them, Captain Souza e Silva, followed the scoundrels to Cirado Hill, where the chaplain must be held captive. The car they used had been stolen that morning in the Tijuca district. I also learned from Brito in the 12th Precinct about the problem your brother had there on the border. Brito had already warned me of the possibility that a kidnapping might occur. In this way, it wasn't difficult to find out that he's in the hands of Serginho from Cirado Hill. We're carrying out intelligence work, with the help of your Federal Police colleagues here in Rio and of the Drug Enforcement Department, with a view toward precisely locating the bandits' hideout, in order to plan the chaplain's rescue."

"Chief, my superior officer in Foz de Iguaçu authorized me to be at your disposal, assisting in the investigation of the kidnapping."

"All assistance is welcome, Eduardo. I'm going to call Detective Gilberto to introduce you to the other members of the team and bring you up-to-date regarding the steps taken until now."

Detective Gilberto was a man in his thirties, with a young boy's features He must have been one of the new crop of police officers who recently graduated from the Police Academy. He took Eduardo to a spacious room, where another six policemen were working, seated at their desks, some with computer terminals, and introduced them one by one. The man that seemed to be the chief invited Eduardo to have a small coffee in a corner of the room, and told him, "Eduardo, the situation is very difficult. We know your brother was kidnapped for revenge, and it's even possible he's already been killed. What I'm going to tell you now, and I'm asking you to keep it secret, may be our only chance to save the chaplain."

He paused to drink his coffee, leaving Eduardo in a state of terrible expectation, and then continued, "It's about a spy we have in Serginho's organization. It all started with a joint project involving the Drug Enforcement Department and our department. Several months ago, one of our detectives was prepared to join the Cirado Hill gang, which, besides the drug traffic, has been accused of several kidnappings. It was a meticulous project, which required much planning. I don't need to tell you the risk our man is running. Tomorrow he'll make contact, which will be accomplished with enormous care. The information we'll receive will be crucial for planning our raid on the hideaway. Pedro is the name of this detective. He holds the position of manager of a drug sales point and is trusted by Serginho. At eleven o'clock in the morning we'll know what to do. I advise you to go home and come back here tomorrow, a little before that time."

Eduardo accepted the advice, said good-bye to all of them, thanking his colleagues for their efforts. He picked up his suitcase and went out to hail a taxi to Copacabana.

His mother gave him a long hug, since she hadn't seen him for six months. In the kitchen, serving Eduardo's dinner, she listened attentively while her son told her everything that had happened in the Kidnapping Investigation Department and also about the information they expected to receive the following day, but omitting, for obvious reasons, the part about the spy. His mother commented, "I've been praying a lot, my son, praying to God that it all ends well and that Reinaldo can come back to us, safe and sound. I already knew we're living in a violent and cruel world, but I was hoping our family would be spared this torment."

"That's right, all we can do now is to pray. Only tomorrow we'll know what path to follow. I'm going to phone Sílvia, bring her up-to-date on what's happening and ask about the children."

After dinner, he made the call to his wife. He conversed with his mother for another half hour and then went to sleep in the same room that was being occupied by his brother.

Reinaldo woke up and thought, very pleased, that even in the situation he found himself in, his dream wasn't abandoning him. Already completely lost with respect to time, he hadn't the slightest idea what day and time it was. He smelled food, and saw, near the door, a food take-out carton with rice, beans, steak, french fries and mayonnaise. Alongside was a plastic spoon and another plastic bottle of water. He was very hungry. He ate all the food and drank some water. He couldn't understand why he hadn't awakened at the time when they opened the door.

He must have been in a deep sleep. The recollection of his imminent death made him suddenly shaky. Couldn't all that be a dream? No, unfortunately it was very real. He recalled sadly that Jean was also heading for his last hour. Would it be a coincidence? Some say coincidences don't exist, the correct word for them is fate. Would he, the dream and Jean all die at the same time? He stretched out on the mattress and closed his eyes. He began to pray, and continued for a long time. On opening his eyes, the sun's brightness almost blinded him. He was arriving on horseback in front of a large camp made up of tents that extended out as far as he could see, to the south of Seforia castle . . .

THE LONG-AWAITED HEIR

Such a large Christian army had not gathered together in the Holy Land for many years. There were around 1,200 knights, 4,000 sergeants and turcopoles, 17,000 infantry soldiers, ranging from professional crossbow-men to recruits without any military experience. The Christian army totaled around 23,000 combatants, while Saladin was marching with 45,000 Saracens toward the Christian camp. Of the latter total, 12,000 were cavalry troops, mostly excellent professional soldiers. The sultan's forces came from what are presently the territories of Egypt, Syria, Turkey and Iraq. The meeting place of these troops was in Tal'Ashtarah, a region with much grazing land and water. Around 30 kilometers separated the two army camps.

On June 27, Jean had already adapted to the life in the Christian camp. The Templars tried to follow a normal routine, maintaining the scheduled times for taking care of their horses and their camp, saying their prayers and having their meals. The sector reserved for the Knights Templar was divided into several chapters of the Order, the most important being those from Acre and Jerusalem, which had the largest numbers of knights and sergeants, and where the Grand Master and his main officers were encamped. On that afternoon, right after reciting the none, Jean's thoughts went back to André, his beloved son. He recalled the day of his birth; five years had already passed.

When the birth pains began, everyone in the castle oscillated between happiness and concern. It was still morning of a beautiful summer day. The frustrating recollection of the previous childbirth, two years earlier, was still strong. Melissande had become pregnant for the first time soon after the wedding. An abortion in the beginning of her pregnancy had frustrated the couple's dream. The second pregnancy occurred without any problem, and everything seemed to be going well when a beautiful little girl was born. But the infant died before a week had passed since her birth, causing her parents much pain and suffering. The third pregnancy also proceeded normally, and this time a handsome, robust boy was born. André was growing, week after week, with excellent health. Melissande had prepared herself a lot to receive her son. She was strong and healthy, with plentiful breast-milk, and the child's development caused admiration on the part of all the ladies in the castle. André was baptized in the chapel, a month after his birth. It was a simple ceremony, with the presence of the maternal and paternal grandparents. At the alter, the godparents, Jean's sister Marie and Melissande's brother Robert, were exultant and deeply conscious of their important role. They brought a couple of magicians from Orléans, who entertained more the adults than the few children present.

They were almost two intensely-lived years which went by very rapidly. Jean recalled every moment, every peal of laughter of his so long-awaited son. The scenes came back to him in their sequence, each new cute little trick, the first time his son sat down, the first tooth, the first word, the first steps.

When André reached his first birthday, they organized a big party, and all the relatives attended. The baby's parents were besides themselves with happiness. "André shall be the most famous knight in the whole kingdom", his father used to say.

"Perhaps he shall not be the most famous, but he shall certainly be the most handsome," his mother used to say.

That year spring had begun earlier, the gardens were full of flowers and nature's beauty was overflowing. A big tent was set up in the castle patio to shelter the guests during the exquisite dinner that was offered them. Lute players performed the favorite songs of the day. A magician and a clown amused the children present, as well as the adults with childish souls. The atmosphere was extremely joyous. André was the image of hope, beautiful in his blue silk baby clothes with gold embroidery, a present from the Duke and Duchess. It was an unforgettable day.

Life in the castle followed a routine that was almost boring. Four knights, vassals of the Marquis, were living there: Giles, the oldest, was the castle supervisor, responsible for the general administration; Dennis, the captain of the guard, who was nicknamed "Bear" because he was very tall and strong; Eudes, the youngest, who was Dennis' lieutenant; and Ferdinand, the cheeriest and most communicative, who held the post of tax collector and once a month accompanied Jean on his visits to the two towns in the Mont-Rémy fief. These visits were for the purpose of collecting money from the tenants who rented the land and practiced crafts. Jean always acted fairly, never condemning his subjects to death, a power he possessed but never utilized. He used to travel every month to Orléans, where he would pay homage to the Duke and take advantage of the trip to visit his parents and brother and sister. His brother Gilbert had already been knighted and was his father's assistant in his capacity of Master of Arms in the Duchy. These duties included the administration of the Duke's arsenal and the military training of the professional soldiers that made up part of the troops maintained by Anjou. During these visits, Jean used to buy, in the variety of shops in the large city, many presents for his beloved wife and toys for his son. He would rarely stay away from Mont-Rémy for more than two days.

Summer was pleasant, the day had dawned radiantly, with a blue sky and few clouds. As was his habit, Jean would be leaving, accompanied by Ferdinand, for his monthly visit to his fief. Then he'd go on to Orléans, where he'd stay for two days. He had a meal in the company of Melissande and his son. His wife asked him to bring two pieces of velvet cloth to make a dress she had in mind. André was laughing and playing with his father, preventing him from eating calmly. A little later Ferdinand arrived and said, "Sir, everything is ready for our departure. They have already brought your horse."

Jean hugged and kissed his wife and son. He could never have imagined that he was seeing them for the last time.

Pierre's voice once again took him away from his sad thoughts: "Sir, Grand Master Ridefort is calling all the Templar officers for a meeting in his tent."

With the death of more than 80 knights in the combat at the Cresson springs, on May first, Jean had been promoted to the position of officer, a rank which was conferred upon the more experienced knights. Since that disaster, the atmosphere in the Order was one of great apprehension. The belief that the Christian army was better in combat than the Saracen army fell apart. On arriving at Ridefort's tent, Jean encountered around fifty knights, most of them unknown to him. He stayed near his brothers from the Acre chapter, who were headed by the knight Lagéry.

The Grand Master took his position in front of the group, which immediately became silent, and said, "Brothers, the most difficult hour for the Christian knights in the Holy Land is nearing. We have to defeat the Saracens, or all our work shall be lost. The Templars shall fight all together in the rearguard of King Guido's army. We have received news from our advance patrols that the enemy has crossed the Jordan river this morning with the vanguard of his troops, and is sacking the region of Nazareth, the Sea of Galilee and Mount Tabor. The King shall call his council today to decide on our army's movements. The brothers should be prepared to break camp at any moment now."

Lagéry raised his arm and asked leave to speak, which was granted by the Grand Master, and suggested, "Sir, would it not make more sense to wait here, in this strong position, with plenty of water and grazing land, to confront the Saracens, who would be coming from the desert, thirsty and tired?"

"No, Lagéry. We must not show them any fear, they are the ones who should be fearing us. We should march against the Saracens and destroy them as quickly as possible, thus avenging our brothers who died in Cresson. This shall be my advice to the King. The meeting is adjourned. Go back to your tents and wait for my orders!"

THE SPY

Searching for the place where Reinaldo was being held captive, "Crazy Guy" was looking for some kind of strategy. He wrote down in his notebook the total amount of the drugs sold at his sales point the previous night. Between cocaine and marijuana, it came to R$865,00, not bad for a Thursday. He prepared the money and the merchandise that was left over to take to Serginho. He breathed deeply and began to climb up the hillside slum. It was early and he encountered many slum-dwellers on their usual way to the bus stops where they'd catch the bus to go to work. At times, he thought he was really crazy, as his nickname suggested. Volunteering to be a spy was really something crazy. If he were caught, he'd suffer terrible torture and have to beg to be killed. He'd taken on all this risk in order to be promoted to the rank of detective, after the mission was over. It was a good thing he wasn't married nor had any children. He had grown up in an orphanage and had succeeded in improving his life through his own efforts. Black, poor, his life seemed more like an obstacle race. He had studied law and with great sacrifice graduated from law school. He joined the Police Department after passing a civil service examination. Then he attended the Police Academy, from which he graduated two years earlier, at the age of twenty-eight.

Until now he'd being doing good work. The amount of evidence that he'd already gathered together and sent to his chief was more than enough to do away with Serginho's gang. Everything was ready for the final raid on the gang, when this kidnapping case appeared. The situation became complicated. He hadn't yet succeeded in discovering the hiding place, the key piece of information for rescuing the hostage. He'd heard the day before a comment by Serginho's main lieutenant that the priest would be executed on Sunday. This meant he had 48 hours to discover the hiding place and transmit the information to his police colleagues. On reaching the top of the hill, where his chief's office was located, he reported, "I brought the day's work, chief!"

"Speak up, boy!" said the gangster. The spy approached and placed the money and the drugs on the table."

Reinaldo woke up alarmed. During a few seconds, he felt completely lost, without recalling where he was, without knowing what day or what time it was. His other life seemed to be safer. At least there he'd have the chance to fight for his survival. Everything was heading toward an obscure ending, completely senseless. His only hope was in the comfort of his faith. He prayed constantly, not through fear, but rather to feel integrated with divine grace, another link in the great chain of the Holy Ghost. The cubicle already had a terrible smell, coming from the bucket reserved for his physiological needs. He placed the bucket near the door, in the hope that they'd take it away when they brought him food. He tried to do a little calisthenics in order to maintain his muscles in shape. He thought about his mother, who must be suffering a lot. He also thought about Jô. Apparently she hadn't suffered any violence, since he and he alone was the target of the attack. At this point, his brother must be in Rio, helping the local police in the investigation of the kidnapping. He sat down on the mattress, closed his eyes and began praying again.

In Reinaldo's home, his brother Eduardo awoke early, got ready and went to the kitchen to meet his mother.

They had breakfast quickly, in silence. Eduardo noticed his mother's frightened look, which broke his heart . . . She commented that Aunt Glorinha was coming from Nova Friburgo in the mountains in order to provide company for her, and that same day she'd visit her doctor, since her state of anxiety didn't let her sleep. Her son took leave, promising to phone her as soon as he had any news, and left in a hurry.

He took a bus on the corner, heading for the Barra da Tijuca district, and was enjoying the view of Copacabana, Ipanema and Leblon beaches before reaching the tunnels. He got off the bus at the beginning of the main avenue and walked to the police station. It was ten thirty when he entered the building. He greeted the station chief and went directly to the detectives' room. He said good morning to everyone and went to look for the man in charge of his brother's case who, at that moment, after conversing with another detective, said to him, "Eduardo, come here. This is Detective Brandão, from the Drug Enforcement Department, who's going to head the team responsible for raiding the hiding place, as soon as we discover its location."

And turning to the detective, he then explained, "Eduardo is from the Federal Police, and he's the victim's brother."

Eduardo and the detective shook hands. Fábio, the man in charge of the case, continued, "Eduardo, I've just canceled the order to tap your mother's phone. We've arrived at the conclusion that there won't be any calls asking for ransom, for obvious reasons. Furthermore, we already know the kidnapper's identity and the reason for the kidnapping, and I'm sure that in a little while we'll know the exact location of the place where your brother is held captive."

At that moment, the boyish-faced detective entered hurriedly and said, "Pedro's on line 2, Chief!"

The chief answered the phone immediately, saying "Yes, Pedro, this is Fábio, go on."

"I haven't been able to discover the hiding place yet. The gang has scheduled the priest's death for Sunday at noon. I'll call tomorrow."

The telephone was hung up on the other end of the line, without Fábio being able to say anything. They all looked at him, awaiting the news. He told them, "Nothing. He hasn't discovered the address yet. He only said they've scheduled the victim's death for Sunday at 12 noon. He's going to call again tomorrow at the same time. I know, Eduardo, there are only 48 hours left. Every time Pedro calls here represents a serious risk that he'll be discovered and killed, besides the loss of all our work. Even though he discovers the address today yet, the information can only be transmitted tomorrow. I'm sorry, but we're going to have to wait. That's all we can do."

Eduardo understood the situation and without being able to do anything either, took leave of the detectives and said he'd return the next day. He walked to the corner and took a bus to Copacabana.

Jô had been very shaken up by Reinaldo's kidnapping. In a certain way, she felt guilty for having exposed him, involuntarily, to the violence of the Rio nights. She didn't know yet the complicated cause of the occurrence. She gave her testimony in the police station, and was following the progress of the investigation, phoning daily to Reinaldo's mother, who also knew little about the case. Jô couldn't do anything more than pray to God to help her very special friend. At two o'clock in the afternoon of that Friday, she called Reinaldo's mother again, wanting to know the latest news. A man's voice answered the phone. Jô said she'd like to talk to Reinaldo's mother and identified herself.

His mother had already told Eduardo about his brother's meeting with his old girlfriend, and therefore Eduardo wasn't surprised and asked her how she was feeling. She replied, "Very shocked by what happened, I'm taking tranquilizers. It's a pity that we meet again, after so many years, in such afflicting circumstances. I'm glad you came from Foz de Iguaçu. Have you heard any news? Has there been any call asking for ransom?"

"Maybe tomorrow something new will arise. At least, that's what the police promised me. In any event I'm happy to learn that you're alright and that you've been in contact with us again. My mother went to the doctor with my aunt Glorinha. She also hasn't been able to sleep and is very anxious."

Jô said good-bye trying to give encouragement to the family.

Reinaldo had just eaten and drunk a little water from the bottle. The same youth that had followed him, and that had participated in the kidnapping, had brought the meal in the take-out container with plastic knives and forks. They'd changed the bucket that had served as a latrine for another clean one. The chaplain tried to talk to him, but he didn't receive any reply. He looked at his wrist, out of the habit of seeing what time it was. He forgot that he didn't have his watch. He didn't know how much time had already passed by, but he felt that his hour of reckoning was approaching. His faith was becoming stronger to the extent that the prospect of his death was being transformed into reality. He knelt down, recited the Credo and asked God for forgiveness of his sins. Finally the Lord had shown him the path; he didn't have any more doubts regarding his priestly vocation, and if he were spared, would devote his life entirely to the priesthood. He was feeling light, calm, content. "Oh Lord, Your sea is so immense and my ship is so small". He laid down and thought about his life in the Holy Land. There also he was heading for death, without any fear, in the Lord's peace and anxious to encounter Melissande and André again. He closed his eyes, concentrated and a little while later, he was in Seforia . . .

SEA OF GALILEE

During the War Council meeting held on June 29, King Guido decided that the army would remain in Sephorie, following the suggestion made by Count Raimundo of Tripoli. Saladin's army continued marching toward Sephorie, along the southern shore of the Sea of Galilee. On June30, the Saracens crossed the Jordan River and made their camp at Cafarsset, 15 kilometers distant from the Christians. In that region water was abundant, and the army had a good supply system which provided the troops with sufficient food transported by camel caravans from Damascus.

Jean learned on July 1 from some Templars coming from the Sea of Galilee that the enemy had sent patrols up to the most advanced Christian positions. The group that he commanded kept their horses in nearby pastures, always guarded by sentinels. Pierre organized the control of the food, assisted by Gaston, who distributed the rations of bread and lamb, and controlled the water, brought from the nearest source. In the morning of that same day, Lagéry sent a sergeant to call Jean. The latter walked over to the tent occupied by the monk, who was waiting for him together with Grand Master Ridefort. Lagéry said, "Jean, the Grand Master wants your group to check the position of Saladin's army. We have been informed that large movements of enemy troops have begun, in various directions, and we need to know what is happening. You shall leave the camp as soon as you are ready. Take water, food and millet for the horses, since the region is a desert. You should travel all the time, including at night, spending the least possible time for resting. You should be back tomorrow, before the terce is recited. Fight only when you have no other alternative. Try to hide from the Saracens. Head for Tiberias, go as far as the castle, which is located on the shores of the lake, and return. Any questions?"

The knight answered quickly, "No, sir. I shall leave now."

The Grand Master was watching, without saying a word. Jean returned to the camp and gave orders for the departure. In a short while, they were all ready and mounted. In a column of two, they headed to the east, toward the Saracen camp. They weren't carrying any luggage. Jean and João went in front, followed by the sergeants and by Pierre and Gaston, who brought up the rear of the column. The road stretched out in front of them, snaking through the arid desert, bathed by a caustic sun. Some time later, grouped on top of a small hill, they saw a detachment of four secular knights, accompanied by ten archers on foot, that made up the Christian advance guard. The knight in command, a Spaniard named Pablo, warned them that from there on they would encounter ever more numerous Saracen patrols. In the dry plain, the sun heated their coats of mail almost unbearably, and the weight of their helmets aggravated even further their discomfort. Their swords, shields and other weapons were tied by straps to their saddles. The sparse vegetation was composed of dry bushes which dotted the landscape on both sides of the sandy road. Small rises of land hid the view ahead of them, making ambushes possible. One of the sergeants named Lehoux, from Burgundy, knew the region like the palm of his hand and guided Jean on the direction to take. When the sun was already on high, they stopped to drink some water, eat and take care of the horses. They were at the foot of a small hill, on a curve in the road. When they were preparing to leave, the monk ordered Pierre to climb up the hill and see what was in front of them. He returned very quickly and ran over to Jean, saying, "Sir, a group of 15 Saracens, on horseback, is approaching along the road. Ten are Bedouins, wearing white cloaks and armed with spears. Five are mounted Turkish archers."

Jean knew the Bedouins were part of the auxiliary troops and not professional soldiers, but the mounted Turkish archers were among the most feared troops in the Saracen army. In any event, there wasn't time for flight, since they would be immediately discovered and pursued. Besides Pierre, four other sergeants had brought bows and arrows. In a few seconds, Jean set up an ambush. He ordered his archers to aim their first arrows at the Turks. Mounted and with their archers at the ready, they waited a little above the slope of the hill. When the Saracen group came trotting around the curve in the road, the arrows flew. The distance was short, but even so, the target was moving, which made aiming more difficult. Three Turks were hit and fell off their horses. Meanwhile, Jean, João, Gaston and two other sergeants galloped downhill with their horses side by side. They had their shields raised and spears thrust out. The Saracens were taken completely by surprise. Instead of galloping forward, in order to escape the attack and take a better position for counterattacking, they braked their horses and turned around to the side from which the Christians were coming. At that moment, another cloud of arrows flew toward them, hitting the two remaining Turks and two more Bedouins. Two of the horsemen that were hit fell, and the other two continued on their horses and still ready to fight. The five Christian horsemen, mounted on their large Frankish war horses, knocked down everyone in front of them as if they were an avalanche. Their swords took resolute aim at the Saracens' bodies, splitting open skulls and cutting off arms and legs. The other five Christian horsemen, who had used their bows, then descended in the same formation as their brothers, and attacked the remaining enemy troops. The Bedouins waited for them with their sharp spears. Some of them broke on the impact with the shields, but there was one that penetrated through an opening in the shield barrier, hitting squarely a sergeant's throat. The struggle lasted less than two minutes. No Saracen escaped alive. The sergeant who was hit died immediately, the victim of a massive hemorrhage. He was still very young, had come from Marseilles and had only been in the Order for a year.

Jean ordered the burial of the dead, while Pierre served as a lookout on the top of the hill. They all said a prayer for the soul of the dead sergeant. They buried the Saracens' weapons together with their bodies, picked up the weapons and belongings of the dead sergeant, tying them to the saddle of his horse, which now would be led by the reins, during the trip, by one of the sergeants. Jean then ordered Pierre to ride well in front of the group. He was to climb up hills, and in case he spied enemies, he was to return and warn the others. In this way they succeeded in avoiding encounters with two more Saracen patrols by hiding behind small hills, which were very frequent in that region.

Some time later, they saw in the distance the tents of Saladin's army's camp. They circled to the north around the region, avoiding three more enemy patrols. When night began to fall, they spied from the top of a hill Lake Tiberias, which in ancient times was called the Sea of Galilee. The walled city of Tiberias was also located there, with its citadel's high tower overlooking the outside walls. They started to gallop in that direction when they noticed, in the sunset's contrasting light, coming along the southern shore of the lake, a large cavalry formation, followed by infantry and siege mechanisms, surely Saracen and ready to attack the city. Jean ordered the group to halt and take shelter behind a rock formation at the side of the road. They dismounted and Jean climbed up the highest rock, from which he could see the entire area. Looking toward the castle, he noticed a horseman leaving the main gate at a gallop. The Saracens didn't take the trouble to pursue him, as if they wanted him to tell the King what was happening. He came directly toward the Templars. When the man was very close, Jean went to the side of the road and called him, saying, "Stop. We are Templars."

The horseman braked his horse immediately on seeing the knight wearing the characteristic cloak of the warrior monks. The Templar took him behind the rocks, where the others were. It was already getting dark, but they could see that he was a young Frankish squire, who explained, "Sirs, my name is Guillaume, I am a squire at the court of Count Raimundo of Tripoli, who is with the King in Sephorie. He departed with his sons and most of his troops, leaving his wife Eschivia in command of the castle. I am going to tell the Count about the attack and ask for help."

"We shall go with you, Guillaume, we are returning to Sephorie and we have already seen that the Sultan sent only a part of his army to attack your city. I believe he is trying to lure our forces to fight on ground which favors him, that is, outside Sephorie."

The other Templars greeted the young squire and then prepared for the trip back to the camp. Night had fallen and under the cloak of darkness and the evening freshness, they rode much faster, always taking care to send a scout well ahead of the group, to see whether the road was free of enemy patrols. They had to make strategic detours twice to avoid the Saracens, but they succeeded in putting them off the track. The squire told the Templars the saga which his lord, the Count, had experienced. Some years earlier, he had been taken prisoner during a combat with the Syrians. Before payment of the ransom, he had been confined for several years in Damascus, where he learned the Saracens' language and acquired many oriental habits. He even established ties of friendship with the Sultan, with whom he used to exchange letters. Jean perceived the possible ramifications that this friendship could have for the Christian cause. During the wee morning hours, the horsemen and their mounts began to show signs of extreme fatigue. Jean chose the ford of a dry river, behind a hill, and there they dismounted, drank some water, ate the rest of the food they had brought and cared for their horses. They rested sufficiently and continued on their way. They opted for a detour to the north, to avoid Saladin's camp. At that moment, João came over to talk to Jean, saying, "Dear brother, we are close to the Saracens' camp. I want your authorization to go a little closer and spy on what they are doing. I kept the clothes of two of the Bedouins and since I have brown skin, I can pass myself off as one of them. Sergeant Lehoux could accompany me, so as not to violate our Order's rule that does not permit us to travel alone."

Jean looked amazed at his friend, admiring him for his shrewdness. He was worried since he didn't know exactly how much of his army Saladin had sent against Tiberias. This information would be very valuable for the King. The new moon was shining weakly, lessening the visibility of objects, whether animated or not. Jean replied, "You are right, brother, go. We shall wait here until sunrise. If you have not returned by then, we shall leave without you."

João galloped southward, following the road that went from Tiberias to Cafarrset. He had put on a Bedouin robe, which covered his whole body and head, and exchanged his big war horse for a smaller animal used by a sergeant. He was holding a Saracen spear, keeping his Templar sword covered by the robe. In this way, it would be difficult to recognize him. Lehoux had done the same, but he didn't have to change his horse, since he rode a smaller horse, similar to the Arabian horses. Further ahead, they came upon an advance post. They passed through without obeying the order to halt given by the sentinel, a Kurdish soldier. Everything happened so fast that the sentinel couldn't take any action, and just shouted and made gestures. They soon saw the camp in the distance. It was a sea of tents stretching out of sight. Thousands of bonfires produced a yellowish light, making possible a good view of the place. In the distance, the Sultan's yellow banner fluttered, announcing his presence. The Turkish archers' banners occupied an immense area of the camp, showing that they would be massively used against the Christians. Day was starting to break, which allowed João to observe everything from a small hill, just opposite the entrance to the camp. The sentinels noticed those Bedouins standing still, before sunrise, looking at the camp, and began to suspect something. "It's time to return", the Portuguese knight thought, and immediately began to gallop back down the road. They circled around the post, making a large curve through the desert, and continued on as fast as they could. The sun had already risen and had become a red ball on the horizon, when they arrived at the meeting point. Their Templar brothers had already left. It wasn't very difficult to follow the trail they left, possibly half an hour earlier. João galloped in the direction indicated by the horseshoe marks made by the war horses. In one of the curves, they came upon a group of twenty Turkish soldiers and some Bedouins. He didn't hesitate for a moment, and continued to gallop towards them. The Emir in command of the group made a sign for them to pass. João continued on, as if he hadn't noticed anything, and was surprised when the horsemen opened a path for them to pass through. The Emir shouted something in Arabic, but João kept galloping ahead without looking back, his back tensed as if awaiting the arrows that would fly in his direction. Fortunately, nothing happened. Further ahead they saw in the distance the dust raised by their brothers' horses, as they returned to the road after avoiding an encounter with the Saracens whom they had come upon earlier. Finally, they rejoined their group.

They arrived at the Christian camp after the terce, and the Knight Templar ran to Lagéry's tent, accompanied by Count Raimundo's squire. The chief immediately took them to the Grand Master. When they entered Ridefort's tent, they saw him seated on a wooden bench, conversing with another monk. On seeing them, the Grand Master turned toward Lagéry, who said, "Sir, our knight Jean has returned from his mission to Tiberias."

"Speak up, brother Jean, what did you discover? Who is that young man accompanying you?"

"Sir, the Sultan continues to stay with most of his army in Cafarsset. He sent around one thousand men to attack Tiberias yesterday afternoon. I believe this is an attempt to lure our forces into combat under conditions more favorable to him. Squire Guillaume was sent by Count Raimundo's wife to look for help. She is besieged in the castle, her husband and sons came to join the army."

"This is very important news. Let us go to the King's tent and inform him."

The King had called a meeting of the War Council, which at that moment was discussing whether they should attack Saladin's army or await the Sultan's attack in Sephorie. They were all there: the King. Reinaldo of Châtillon, the Lord of Karak, Count Raimundo of Tripoli, Balião of Ibelin, the Lord of Ramallah and the Master of the Hospitallers. On learning that his wife was surrounded in Tiberias, Raimundo became very nervous. His sons insisted they should go immediately to rescue her. The King then asked him for his advice, and he replied, "It would be madness to abandon our favorable position here in Sephorie. For the good of the kingdom and the holy places, with enormous agony, I prefer leaving my wife and my castle in danger."

The King and the Council agreed with Raimundo's proposal. The meeting was adjourned and they all returned to their tents.

THE WAIT

Reinaldo hadn't the least idea of how much time had passed since he'd begun to dream. There were moments when his real life seemed to be a dream and reality was in the past, in his life as Jean. He began to laugh at the folly of such thoughts. In addition, Father Demétrio's words about the death of the Templars in the battle of Hattin, on July 4, 1187, came to mind. Everything led him to believe this would be the battle that would be fought now, in his dreams. "What madness! They're, or rather, I'm going to die in the past and in the present!" The situation was so absurd that it most resembled an Ionesco play. He decided to stop thinking about it. He rose, took a drink of water and began exercising, taking care not to hurt his chained leg.

Eduardo had arrived in his mother's apartment at 1:00 p.m. sharp. She was expecting him for lunch. While eating, he told his mother what had happened at the police station, taking care to omit the part regarding the spy and the deadline set for his brother's death. He only told her that the kidnapping had been done by the brother of the drug trafficker killed by Reinaldo on the border, but the police had the means to rescue his brother within a few hours. She became very nervous at the news and asked him to stay home, answering possible phone calls, while she went with Aunt Glorinha to the bank.

At two in the afternoon Jô called to learn the latest news. Some time later, Eduardo phoned his wife in Foz de Iguaçu, to see whether everything was alright at home. And he awaited further happenings.

The Cirado hillside slum was a real fortress. Pedro was in a shack a few meters away from the gang's headquarters. Not even a little bird could arrive there without any alarm being given by the hundreds of boys who served as lookouts for the gang. Various methods were used to warn the drug dealers of the arrival of intruders: firecrackers, kites, mobile phones—a very well-established system. The local community either collaborated openly or remained indifferent, without disturbing in any way the drug traffic operations. Pedro possessed a mobile phone, which was controlled by the gang. Serginho had set up a phone-tapping center operated by three technicians, twenty-four hours a day, which controlled all the calls from the slum. At 11:00 a.m., the technicians changed shifts. It was the only time they turned off the equipment, and then only for a minute, while they performed some minor maintenance. It was exactly at that time that Pedro used to call the police station, on the special phone line they had installed. The risk of something going wrong was very great, but until now it had been working. He'd finally been able to discover the captive's hiding place. At 1:00 p.m., the take-out lunches for the gang used to arrive. Each one picked up his take-out lunch and went to eat wherever he wanted. Pedro saw when Gato, Serginho's cousin and one of his trusted henchmen, picked up two take-out lunches. Pedro had already noticed Gato doing the same thing the day before and then walking down the hill. Then he had a sudden inspiration. It was almost obvious that the guy was in charge of the hiding place. Pedro followed him, as discreetly as possible, taking along his food, as if he were going to eat some place. He didn't walk more than five minutes. Gato stopped in front of a small house on Ilhota Street and knocked on the door using a type of code. Pedro sat down on the curb, behind a wheelbarrow, at a good safe distance. He pretended to be eating his lunch calmly. He saw three men leave the house—they must have been the guards—and walk up the hill. They were probably going to have lunch, while Gato was guarding the victim. His presence went unnoticed. The gang had around 140 members and not all of them knew each other, since almost every month there were one or two deaths, which required constant replacements. Every afternoon Pedro used to sleep a little, in order to take up his position, at 11:00 p.m., more rested. He felt a great anguish. He didn't see any way of transmitting the information to his police colleagues before 11:00 a.m. the next day. Every minute that went by was precious. He was so nervous that he was perspiring. He had already seen two executions of gang members. The torture was merciless and the killing even worse. They were burned alive, with three old tires pulled down over their heads and then set on fire. The drug traffickers couldn't leave the hillside slum without authorization from Serginho himself. He recalled that one of his chief's manias was boasting that he took care of the health of all the members of his gang and their families. The week before, when one of them got sick, he'd ordered one of his lieutenants to take him to a clinic in the Vila Isabel district, which used to care for the gang members. The guy had to be hospitalized, because he had the dengue. Pedro didn't think twice. He went to the gang headquarters, looked for Serginho and took a chance, saying, "Chief, I'm feeling sick. It's serious! My head aches like it was going to explode, I'm feeling nauseous and dizzy. Please, help me!"

He sat down on the floor and held his head, making faces full of pain. The chief contemplated the scene for a few moments, let out a curse word and ordered a trusted gang member to take Pirado by taxi to the doctor in the Vila Isabel clinic, shouting, "F—! This guy has to be back in half an hour to open the drug den. Get going!"

The gangster that was accompanying Pedro was from the state of Bahia, around 35, white, strong and mistrustful. They took a taxi at the bottom of the hill and went to the clinic. There they received immediate attention. The gangster entered the doctor's office with Pedro, which would upset all his plans. But luckily, while he was being examined, the guy said he was going to the bathroom and left the room. It was the moment Pedro was waiting for. He asked the doctor if he could use the phone, and called the police station, It was already 5:45 p.m., and many policemen had already gone out, leaving only those on duty, who took a long time to answer phone calls. When they finally answered, the doorknob began to turn. Pedro couldn't say anything and hung up. He wasn't caught red-handed by a fraction of a second. The doctor continued the examination, diagnosing just a minor illness, perhaps indigestion, and prescribed some medicine. Back at the hillside slum, Pedro was unable to disguise his frustration. Everything had gone wrong, after so much work. He went to his shack, assuring the gang member that he was feeling better and would take up his position later. He laid down again and looked at his watch; it was 6:45, and he hadn't been able to transmit the information.

The chaplain spent those interminable moments in prayer and thinking about his relatives and friends. He wasn't thinking about Jean, nor about the people in the Holy Land. He was restless, one moment he was getting up, another he was lying down, and another he was doing exercises. Then he decided to lie down again, close his eyes and not think about anything. He relaxed and fell asleep. The regression began, minutes later. The sensation was that of having awakened in some other place . . .

THE CONFESSION

J ean returned to the camp and joined his subordinates in prayer and a meal. At sundown they went to bed, since they had been awake all during the previous night. On that night, July 2-3, Grand Master Ridefort went to King Guido's tent and succeeded in convincing him that Court Raimundo's suggestion was pure cowardice. The army should march toward Tiberias as soon as possible, in order to liberate the city and attack the Saracens.

Before sunrise, on July 3, the King gave an order for the army to march immediately. Bugles sounded in the various sectors of the camp. The fires were put out, the tents were dismantled and the march began. The order had been so sudden that most of the combatants didn't even have time to provide themselves with water from the sources in Sephorie.

The first division of the army, which was commanded by Count Raimundo, marched in the vanguard, the cavalry in the center, with the infantry surrounding the great mass of horses. Then came the division of the King and the Lord of Karak, Reinaldo de Châtillon. Close to the King, the Bishop of Acre carried the banner containing Christianity's most sacred relic, the Holy Rood. The cavalry and the infantry followed the same arrangement as that of the vanguard division. Lastly came the division of Balião of Ibelin, with the two religious orders, the Hospitallers and the Templars, bringing up the rearguard. Lagéry's company was on the right flank of the division's large square formation. As the march went forward, they were leaving behind the water sources and the green vegetation. The land's relief was changing dramatically; now they were facing gnarled bushes, sand and rocks, which made up the way that was darkened by the dust cloud they were raising. The hot sun burned relentlessly. Jean was riding with his group, stopping from time to time in order to accompany the infantry's slower pace. João rode at his side and further back were Pierre, Gaston and the other five sergeants. They were all sweating profusely.

The first attack came from behind a nearby hill. A group of approximately twenty Bedouins, armed with bows and arrows, galloped up to a safe distance and sent a cloud of arrows toward the Christians, fleeing immediately afterwards. Two infantry soldiers were hit, one of them seriously. The knights raised their shields and parried the falling arrows, so that none of them was wounded. The order was to keep in formation and not pursue the attackers. The attacks were repeated several times, creating panic and demoralizing the Christian soldiers. They learned later that the other divisions had also suffered successive attacks. Lagéry sent for Jean and the other officers in his company. Jean rode up close to the commander, and together with his brother officers, learned from the experienced Templar they would soon be reaching Touraan, a small Syrian town. There was an everlasting source of water there, and surely the army would receive orders from the King to stop for a rest and supply themselves with water. They were almost without any water at all for the men and the horses. The officers should maintain discipline and organize their subordinates for going to the water source. Lagéry's company would be the last one to obtain a water supply. Food was also scarce. At that moment, a messenger from the King came to tell them that the vanguard division had encountered the center of the enemy army, and was engaged in a violent, generalized combat with the Sultan's forces. He added that there wouldn't be any time for the stop at the Touraan water source. Some units succeeded in obtaining water, but most went ahead without the precious liquid.

Jean's group was bringing along two horses laden with weapons, food and two sheepskin bags filled with water, of which one had already been totally used up. Jean commented to João on the King's decision to march on Tiberias, "Brother, I have a feeling that King Guido's decision will lead us into a very difficult situation. We are going to need a miracle."

"But if we arrive tonight at the lake, we shall have water, and after resting, tomorrow morning we shall be able to fight well, even though we are outnumbered," replied the Portuguese knight, trying to be optimistic.

"I doubt the Sultan will let us reach the lake. The struggle will get harder and harder. It is just that they have lots of water and we do not. Tell the sergeant in charge of the cargo horses that we shall only drink and eat tonight."

Starting at the beginning of the afternoon, the Saracens began to attack in larger numbers, with professional troops. The mounted Turkish archers and the Syrian cavalry launched a great attack, involving more than eight thousand horsemen. The rearguard, where Jean and his brothers were, suffered great harassment. The monk kept his men side by side, with their shields forming a barrier. They attacked with their large horses the increasingly numerous hordes of Saracens. The struggle was fierce on both sides. Fatigue was already weakening them all. Keeping their shields in position, raising and lowering their swords forcefully on their enemies in itself required a great effort. Thirst and heat added to the Templars' torment. Up to then they hadn't suffered any wounds. Their steel coats of mail protected them against all those blows that penetrated the shield barrier. Regardless of the combats, the army continued advancing, but now the advance was very slow. The vanguard division, encountering strong resistance to its advance, had changed its course to the left, seeking to circle around the powerful Saracen forces in front of them. Count Raimundo intended to reach the water sources of Hattin, in a Syrian town with the same name, that same night, and on the next day go on to the Sea of Galilee, which was six kilometers from that point. Close to the town of Hattin, there was a rise in the ground with two hills in the form of horns, which were called the horns of Hattin. Saladin perceived the Christians' maneuver and ordered Emir Taqi al Din, commander of one of the Saracen divisions, to march rapidly to Hattin and occupy the town, thus preventing the Christians from reaching the water source. The Emir carried out the maneuver successfully. At the same time, Emir Gökböri's division attacked heavily the Christians' rearguard division, bringing it to a complete standstill. Sunset was approaching and the King had no other alternative than ordering the army to halt and camp on the hills in front of it, the horns of Hattin. Meanwhile, in the rearguard, Balião of Ibelin, in a final desperate effort to break the encirclement, ordered a general attack by the Templars and Hospitallers against Gökböri's division.

Grand Master Ridefort called all the officers together and ordered, "All the Templars shall participate in this attack on the Saracens. Close your ranks and we shall charge toward the enemy. Our infantry shall come following us, covering our rearguard."

Then the Templar gave the Order's famous battle cry: "It is God's will!" The cry was repeated by all the Templars and echoed through the desert. They all ran to their posts and began to ride toward the enemy.

Jean kept his group in their correct position, within Lagèry's company. At the right end, the most vulnerable, was Pierre, with João at his side; afterwards came Jean, Gaston and the other sergeants, all Franks. The gallop of the eight hundred Knights Templar and sergeants and the thousand Hospitallers picked up speed. The sound of their battle cries, their banners fluttering in the wind, with the emblazoned cross of Christ, made for a spectacular scene, contrasting with the reddish backdrop of an indescribable sunset. The Saracen Gökböri division had 2,000 *tawashi* horsemen, 1,500 Mameluke *qaraghulam* horsemen and 1,800 Turkish horsemen from Mosul, all elite soldiers in the Sultan's army. The Christian cavalry was followed by the infantry soldiers, who were protecting the cavalry's rearguard. The Saracen infantry, with their archers and axmen, attacked the Christian infantry on both flanks, taking advantage of their numerical superiority.

Jean felt the speed of his horse increase and made a great effort to keep in line with his Templar brothers. The clash of the two armies made a noise similar to a peal of thunder. From then on there were only shouts, bodies of men and animals falling to the ground and blood staining the sand, mixed with the noise of the steel weapons clanking on their impact. The first ranks of the Saracens were being destroyed and the Christians' advance continued. However, the Saracen soldiers showed no fear and didn't retreat an inch. Little by little, the attackers' speed was diminishing. The Knight Templar was almost breathless and his arms hurt, one from parrying so many blows with his shield that protected the knight on his left, and the other from the incessant blows he struck with his sword. Suddenly he realized that the line of knights had broken up and he was alone, surrounded by two Syrian horsemen. He parried the spear thrust of one of them and succeeded in striking a blow with his sword between the other's shoulder and neck. The blade penetrated deeply into the flesh and momentarily got stuck. The other horseman took the opportunity to attack him again, and his spear was coming directly toward his chest, since his shield was turned aside to the rear. Jean felt his mortal hour had arrived. In that fraction of a second, he saw a horseman arrive like a bolt of lightning and knock down the Syrian, turning aside the latter's spear. It was Pierre, who shouted, "Let us go back, Sir. The lines were undone and we need to reorganize ourselves."

They galloped as fast as they could back to the higher ground, while the Saracen infantry, which had already forced the Christian infantry to retreat, attacked the fleeing knights with arrows and axes. Now almost exhausted and dying of thirst, they succeeded in returning to their defensive positions, at the high point of the raised ground at the foot of the two hills of Hattin. Night began to fall, and as was their custom, the Saracens interrupted the combat, since they weren't used to fighting in the dark. Jean and Pierre dismounted and fell on the ground in a half-faint. Around them, several groups of survivors, with many wounded, rested from the combats. In the distance, the Saracen army was beginning to set up their camp for the night. Drum rolls and prayer shouts were heard. Now more recovered, Jean asked Pierre, "Where are the others?"

The squire lowered his head and answered in a bitter voice, "Sir, only the two of us and sergeants Gaston and Armand have returned. The other five Templars in the group fell during the attack. I saw when João, the knight, fell, after his horse was killed by arrows. Then a group of axmen fell on him and killed him."

Jean felt a deep sadness on learning of his friend's death. He knelt down and prayed for his soul, and Pierre imitated him. He had taken a liking to the young Portuguese. He was sorry he hadn't been able to accompany his friend to the Kingdom of God. They lit a bonfire, with the help of Gaston and Armand, a young sergeant born in Rheims. Gaston had brought the cargo horse, and they could care for and feed the animals that were in a deplorable state. They divided among them the little water that was still left and ate the last pieces of bread. The Bishop of Acre began to celebrate mass in front of the holy relic, in torchlight, and the survivors knelt down and contritely accompanied the prayers. All of them confessed, the Templars doing so with their warrior monks. When Gaston's turn came, the youth began to cry convulsively and asked Jean to call Pierre, since what he wanted to tell was important for him also.

"Sir Jean, I came to the Holy Land as a pilgrim, to seek forgiveness for a great sin which I committed. God, in His wisdom, put me in the presence of the one I offended seriously. I participated in the group of bandits that attacked your family, in your castle, and I helped to set the chapel on fire, killing the innocent people that were inside. At the time she was closing the vestry gate, your wife begged me to save her boy, your son. I was much grieved over her suffering and hid the little one in a cloth bag, that I carried away with me in my flight. I gave the little boy to my aunt and uncle, who had no children, to raise.

When I left France, he was well, a strong healthy boy. I kept this secret until now out of fear and shame. But I need your forgiveness and that of God, since it is almost certain that we are all going to die."

Jean sobbed, embraced by Pierre, who also couldn't contain himself. He was unable to organize his thoughts in a coherent way, with his feelings so confused now. He moved away and sat down, putting his head between his legs. He was trying to think what to do. After a while, he rose and returned to Pierre and Gaston. His voice showed great affliction as he said, "Pay close attention to everything I am going to say. Gaston, I forgive you for the sin you committed against the Law of God and against my loved ones. I am going to consider your confession also as a religious one and I absolve you in the name of God. The happiness on learning that my son is alive is only incomplete due to our tragic situation and due to my vow to the Order, which I must fulfill. I want Pierre to vow to obey all my orders, and to fulfill his vow, even if this makes him break his vow as a Templar. André's future depends on this. Gaston and I, tomorrow, during the struggle, shall do everything possible so that you survive and escape from here alive. You must leave the Holy Land and return to France, where you shall look for my parents and my brother, tell them everything that happened and take them to André, their grandson and nephew. Try to protect him, like you have protected me, giving me your sincere devotion and friendship, during all these years. Wherever I may be, in the way chosen by God, I shall always be with you."

Pierre looked at him and said, "I give you my vow, my lord Sir Jean de Saumur!"

Jean rose and went close to the relic of the Holy Cross, to pray and wait for sunrise.

A little while afterwards, Count Raimundo went to confer with King Guido in the royal tent. On learning of the defeat of the Templars and the Hospitallers, he went into despair and shouted, "My God, the war is lost. The Holy Land shall be taken away from us."

THE EVE OF
THE EXECUTION

Reinaldo woke up in tears. He'd been carried away by strong emotion. João's death, the revelation that André was alive and the imminent battle with the Saracens set off within him a whirl of dizzying thoughts and feelings. His death sentence was one more complicating aspect in that confusion of traumatic events he was experiencing. He rose, did a little more exercise and began to pray.

He felt very bad physically. The lack of any bath, the precarious hygienic conditions, the chain on his right leg, which made his blood circulation more difficult, the light that was permanently turned on, all were contributing to a growing malaise, which had culminated in a strong headache and nausea. He'd been feeling this way since he'd eaten the food they'd brought him, a few hours earlier. The drug traffickers unintentionally were helping Reinaldo to know the date and, consequently, the time of day. The take-out lunches furnished all the information. He noticed that on the cover of the container, besides the name of the supplier, "Engenho Novo District Hot Lunches", there was a small stamp with the date. On that day, for example, the stamp showed August 26. This being the third meal he'd received, therefore the previous ones had been on

Thursday, August 24, and Friday, August 25. The time must have been between 1:00 and 2:00 p.m., since the food was still warm when it arrived. That meant, also, that there were 24 hours left until his execution. His biological clock was even working well, since he was falling asleep at what must have been approximately the beginning of the night. He decided to remain lying down, and in order to pass the time, he tried to recall events that had occurred during his childhood and adolescence, things he hadn't thought about for a long time.

Eduardo woke up early. It was Saturday, August 26. He felt a sudden shock on recalling there was little more than a day left until his brother's execution. They had to learn today, by any means, the address of the hideaway. On entering the kitchen to have breakfast, Eduardo noticed that his mother was very down-and-out, with big bags under her eyes, a sign that she hadn't slept. Even so, she had enough strength to prepare her son's breakfast.

Right after breakfast, he took leave of his mother and went to Avenida Atlântica to catch a bus for the Barra da Tijuca district. He arrived at the police station a little before 10 a.m. The detectives were in a meeting with their chief, Fábio, and with detective Brandão from the Drug Enforcement Department, discussing his brother's case. The chief detective invited him: "Sit down with us, Eduardo."

He greeted all of them and sat down in the empty chair beside the chief. The latter informed him they had just decided to await Pedro's contact, at eleven o'clock, and then plan the action for rescuing Reinaldo. They closed the meeting and went to drink a small coffee before going back to work. At eleven sharp, the spy called and reported, "I got the address. Make a note: 344 Ilhota Street; its here in the Cirado slum, just starting up the hill. There are three guards."

Fábio noted down the address on a piece of paper, handing it to Brandão. Right away a great commotion began in the police station. The whole team was armed with FAL rifles. Bullet-proof vests were distributed to the policemen, as well as ammunition for pistols and rifles. Eduardo was included in the group, and received a bullet-proof vest and a rifle with ammunition. He'd also brought with him his service gun, a 9 mm pistol. The plan for rescuing Reinaldo was based on the assumption that the victim's life had to preserved at all cost. Accordingly, the action had to take place with maximum surprise. The time chosen for arrival at the hiding place was 3:00 a.m. on Sunday, when the activity in the area would be very slight. They decided that the means of transportation to be utilized would be an ambulance from the Vila Isabel clinic, which might occasionally enter the Cirado slum on more serious cases, duly authorized by Serginho. At night, the drug traffickers used to set up a barrier with five armed men at each one of the two entrances to the hill complex. The police obtained from the Municipal Government an ambulance having the same characteristics as the ambulances belonging to the clinic. It was already in the police station garage and was being painted in a way similar to those of the Vila Isabel clinic. Two detectives from the Larceny and Theft Department, specialized in opening locked doors, were already prepared to accompany the action. Their work would be extremely important: opening the door of the hiding place in less than ten seconds, without making any noise. Five detectives would then invade the place. They were specialists, with a high level of technical training. They were equipped with night vision devices, bullet-proof vests, guns with silencers, material for breaking down doors and cutting chains. They'd already memorized Reinaldo's face by studying photographs brought by Eduardo, at Fabio's request. A police doctor, with resuscitation equipment, also formed part of the group. A total of 11 men would go in the ambulance. Two, dressed in white as though they were employees of the clinic, would go in the cab with the driver, and the rest would remain hidden in back. All the personnel involved in the operation would remain in the police station until the time of the action. They'd have take-out lunches from a nearly restaurant. Their families would be told that they'd be on duty that night, including Eduardo's mother.

His mother heard the telephone ring and ran to answer it, wearing her heart on her sleeve. Her son said, "It's me, mom. Forgive me for calling only now. I've got good news. If all goes well, tomorrow afternoon everything will be resolved. Don't say anything to anybody. I'm going to remain on duty here in the police station and I won't go home to sleep. Pray a lot. I have to hang up."

She hung up and heaved a great sigh. Something in Eduardo's voice told her that, God willing, everything would turn out well. Jô would probably call in a little while, like she did every day. She'd say she still didn't know anything, following Eduardo's recommendation. After cleaning up the kitchen, she decided to go to church with her sister and pray, as her son had suggested.

Eduardo looked at his watch, it was 6:30 p.m., and night came rapidly. The weather was good, it almost seemed like summer. It wasn't very hot—the temperature should oscillate around 77° F. As the hours passed by, the anxiety in his chest increased. He'd already participated in countless actions, some very dangerous, risking his life, but none of them had involved anyone from his family. The whole teams had already gone over the plan several times. Searching in the Internet, they found photographs of the slum in a newspaper site. Through enlargement of the photos, they obtained the exact place of the hideaway, which made it possible to give precise guidance to the ambulance driver. Now it was all a question of waiting and carrying out what had been carefully planned.

Reinaldo began to feel sleepy. He laid down and used the trick of putting the pillow over his head, thus lessening the clarity which bothered him so much. He tried to relax and not think about anything. At that luminous moment he heard the bugles of the Christian camp, which ordered the formations to prepare for combat . . .

THE HORNS OF HATTIN

J ean had spent the whole night thinking. The events of his life marched through his memory; moments of happiness and moments of pain alternated continuously. His thirst was unbearable. His dry mouth began to make him dizzy. He rose and went to care for the horses. There still remained a few handfuls of millet, which he distributed among the animals. The night of rest had restored a little of their energy. The big drama was the lack of water. There wasn't even a drop left, neither for the men nor for the animals. The sun shone in the sky, announcing another day of extreme heat. From the top of the hill, the Sea of Galilee could be seen. And between them and the water was half of the Sultan's army. Jean began to smell something burning, and looked at the ravine, at the foot of the hills, noting that the brush was on fire. A dense cloud of smoke headed in the direction of the Christian camp. It was only then that he realized what the Saracens' diabolic maneuver was. They set fire to all the dry vegetation in such a way that the wind would carry the smoke toward the hills. The unbearable heat, the lack of drinking water and food, and now the suffocating smoke, made the troops' situation untenable. From his place up on the hill, the knight saw the agglomeration of infantry soldiers, mostly of Italian origin, disheartened, tired, hungry and thirsty. With no little sacrifice, they were trying to regroup for the struggle which wouldn't be long in recommencing. The cavalry, almost entirely spread around the slopes of the two hills, was also scattered through the plain. Due to the casualties suffered during the previous day's combats, the units had shrunk in size.

Grand Master Ridefort had survived the ferocious combats and continued in command of the Order. He sent messengers to call all the officers. Jean headed for the group which gathered in front of the royal tent. The nobles also arrived, joining the King. They were all there: Count Raimundo, Reinaldo, The Lord of Karak, Balião, the Lord of Ramalah, the Grand Master of the Hospitallers and other less important knights. They decided on a radical attack against the center of the Saracen army. The cavalry would go in front, followed by the infantry. They'd try to break through the enemy lines and reach the Hattin water sources, which were closer than the lake, and where the army could provide itself with water and then take up defensive positions near the village. On Saladin's left flank, a large formation of Bedouins had taken up position. An Italian noble then asked why didn't they attack this formation, which being weaker, would give ground more rapidly and would open a path to the lake. Ridefort answered that as soon as they were involved in the attack the enemy's elite divisions would attack their flanks and destroy the Christians. In the center of the enemy line, they could make out the three Mameluke regiments of the Sultan's personal guard, the Halqa, with their yellow uniforms and banners. To the right of those regiments, there was a large Kurdish elite unit, in black uniforms. These troops' spear blades scintillated in the sun, as if challenging the Frankish warriors' courage. The Christian rearguard would again attack the powerful Gökböry division, which was on the left flank. The remaining Templars and Hospitallers would join in the vanguard of the attack. The battle cries resounded through the desert: "It is God's will!"

Jean, Pierre and Gaston were riding together, in a line of thirty Knights Templar. They were armed with spears, in an attempt to destroy the defense lines of the Saracen regiment in front of them and open a path for the lines of Templars that were following them. They began to gallop and the long row of spears seemed to be flying toward the enemy line. Jean held his spear and shield as firmly as he could in his arms, and saw the mass of Saracen cavalry approaching. The shock was violent. The speed of the attack and the strength of the large war horses destroyed, like a battering ram, the Saracens' first lines of defense. Little by little, the enemy's reaction was increasing and it became difficult to maintain the formation. The scimitars began to forcefully hit the shields, which were kept in a closed position. They got rid of their spears, useless in this type of combat, and drew their swords. The struggle which followed was extremely violent. The enemy's numerical superiority and the weakness of the Franks', almost all of them suffering from dehydration, made the scale tip in favor of the soldiers of Islam. The Templars' lines broke up, and with them their best defense, the shield barrier. Each Frankish knight was being surrounded and attacked by two, or sometimes three, enemy warriors. At this moment, Jean, who didn't lose sight of his two companions, ordered them to retreat. They rode back to the hills and halfway there, they noticed a large group of knights, with the colors and coats of arms of the earldom of Tyre, galloping toward the end of the Saracen right flank, made up of Bedouins.

"It's Count Raimundo", shouted Jean.

He soon noticed that the noble was going to break through the Bedouins' line and flee toward the lake. He ordered, "Pierre, go with them and keep your promise."

The squire didn't wait a second and galloped toward the group. They saw when he joined the knights from Tyre, and they all disappeared on encountering the white line of the Bedouins. The latter broke up so rapidly that it seemed like they were opening the way for the Christians.

Ridefort was among the knights that retreated from the attack. The Templars' banner was waving, calling on the survivors to gather together for a new charge. Balião's Frankish knights, the Hospitallers and the Templars again formed a line and this time the target would be the yellow banner in the center of the Saracen formation: Sultan Saladin himself. The bugle call gave the command for the beginning of the desperate charge. The line of knights began to trot, then went into a half-gallop and, at the sound of the battle cries, began the final gallop. The Halqa guard regiments began to be destroyed, and for a few moments, it seemed that the suicide attack would be successful. At that decisive moment, the Kurdish regiments attacked the flanks of the Christian lines. It was the final blow. One by one, the Christian knights were being knocked down from their horses. The Saracen infantry finished the job. Axmen fell upon the bodies of those who were still trying to get up and with violent strokes, killed them unceasingly.

Jean and Gaston continued fighting, side by side, helping each other. The lines were already broken. The two Templars instinctively tried to retreat and stay close to the survivors who were still fighting. After much effort, they succeeded in returning to the hills. Almost all were wounded. There were around 300 survivors among knights, sergeants and Turcopoles.

The Grand Master was still among them. They were what was left of the Order of the Knights Templar in the Holy Land. They decided to dismount, since their horses were showing signs of collapse. Their widespread front hooves and lowered heads were signed indicating that the animals had reached the end of their physical resistance. Jean noticed that Gaston was bleeding through his coat of mail, due to various wounds. He himself felt much pain from the blows on his coat of mail. They sat down on the ground to rest. They were shocked, looking down at the plain below. Bodies of knights and horses covered a large part of the ground. The Christian infantry had been viscerally attacked and destroyed by the combined Saracen cavalry and infantry. The latter would soon move up the slopes to attack the last Christian bastion, the King's tent and the banner of the Holy Cross. A few dozen knights gathered together, on foot, around the tent, for the last combat. Jean, with great sacrifice, rose and shouted, "Let us go, Gaston. We vowed to defend the cross of Christ until death. We must keep our vow!" The young sergeant rose and accompanied the knight to the King's tent. There they learned that Balião of Ibelin had escaped with a group of knights heading toward Sephorie. The Bishop of Acre had been killed by arrows and the holy relic had been taken by two priests to the highest part of the hill. The infantry, further down, was no longer an organized formation. Most of them had been slaughtered or had fled downhill in despair. The combat finally reached the place where they were. Gaston was one of the first to fall. A Kurdish horseman, all dressed in black, thrust his spear into the sergeant's neck, but was killed by Jean, who buried his sword beneath the enemy's right armpit. The final combat cost the Saracens dearly. Two emirs, one of them being a nephew of the Sultan, were killed in the bloody combat which followed. The Christians were fighting desperately to defend the King and the holy relic. A bugle call interrupted the combat, since the Kurdish regiment that was attacking them had suffered heavy losses and was withdrawing. The short truce was only a brief interlude in the Christian tragedy. Soon afterwards, another Saracen bugle call ordered the attack by a Halqa Mameluke regiment that replaced the Kurds. The Sultan had sent his personal guard to finish the battle and assure what would be his greatest victory. The end came rapidly. The defenders of the cross barely had enough strength to raise their swords. Emir Taqui al Din personally cut the ropes of the King's tent, which fell to the ground, and with it, the symbol of the last center of resistance of the Latin knights. The Mameluke officers disarmed the surviving knights and took the King and the nobles to the Sultan. All the combatants wearing Templar or Hospitallers uniforms were tied up and separated from the rest. The ordinary combatants were taken to Damascus, where they'd be sold as slaves. The surviving Turcopoles were killed by their captors at the time of their surrender, since they were Syrians by birth and thus considered to be traitors to the faith. The relic was taken and delivered to Taqui al Din. Jean had survived and was led, tied up, together with his Templar and Hospitallers brothers, to a small clearing at the foot of the hill. All told, there were about 230 survivors of the two orders, between knights and sergeants. One of the last to arrive was Charles of Toulon, the Grand Master's aide-de-camp. He had been in the Holy Land for 12 years and spoke Arabic well. He told Jean that he'd accompanied the nobles to the Sultan's tent. All of them were well treated, and Saladin ordered sweetened cold water to be brought for everyone. At that moment, an emir recalled that among the nobles was Reinaldo de Châtillon, who had tried to invade Mecca. The Sultan then snatched the glass from his hand. According to the Arab tradition, a prisoner who received water or food from his captor could no longer be killed. Right afterwards, he ordered one of the Mameluke officers to decapitate the noble, which was done immediately, to the horror of the other Christians. Charles had also heard the Sultan himself order the execution of all the Templars, with the exception of the Grand Master. The Prophet's religion didn't permit the killing of prisoners, but Saladin had alleged that those warriors were too dangerous for the Islamic faith and he wouldn't permit them to fight again against his people. The executioners would be volunteers.

Many religious men, Egyptian Sufis that were accompanying the army, volunteered for the task. The Templars would be permitted to renounce their faith in order to save their lives. The Kurdish soldiers began to untie the condemned men, taking them to a small rise in the land, where many executioners with scimitars were waiting to begin the decapitations. The monk knelt down and began to pray. First, for the souls of the friends who had departed, asking God to protect Pierre and help him find his son and deliver him to his parents. Finally, he asked for forgiveness for all his sins and recited the Credo. Suddenly, he felt great happiness. He recalled that he was going to encounter his beloved Melissande. He couldn't contain a smile of joy. Some Saracen slaves were distributing water to the prisoners, many of whom had to be helped by their brothers, since they could hardly walk, due to their wounds. The executions were accompanied by shouts of rejoicing from the Saracen combatants who came to watch the event. Sunset was near, and those in charge wanted to finish the job before nightfall. The heads were picked up by the slaves, to be taken later to

Damascus as trophies. The monks' blood stained the sandy soil dark red, while the bodies were dragged by the slaves to a small depression in the ground. A Kurdish soldier approached Jean and cut the rope which bound him to his brother at his side. The monk rose and walked toward the place of the executions. A Mameluke combatant, in a yellow uniform, moved away from the others and came up to him, with his scimitar unsheathed. Jean, who was praying in a low voice, raised his eyes toward the executioner and was frightened by what he saw. The man who looked at him hatefully was the bandit chief whom Jean had defeated in Nablus. It was he, Al-Ashfar, as ambassador Usamah had told him. The scar from the arrow wound inflicted by Pierre still appeared near his neck. The two Kurdish soldiers forced the Templar to kneel in a great puddle in the ground soaked with blood. One of them asked, in heavily-accented French, "Do you renounce your religion, Templar, and accept the word of the true God and His prophet?"

Jean raised his eyes to the sky, and with his hands joined together, shouted out loud, "I believe in God, His son Jesus Christ, in the Holy Spirit and in the Holy Mother Church!"

The Mameluke, his face twisted with hate, raised his scimitar up high and brought it down violently.

AUGUST 27

Reinaldo felt inexplicably calm, a sensation of intoxicating peace. It was an intriguing phenomenon. Shouldn't the opposite be the case? Shouldn't he feel sad over Jean's death? Or better still, over *his* death in another life? He knew in his heart that the Templar monk's strongest desire was to die. To die for his faith, for his beliefs and, in this way, join his beloved in another life. Wouldn't it have been better to survive in order to find his son and help him to grow up, to become a man? The monk was bound by his vow and had already become accustomed to the idea that he'd die fighting, keeping the promise he'd made on entering the Order. It was his fate and he knew it. And now? His dreams in which he was Jean would end. He wouldn't know about Pierre and his encounter with André. He tried to come back to the present.

He rose and took a drink of water. He felt gooseflesh on his neck. It must already be Sunday, the day of *his* death. At least Jean had known the reasons why he was going to die. He knew, obviously, that the drug dealer was going to kill him to avenge his brother. But why had he, a priest, become a killer, starting off a process of violence? This question remained unanswered.

Eduardo looked at his watch again. It was two o'clock in the morning. The entire police team was ready. They'd get into the ambulance at two fifteen sharp. The man in charge of the action, detective Brandão, went over the last details of the plan. Detective Fábio, with other policemen, would stay in the police station accompanying the unfolding of the action by means of the mobile phone. Eduardo took advantage of the remaining minutes to have a small coffee and a glass of water. He was feeling neither sleepy nor tired, just somewhat anxious. As soon as he finished drinking the water, he heard the call for departure. He grabbed his rifle and ammunition, put on his bullet-proof vest and got into the ambulance. The nine policemen arranged themselves as best they could, four on one side and five on the other, in the rear of the vehicle, which had been adapted for the action. The driver went along Avenida das Américas, heading for the Jacarepaguá district, where he entered the Grajaú/Jacarepaguá road. From the Grajaú district, they went on to the Engenho do Dentro district, arriving a little later at the Cirado hillside slum. Detective Brandão, seated beside the driver and dressed in white, pretending to be the doctor, warned his colleagues in back, "Pay attention, men. We're arriving at the Cirado slum."

On the corner of the street going up the hill, they saw the group of five drug dealers armed with AK-47 rifles that guarded the entrance to the slum. The place was well-lit, since they were beneath a lamppost. The street was deserted, except for the criminals passing through the area. The ambulance driver slowed down, stopped close to the group and said, "Good evening, chief. We're answering an emergency call. It's at number 18, Comprido Street. That street is at the end of Ilhota Street. It was the reference point they gave us. It's authorized by Serginho, the chief."

The policemen were prepared for an inspection of the rear of the ambulance. If it happened, they would use the guns with silencers, ready to neutralize the five bandits.

The drug dealer who seemed to be the chief of the group, and had a sleepy look, turned to one of his men and said, "Ratão, you go with them and stay with them all the time until they leave. Get moving!"

Brandão jumped out and let the criminal sit between him and the driver. The gun barrel was placed uncomfortably at his head. The ambulance continued on its way. A few minutes later, it entered Ilhota Street. The driver paid attention to the building numbers and stopped right in front of the hideaway. Before Ratão could react in any way, he was immobilized by the two policemen at his side, and a third, getting out of the rear of the vehicle, put handcuffs on him and gagged him with adhesive tape. Meanwhile, the two men responsible for opening the street door finished their task, which took less than ten seconds. The five invaders ran into the house.

Serginho didn't like to leave the Cirado slum, because he felt like a fish out of the water. But he couldn't turn down the invitation to the wedding party of Gato, his cousin and only relative left, besides his aunt. He'd bought a penthouse apartment in the Tijuca district for that aunt, his dead mother's sister, where the party would take place. Everything was carefully prepared for that night. It was already three o'clock in the morning and he was returning to the Cirado slum. They always went out in two cars, with two men in each one, all heavily armed. These men were chosen from among his most loyal subordinates and were responsible for his security. Since it was a calm outing, they weren't wearing bullet-proof vests. The cars approached the entrance. Serginho noticed something wrong, since there was a man missing at the roadblock. They stopped, and the chief asked, "What's going on?"

The bandit that headed the group noticed the chief's tone of voice and answered quickly, "Everything's OK, chief. It was just the ambulance that you authorized to enter. I sent Ratão together with the doctor."

Serginho felt his chest explode with hate. He needed to think rapidly, and shouted, "It's the police! You two come with me. The others stay here, and if the ambulance comes, shoot them. Tell the men that are in the office to come down quick. Let's go."

When the five policemen entered the house, they found all the lights turned off and immediately turned on their night vision equipment which allowed them to see in the dark. In the front room there were three folding beds in a row and the guards were sleeping calmly. Besides the guns with silencers, they were also carrying pistols with tranquilizers, which were utilized right away to keep the guards sleeping even more deeply. Handcuffed, gagged with adhesive tape and carried out to the ambulance, they were placed beside Ratão. Meanwhile, another two policemen broke down the door to the room where Reinaldo was held captive.

Thinking about the tragic events he had witnessed in his dreams, the chaplain heard a noise at the door, which opened with a loud crack. The operation was very quick. The two policemen took him rapidly out of the house. At the door they met Eduardo, armed with a rifle. The five policemen who had invaded the hiding place walked toward the rear of the vehicle. Reinaldo and his brother were among them. The driver and detective Brandão were waiting, already seated in the cab of the ambulance, and the two remaining policemen together with the doctor had already gotten in. At that very moment, they heard the noise made by two speeding cars which turned a curve and entered the street. On both sides of the car in front, AK-47 rifles opened fire. A fraction of a second earlier, the policemen threw themselves to the ground and took shelter behind the ambulance. Eduardo threw Reinaldo under the vehicle and laid down alongside him. Brandão and the driver, trying to get out of the cab, were hit and fell to the ground. The cars braked right in front of them and the drug dealers began to get out. That's when the rifles of six policemen, Eduardo among them, opened fire. The seven bandits were hit. Five fell and two continued to walk toward the ambulance, firing. Serginho was one of them. One of the policemen dropped the other bandit with a burst and Eduardo shot Serginho in the chest. The bandit chief fell dead. He was lying prostrate almost beside the ambulance, and everyone heard Reinaldo's terrified exclamation, "I saw that expression a little while ago. Al-Ashfar!"

In the commotion that followed, nobody paid any attention to those words. Brandão, despite being seriously wounded, shouted, "I want three men in Serginho's car. They'll go in front and neutralize the guys at the roadblock. We'll follow behind, in the ambulance. Quick!"

Three detectives from the elite group got into Serginho's car and sped off toward the exit from the slum. The doctor ordered the wounded men to be placed in the rear of the ambulance. The other two men from the elite group got into the cab and drove toward the exit. The car in front arrived quickly at the roadblock. There, the two bandits on guard took a few seconds until they realized that the occupants of Serginho's car were policemen. A burst from the gun of the detective seated beside the driver knocked down the two bandits. The policemen stood still for some time, while the ambulance passed. Fortunately, the drug dealers that were coming down the hill to help their companions had not yet arrived.

The policeman who was driving the ambulance and had been shot, lost his life even before the doctor tried to save him. He'd been wounded in the head, and didn't have any chance to survive. Brandão had been shot twice, once in the left shoulder and once in the left forearm. The doctor gave the policeman first aid, as the latter asked every moment about the progress of the operation. One of the men who had opened the door of the hiding place was making contact with the police station by means of a mobile phone, and gave all the information to Fábio. After listening to the doctor, the detective chief ordered them to take the same return route and when they arrived in the Barra da Tijuca district, take Brandão to the hospital emergency ward, which would already be prepared to receive him. The police doctor and one of the detectives from the group were to accompany the wounded man to the hospital.

Reinaldo, very shaken up by everything that had happened, stayed beside his brother, without saying anything. Eduardo had embraced his brother and also wasn't saying anything. He broke the silence to ask the doctor to lend him his mobile phone and called his mother, who answered right away after the first ring. He passed the mobile phone over to his brother, who said, "Mother, I'm OK, thank God! After everything is finished at the police station, we'll go home."

The ambulance arrived at the hospital, which was already expecting Brandão, and after leaving the wounded man and the body of the dead driver, they went on to the police station, arriving at four fifteen in the morning. The prisoners, after being identified, were taken to the jail. After filling out their reports, the policemen were allowed to leave. Eduardo and Reinaldo returned home in a police car.

On arriving home, there was a very emotional moment, with many hugs and kisses. Their mother and aunt couldn't contain their happiness. The priest was anxious to take a long hot bath and shave, after all that he'd been through. A generous breakfast, affectionately prepared by their mother and aunt, awaited them. It was 6:30 a.m. on a cold, rainy Sunday. After breakfast, Eduardo asked them to forgive his haste, since he had to go to the airport and catch the 11 o'clock flight to Foz de Iguaçu. He was anxious to see his wife and children again.

Reinaldo thanked him effusively.

Eduardo packed his bag and took the first taxi that passed by the building door, heading for the airport. Their mother, now greatly relieved, had sat down in the living room, hugging Reinaldo and didn't stop kissing him. Then the priest invited her to go to mass to pray and thank God for having rescued him.

Before they left, Reinaldo's mother phoned Jô and Souza e Silva to give them the news. She felt that they were relieved. Then mother and son got dressed, in order to take Aunt Glorinha to the hack stand so she could get a cab to the bus station. The cold mist forced them to dress in warm clothing and take an umbrella. They preferred to walk along Avenida Nossa Senhora de Copacabana, which offered more protection from the wind. They arrived at the church a little before the eight o'clock mass. They were able to find empty seats.

Up to that moment, Reinaldo hadn't met his two friends who were priests, Sílvio and Demétrio. When the mass began, he noticed that Sílvio was taking part in its celebration. Reinaldo prayed contritely for the souls of all those who had died, both in the past as well as in the present. He also asked God to help him find the meaning of all those events in which he'd been involved, as Jean and as Reinaldo.

When the mass ended he went to the vestry, accompanied by his mother, and there he found his friends, greeted them and introduced his mother. He didn't make any comment regarding the kidnapping.

They returned to the apartment along the same route, beneath the same drizzle and feeling a little cold. They read the Sunday newspaper and afterwards went out for lunch in the Italian restaurant conveniently located on the ground floor of the building. A red *Chianti* wine helped to warm them up. More at ease, the chaplain told his mother all the details of the kidnapping and the dreams. At the conclusion, she commented, "Look, son, I think I'm going to order another bottle of wine in order to assimilate all that confusion."

Reinaldo laughed a lot at the unexpected comment and replied, "Mother, you're already a little high, but it's not such a bad idea. After all, we've plenty of reasons to celebrate!"

They ordered another bottle and began to talk about other things. After a long conversation, they returned to the apartment. Reinaldo went to his room to sleep a little. He had missed his comfortable bed. He slept until the evening. He didn't have any dreams.

On awakening he went to savor the snack his mother had prepared for the two of them. She was saying, "Your brother phoned from Foz de Iguaçu. He arrived there OK. I took the opportunity to call your cousin also, to give him the good news. I'd told him about your kidnapping and he called every day for the latest news. He said he had a friend, a doctor, who works with regression and past lives. It seems they want to schedule a visit for you, son. Call him tomorrow morning, until ten o'clock, when he's usually home, OK?"

After cleaning up the kitchen, they went to the living room to watch television. They watched a movie on cable TV. His mother began to snooze in the middle of the film. She ended up saying good night and went to sleep. Reinaldo didn't feel sleepy and watched a second movie, until sleep came. Then he went to his room and slept deeply, without any dreams. He woke up early. It was still dark, the day had dawned rainy and cold. He recalled it was Monday. He stayed in bed a little longer, before taking heart and rising. He went to the bathroom, got ready and then went to the kitchen, where he found his mother seated, eating her breakfast, and greeted her, "You're getting up early, aren't you?"

"That's what happens when I go to bed so early, son. I'm a little out of control due to the sleepless nights I had up to yesterday. I'll be back to normal very soon. Sit down, I'm going to serve you your breakfast."

They conversed about the recent events. His mother asked, "And then what? Did you have any dreams?"

"No, I had a deep sleep and if I dreamed anything, I don't remember it. I think that with Jean's death, my dreams about life in the past ended. Theoretically, I could dream about another life, since, according to what I read in some books, people can reincarnate several times. However, I wouldn't like this to happen. The experience I had with Jean was very striking and I still haven't been able to evaluate or understand well what happened to me."

Reinaldo's mother took leave of him. She needed to go out and take care of some matters. After his mother left, Reinaldo phoned his cousin Luís. He thanked him for his interest in his case and asked about the visit his mother had mentioned. His cousin replied, "Can you go to my office now? A friend of mine, a specialist in regression, told me he'd be available this morning. I'm going to set up a meeting in my office."

Reinaldo got dressed, put on a coat, walked for a while and arrived at his cousin's office. The doctor hadn't arrived yet. He stayed in the waiting room, after speaking with the receptionist. Fifteen minutes later, he saw his cousin arrive, accompanied by a man around 35, short, fat and wearing glasses. He must be the doctor he cousin had mentioned. Luís embraced his cousin, very moved, which was a natural reaction after the ordeal Reinaldo had undergone. He introduced his colleague, Dr. Carlos Sampaio de Lima. They entered the office and Luís asked him to lie down on the divan at the rear of the room and relax. The doctors sat down on the armchairs alongside.

Luís explained that his colleague was already familiar with all the details of the case. Then Dr. Lima turned on a tape recorder, placing it on a little center table. Luís turned down the intensity of the room lights.

Reinaldo began talking softly, "With a very smooth voice, the doctor asked me to close my eyes and breathe slowly and regularly, thinking only about my breathing. For a few minutes, that was all I did. Then he asked me to relax all my muscles, one by one, which I did also. I began to feel drowsy and a great internal peace. It seemed I was flying in a dark, starless night. After a few more minutes, he told me he was going to count up to five and when he finished counting, I should return to my past and tell what I saw. I followed his counting and when it ended, I saw a light which was approaching very rapidly. And when that light was very close, I saw a group of people, all dressed in white, arranged in a semicircle in front of me."

THE GUIDES OF
THE LIGHT

"I was approaching the group, as if I were flying. Those people were making friendly signs. I felt a strong emotion on recognizing some of them. They were all there: my father, my maternal grandmother, Pierre, João, and four more people, two men and two women whom I didn't know. One of them, a very old black man, came forward from the group and began to speak. The most unbelievable thing was that his words were coming out of my mouth, in a hoarse voice that I myself was hearing, as though it were another person talking to me. The Portuguese words were spoken with a strong foreign accent, whose origin it wasn't possible to distinguish. He was addressing me, as if I were Jean:

'Jean, my son, we are your guiding spirits. And I am the only guide who is going to communicate directly with you. I shall speak on behalf of the others. You lived five other lives before being reincarnated as Reinaldo. Pierre succeeded in returning to France and found André. They lived long lives and André became the Marquis of Mont-Rémy, married and had many children. André is reincarnated in a person very close to Reinaldo, Lieutenant Alves, who was in command of the platoon on the border. We intervened, by means of

Reinaldo, to save your son's life. André's mission on this earth is not concluded yet. The man who was going to kill him was the brother of Serginho, the reincarnation of Al-Ashfar, your executioner. Reinaldo's attitude was not one of violence, as he thinks and is ashamed about. It was the noble purpose of a father who was saving his son's life. Since our intervention was very traumatic, we decided to tell Reinaldo everything by means of his dreams. The events concerning the drug dealer and Al-Ashfar are out of our control, since they belong to the Dark Side. The entire universe is involved in the struggle between Light and Darkness. Your spirit, Jean, must still evolve a lot in order to encounter the Light. When this happens, there shall not be anything but love in your heart. Your spirit will give off the light that shall bring peace and fondness to all those around you. Melissande is not here with us, but is incarnated in a child in Ethiopia who is living in very difficult conditions for survival. Your wife has already attained a very high degree of light and chose a life of great suffering to progress even further. Now that you know the reason for everything that has happened, you should return to your present life, as Reinaldo the priest, help your fellow men and show your brothers that they should seek spirituality as the main goal in their lives. We shall meet again when your mission is finished.'

"At this point, he fell silent and returned to the middle of the group. Then the light became stronger and following this, I returned to the hypnotic state. Dr. Lima asked me what I was seeing now. I answered that I wasn't seeing anything, just flying in a pitch-black night. Then he counted backwards from five to one and awakened me from the hypnosis. I felt myself lying on the divan and looked at the doctors. They were serious and silent."

Dr. Lima was the first to speak: "I've already witnessed many extraordinary experiments in regression. However, this was the most complex. I'm going to have to listen to the tape calmly and think about what this represents for my scientific convictions. For Reinaldo, I believe everything has been clarified."

He became silent and looked at Luís, who said, smiling, "All that comes to my mind now is Shakespeare's phrase in *Hamlet*: 'There's more between heaven and earth than our vain philosophy imagines'—to which I'd add: and our still incipient science."

The chaplain sat up, smiled at the two doctors and added, visibly moved, "Thank you from the bottom of my heart for what you've just done for me. Everything is very clear now. I'm finally seeing the right path to follow. What was complicated has become simple and my doubts have straight away been dissipated."

The visit came to an end and Luís said he'd send a copy of the tape to Reinaldo. The chaplain said good-bye to the doctors and walked back to the apartment. His mother had already arrived, and when she heard the door open, she ran to hug her son, saying, "Did everything go alright? Tell me right away what happened."

Reinaldo closed the door and led her by the arm to the living room sofa. He told her in detail everything that had happened in the doctor's office. His mother began to cry softly when her son mentioned her late husband. She interrupted the account to ask, "How was your father, I mean, how was his physical appearance?"

He thought a while before answering, "He was the same way as when we had that luncheon on my eighteenth birthday. I always remember him on that day."

He continued his account of the regression, and when he finished, he let out a long sigh and said, "That's it, mom. Now I know the reason why all that happened. I've found my path again in life and I don't have any more doubts about my priestly vocation. I've found what I came to look for here. I must return to my parish as soon as possible."

His mother stared at her son for a long while, without saying anything. Then she hugged him and said, "I'm glad for you, my son. What happened was a real test of your faith. At my age, no event, as strange as it may seem, surprises me. My mother's heart would like to keep you here, close to me, for a longer time. But you have your mission to accomplish. When do you intend to travel?"

He thought a little before replying, "Wednesday morning, I think. I intend to arrive in São Gabriel before nightfall."

She looked at the clock and said, "Would you like to have some barbecue in the Leme district?"

They went walking slowly along the boardwalk, taking advantage of the improvement in the weather and the timid sun which had come out. They helped themselves to the generous selection of different meats, accompanied by excellent draft beer. On the way back, they stopped at the airline office where Reinaldo bought a ticket to Manaus on the flight leaving Wednesday morning. He'd buy the ticket from Manaus to São Gabriel when he arrived in the former city and embark for a few more hours flight in a Bandeirante model aircraft.

On arriving home, his mother went to her room to rest, and Reinaldo sat down in the living room to read the newspaper. Then he remembered to call Jô, thanking her for everything and taking the opportunity to say good-bye. He ended the call promising to write always. He did the same with Captain Souza e Silva, his father's good old friend. He phoned to thank him for his important help during the kidnapping and said good-bye cordially. He also called Detective Brito, from the Copacabana police station, Eduardo's friend who had been so helpful, summarizing everything that had happened, and thanked the policeman for his help.

The afternoon passed quickly and night fell. Reinaldo's mother prepared supper. They watched movies on cable TV until sleep came. When he went to bed, he felt a great longing for the dreams, mainly for the friends that were lost in the mist of the past.

He woke up and felt a happy sensation brought on by the sunny morning. He rose rapidly, got ready and went to have breakfast with his mother. He talked her into taking the usual walk. And the two went along Avenida Atlântica, walking in the midst of hundreds of people who were having their daily exercise. On their return they found a message on the answering machine asking Reinaldo to phone the Police Kidnapping Department in the Barra da Tijuca district. He called Detective Fábio, who asked him to appear there in order to give routine testimony needed for the police investigation. After taking a bath, he went downstairs and took a bus to the Barra da Tijuca.

He arrived before 11:00 a.m. and went directly to the detectives' room. He was greeted by all those that had participated in the action. Pedro, the detective trainee, was present and was introduced to Reinaldo, who thanked him for his work in discovering the hiding place. His promotion to full detective was guaranteed and would occur at the end of the month, for merit. The chaplain then found out that the action had continued the day following his rescue. Serginho's gang had all been arrested and the drug traffic in that region had been disrupted. He recalled the policeman who had served as the driver and had been killed. He took note of his name in order to have a mass said for his soul. After his testimony, which took around half an hour, he told them he was going to travel to São Gabriel the next day and said good-bye to the policemen. He returned to the apartment and had lunch with his mother. He remembered that he hadn't said good-bye to his brother priests in the Copacabana parish church and decided to go there. It was five in the afternoon when he entered the vestry. He found Demétrio conversing with another priest whom he didn't know. After introducing them, Demétrio asked to be excused and called his friend aside for a private conversation, asking, "You have a mysterious air, Reinaldo. What happened?"

They sat down on one of the benches in the vestry and Reinaldo told his friend everything that had happened since the last time they had met.

Demétrio listened to it all, silent and attentive. When his friend finished his story, he still waited while before saying, "Brother, it's very impressive. I told you once that depending on the outcome of your dreams, I'd begin to believe in reincarnation. Now I'm forced to believe in it. I think that it all begins to make sense. And what are you going to do?"

The chaplain smiled and answered, "I'm returning tomorrow to the Amazon region and resuming my religious life and my military duty. I wanted to say good-bye to you, since I'm going back to my mother's apartment and spend my last hours here in Rio with her."

Demétrio told him that Sílvio had traveled with a group of parishioners to Aparecida, to visit Our Lady's Sanctuary. After giving his friend a long embrace and leaving his regards to

Sílvio, Reinaldo returned to the routine of life. At night, after supper, he packed his suitcase and went to bed.

He had a good night's sleep, and awoke after having had normal dreams. He prepared for the trip and after breakfast, he and his mother went down together. At the building door, he took a taxi to the airport, after a good-bye kiss and a long hug. His mother didn't cry and asked him to come back again the following year.

BACK TO THE AMAZON

He took advantage of the flight time to Manaus to read a little. In the airport bookstore he'd bought a weekly magazine, which would provide distraction during the trip. In the Manaus airport, he was able to buy a ticket to São Gabriel da Cachoeira. The flight would leave an hour later. He arrived in São Gabriel at 7 p.m. At 8 o'clock, he already was in his room in the barracks. After a long bath and a light supper in the officers' mess, he went to sleep, exhausted.

He woke up at reveille. He was already unaccustomed to the sound of the bugle. For a moment, this made him recall sadly the bugles at the Battle of Hattin. He jumped out of bed and went to the bathroom to get ready. His roommate was on duty on the border. He looked at the calendar on the wall and saw the last day that appeared: August 16—the day he'd traveled to Rio. It was now August 30—two weeks had gone by, two weeks that seemed like two years to him. After getting ready, he looked at himself in the mirror. The uniform was a little tight, as a result of those meals the last few days. No one would understand why he'd taken only fifteen days leave, of the thirty days he was entitled to. "I think I'll pretend to be a madman and say I missed the barracks. They're not going to find that very amusing and they'll think the priest really went crazy. Well, forget it."

He appeared at the officers' mess for breakfast. All the officers greeted him, "How are you, Chaplain, is your leave already over? You came back early."

Later he reported to Colonel Peçanha, and said, "Colonel, I'm returning from leave. I know its not over yet, but I've already resolved everything I had to resolve and I want to go back to work."

"Welcome, chaplain. Your brother phoned me and told me everything that happened. I hope you've recovered from the trauma."

"Thank God, I'm completely recovered, Colonel. Once again, thanks for warning me of the danger."

"Yes, but by the looks of things, my warning didn't help. Well, let's go on to what matters. You can't interrupt your leave this way. It can only be interrupted if your duty requires it. Let's do the following. You can stay in the barracks and perform your religious duties, including the celebration of masses, here and on the border, if you wish. Officially, you're on leave. If you decide you want to go, there'll be a helicopter going to the border post Saturday afternoon. There, you can celebrate mass Sunday morning and be back here the same day, after lunch, when there'll be another supply flight. Another piece of news: I've withdrawn the request for your decoration for bravery in combat. On conversing with the Bishop at a ceremony at the Municipal Government office, he explained to me that it would be inappropriate for a chaplain."

Reinaldo was pleased at being able to resume his religious activities and accepted the offer, "Yes, Colonel, I'll go. I'm also grateful for your action with regard to the decoration. It's better this way."

On leaving the Colonel's office, he encountered Lieutenant Alves, who was waiting to talk to the commanding officer. The chaplain tried to contain the emotion he felt on seeing him. The officer said, "Chaplain, what a pleasure to see you again. I want to thank you for what you did for me on the border. My wife and I would like to invite you to have dinner at our home, one of these nights, as soon as we can set a date."

"I'd be very pleased. We'll be able to schedule it for next week. Thanks, Lieutenant. Are you already recovered from your wound?"

"Yes I am, I was lucky to have put on my bullet-proof vest as soon as the combat started. The bullet perforated the protection but didn't cause much damage and the wound wasn't very deep. I'm going in to talk to the Colonel."

They said good-bye and the Chaplain went to the room where he used to work, in order to bring everything up-to-date. During the afternoon he went to the Santa Teresa church to talk with Father Francisco and resume his activities in the parish social programs. His colleague greeted him heartily, "Welcome, brother! You came back earlier from leave! Was it because you missed us or because you don't like Rio de Janeiro any more?"

The chaplain laughed at his friend's joke, embraced him and replied, "Neither one. Or better still, a little for the first reason. But I returned simply because I resolved things more rapidly than I expected."

He spent the rest of the day working in the parish dispensary. There was always a lot of work: cleaning the installations, literacy classes, meetings with youths, visits to the elderly, collection of donations and baskets of food staples and many other activities related to social welfare work. He returned to the barracks only at night. He had had soup in the dispensary and felt a little tired. He took a bath and went to sleep.

The next day he continued his routine duties and in the afternoon went to the Diocese to talk with Bishop Dom José, who received him with an affectionate smile, "My dear Reinaldo, as I can see, you found your answers sooner than we expected, didn't you?"

The two men of religion sat down. The chaplain replied, "Most certainly, Dom José, much sooner than expected."

He recounted in detail everything that had happened since his last visit. The Bishop listened very attentively to it all, without interrupting. At the end, he commented, "Father, your story is very much out of the ordinary. Nevertheless, four years ago I had contact with a case of regression which happened to a priest in Manaus. During a bout of malaria, he began to dream about an Inca slave who had lived in Cuzco in the fifteen century. I followed the case closely, which led me to accept this type of spiritual occurrence. The Church has been studying the matter for some time, but has not yet issued its judgment in this respect. But what about your priestly vocation?"

"I no longer have any doubt in this regard. I want to give myself totally to the Church of Christ and live spiritually. I want to devote myself to helping my fellow men and preach the word of God. Jean's life, with his unshakable faith, was a great source of inspiration for me. Yes, the term is this: inspiration! Courage, enlightenment, revelation."

The Bishop rose and accompanied the priest to the door, saying, "Father Reinaldo, go back to your parish and continue your work. I think your problems have ended."

The chaplain left the old Diocese building, got on his bicycle which he'd left at the entrance, and rode down the cobblestone street. As usual, it was very hot, humid and unpleasant. He pedaled rapidly along the busy streets of downtown São Gabriel up to the Santa Teresa church. A little later he met Father Francisco at the door of the dispensary. They greeted each other happily and went inside to work.

EPILOGUE

It was five o'clock on a Saturday afternoon, September 2, 2000. The Brazilian Army helicopter landed on the clearing which served as a heliport. It was bringing the material needed to supply the platoon which was camped beside a stream, on the border with Colombia. The battalion chaplain came aboard the helicopter to say mass on the following day for the Catholic soldiers that made up the majority of the platoon. After chow in the evening, he walked to the cliff and sat down in his usual place to look at the sky. Sparse clouds, a new moon and a veil of stars decorated the heavens with light. There were the constellations he'd learned to recognize. He thought about everything that had happened and smiled. He was nothing more than a miniscule sparkle in this, God's universe, a fraction of a second of this infinite time. He felt light, happy. He looked upward and saw a comet, an unexpected traveler through the illuminated ether. It was ageless, without any matter, just a twinkling light.